I0761970

not like yesterday

(an ilse beck fbi suspense thriller—book 3)

ava strong

Ava Strong

Debut author Ava Strong is author of the REMI LAURENT mystery series, comprising three books (and counting); of the ILSE BECK mystery series, comprising four books (and counting); and of the STELLA FALL psychological suspense thriller series, comprising four books (and counting).

An avid reader and lifelong fan of the mystery and thriller genres, Ava loves to hear from you, so please feel free to visit www.avastrongauthor.com to learn more and stay in touch.

Copyright © 2021 by Ava Strong. All rights reserved. Except as permitted under the U.S. Copyright Act of 1976, no part of this publication may be reproduced, distributed or transmitted in any form or by any means, or stored in a database or retrieval system, without the prior permission of the author. This ebook is licensed for your personal enjoyment only. This ebook may not be re-sold or given away to other people. If you would like to share this book with another person, please purchase an additional copy for each recipient. If you're reading this book and did not purchase it, or it was not purchased for your use only, then please return it and purchase your own copy. Thank you for respecting the hard work of this author. This is a work of fiction. Names, characters, businesses, organizations, places, events, and incidents either are the product of the author's imagination or are used fictionally. Any resemblance to actual persons, living or dead, is entirely coincidental. Jacket image Copyright zef art, used under license from Shutterstock.com.
ISBN: 978-1-0943-9343-8

BOOKS BY AVA STRONG

REMI LAURENT FBI SUSPENSE THRILLER
THE DEATH CODE (Book #1)
THE MURDER CODE (Book #2)
THE MALICE CODE (Book #3)

ILSE BECK FBI SUSPENSE THRILLER
NOT LIKE US (Book #1)
NOT LIKE HE SEEMED (Book #2)
NOT LIKE YESTERDAY (Book #3)
NOT LIKE THIS (Book #4)

STELLA FALL PSYCHOLOGICAL SUSPENSE THRILLER
HIS OTHER WIFE (Book #1)
HIS OTHER LIE (Book #2)
HIS OTHER SECRET (Book #3)
HIS OTHER MISTRESS (Book #4)

CHAPTER ONE

Kristine's eyelids fluttered and felt like sandpaper. She groaned, the sound creaking through dry and chapped lips. Her tongue dabbed out as her vision slowly returned... She tasted something salty, dried along the edge of her mouth, and it took her a moment to realize what it was.

Her eyes suddenly flared along with a pounding headache. Another ache competed with the pain in her head: her wrists. Still blinking, still wincing, she glanced down at her hands folded in her lap as if they were locked in prayer. A sleek, black rope, like from climbing gear, wrapped around her hands. She stared, not quite comprehending.

The last she could remember... Rock-climbing in Olympic National Park. She'd slipped but caught herself. She frowned, groaning as she tried to recollect... Scrambling on the side of the cliff-face, the grating and scraping of small rocks knocked loose. Then... over an outcropping shelf of stone, a face had appeared. A face with a knife—the man had started cutting her rope.

At the memory, another lance of pain shot through her skull; she stared down at her hands again, shifting in the dark, trying to place where she was...

Muddy walls, slanted and slick. Above her, a glimmer of light, like the mouth of a well. Branches and thick sticks covered the well, visible like the shielding canopy of some treetop. And, next to her, in the side of the mud pit... a metal grate. The thing looked like it had been stolen from some city sewer and then brought to the mountains...

As she shifted for a better look through the grate, her back scraped against the muddy wall. It was then Kristine realized she was naked. A chill erupted up her spine, only partly due to the cold. Her heart hammered, a small yelp caught in her throat as she twisted some more, trying to look for her clothing.

A small whimper of sheer terror croaked from her throat, and she found her bound hands were now trembling horribly in her mud-streaked lap.

As horror welled up within her, along with the prickling sensation across her skin, she finally winced, glimpsing through the metal grate. On the other side of the bars, she spotted a small, wooden bench, as if made in some home carpentry shop like her father had. But unlike her father, whoever had made this bench didn't seem to care for craftsmanship: no varnish, just screws and janky lumber.

But what really attracted her attention were the bottles *on* the bench. As she read the labels, the trembling in her hands got so bad, she leaned forward to try and stop the involuntary shaking.

Terror was now replaced with a slicing, agonizing sense of horror, which started in the pit of her stomach like a fist of ice or a knot and then spread throughout her whole body.

"Dear God...," she murmured beneath her breath. "Jesus, no... please..." Her voice whimpered, the quiet little prayer offered up with no obvious response.

One of the bottles was body lotion. Another was distilled water. And others were unmarked, save a single masking tape label that read, in messy writing, "*detoxifying solution.*"

As the spiders on the wall across from her continued to skitter, her own eyes darted up, crawling past the bottles to examine the rest of the cavern system through the metal grate.

Mannequins filled the room.

She frowned, wincing and leaning forward, her hands still shaking, her breath coming in wild puffs. Her bare body stretched across the muddy ground, and her heart hammered wildly as she peered between the bars, staring into the room on the other side of the pit.

She realized her mistake.

Not mannequins.

Bodies. Human bodies, frozen in place, like stuffed, taxidermy animals. Two women leaned against a wall, stiff as cardboard cutouts, small tea kettles glued to their cold fingers. A woman lay on the ground by a small stuffed dog, as if the woman were playing tug-of-war with a toy in the animal's mouth. Other bodies, difficult to make out from her position, were frozen around the adjoining room.

Now, she did scream. It started as a low, humming groan of terror, but then it burst from her lips in a high-pitched shriek that Kristine didn't even recognize as her own voice. She kicked, scrambling back, slipping on mud, and banging her agonized head against the back wall. As she moved, she yelped in pain, dragging her thigh across a protruding rock embedded in the ground. She felt the new gash welling with blood now, trickling down her leg and mixing with the dirt.

"Oh honey, oh sweetie-pie," a voice suddenly called out in the dark.

Another scream died on her lips. Not because the fear was gone—in fact, she was now more afraid than before. Her whole body shook. But the terror itself seemed to have stoppered her throat. Questions pinged her mind like pinballs: *Who was that? Was he speaking to her?*

"H-help?" she said, her voice shaking uncontrollably. "Help me, p-please!"

But the voice ignored her. Through the metal grate in the side of the muddy hole, she spotted a figure moving now, amidst the stuffed corpses. She couldn't make out features.

But she did notice one thing...

The figure was naked too but unbound. He walked breezily, with no decorum or sense of modesty, strutting around the stuffed figures. He was speaking now, an ornate, folded fan clutched in one hand which he fluttered. His face was cast in shadow.

"A long day, in fact," he was saying. "And yes, Martha, I do intend on returning on time. Haven't you learned to trust me yet?"

Kristine swallowed, her head pounding. Who was he talking to?

"No, no, Olga," said the man's voice, in a rich, soothing tone, like the voice of some talented stage actor. "I just don't have time for that. Texas Hold'em is all I'll play, in fact." A pause, then as if he was on the phone and answering someone she couldn't hear, he called, "Of course not! Of course! Right away, Olga." He patted one of the stuffed bodies on the shoulder, emitting a gregarious laugh, before skipping, in the nude, towards the woman and the hound playing tug-of-war with a sock.

Kristine just stared in horror. As the man spoke, interacting with the taxidermy corpses, she heard something in the distance. A background noise she'd taken for the wind, but now, she realized was too loud, too echoing.

The sound of running water... Her nose wrinkled as she listened to it. Another horrible thought struck her. If they were near a river or something in the national park, no one would hear her screams.

Perhaps that's why she wasn't gagged.

"I suppose later tonight," the man was saying, still waving his fan beneath his chin. "I—hang on," he said, suddenly. The man's pacing form, visible through the bars, stopped in the back of the room. His tone shifted slowly. "Hear that?" he murmured, whispering in the ear of the corpse drinking tea. "Something is outside. A friend? A new plaything? I'll be right back." He suddenly scurried off, stopping long enough to grab something long and metallic which had been resting against the wall.

He disappeared into the darkness, up another tunnel.

Once he was gone, Kristine started to sob, tears loosed unbidden but tumbling down her cheeks, quivering on her chin before dripping to the ground and darkening the dirt.

She needed to get out of here. That psycho would be back any moment. Was he the one who'd cut her climbing rope? Was he the one who'd put her down here?

The sound of running water grew louder now, from down the tunnel where the horrible man had disappeared.

Kristine liked rock-climbing on her own. She knew this national park—knew the area. Her father, the woodworker, had often taken her camping as a girl. They'd spent hours in the woods, fishing, sometimes hunting, tying knots. Sometimes even training in survival skills.

She was an outdoors girl, through and through.

And while this was all horrifying, and terror still pulsed through her...

Kristine swallowed, glancing in the dark towards her leg. Her thigh still throbbed with pain where it had dragged against the rock.

The rock.

A small, little gray nub jutting from the muddy floor.

Hyperventilating, she shifted now, groaning from the pain of movement but pressing her wrists with the rope to the rock. She began to rub her wrists now, though they were still trembling badly, up-down, up-down.

Little fibers of rope began to fall away, small pockets of dust puffed from the motion. Dirt scattered, her hands ached, but she continued to rub against the rock.

The psycho was gone for now—but he'd return eventually. She only had this brief window.

Still, confusion hounded her. Where was she? Why had he brought her here? Her eyes darted to the bottles on the bench, and she swallowed. Perhaps some questions were best left unanswered for now.

The ropes were fraying, a small, burgeoning sense of hope now flamed in her chest. She needed to hurry, to hurry, to—

The rope snapped, and with it a small sob of relief escaped her throat.

But she wasn't free yet. She glanced up, towards the tangled branches and wooden planks blocking the top of the hole. She couldn't reach it from where she stood; it was ten feet high.

She needed something to stand on, to push off.

Her eyes were drawn to the bench by the grate.

Did she have time?

No choice. She had to hurry.

She raced to the grate, pushing and shoving at it. The metal bars were embedded in the mud, but not secured in concrete. It took a few moments but, her fingers scraping and gouging at the mud, she was able to shove the grate, tipping it on the floor of the adjoining room.

Just then, she heard a noise from deeper in.

She bit back a scream and hastily shimmied out from the small, muddy hole once blocked by the grate. The metal bars angled off to the side, with thick chunks of dirt and earth still attached to them.

She reached for the bench, but then realized her mistake.

It was only a few feet wide. Even placed on end, it would never reach the hole.

Panic now flooded her. She heard whistling coming from down the hall... he was returning. The only other exit was in the direction of that noise. But she needed a way to reach the top of the hole!

"Shit," she cursed beneath her breath, her voice barely audible even to her own ears. The sound of running water swished around her, echoing in the strange cavern system.

No choice. She had to move. Sometimes, as her father had often taught her, survival required a willingness to get squeamish.

She lurched forward, nearly tripping over the bench and grabbed the cold arm of one of the frozen male corpses. There were only two men... most of the bodies, by the looks, belonged to women. Glinting, glass eyes stared sightlessly at her. The body was thick, solid and she grunted in exertion as she dragged it back towards the hole in the muddy wall. She shuddered in revulsion, feeling the stiff, cold skin beneath her fingers—almost synthetic... Preserved? Her father hadn't just been an outdoors-man; he'd spent time with friends who'd dabbled in taxidermy.

"Just one moment, my friends!" called a rich, thespian voice from down the other hall. "I found another little buddy."

Tears of fear were streaming down her cheeks, but she couldn't stop now.

She shoved and pushed, angling the taxidermy man through the same gap in the hole she'd shimmied through. She shoved the rigid corpse into her muddy prison pit, wincing as part of his elbow broke off.

Hyperventilating again, shoving with a final grunt of exertion, she pushed the body into the muddy hole.

The sound of footsteps had now reached the main room.

"What in the world...," a voice echoed behind her.

She glanced back, sparing nothing more than a second's attention. The dark figure of the nude psycho was in the mouth of the tunnel, carrying a shotgun in one hand and a dead little, red fox dangling by the tail in the other.

The figure, still in darkness just gaped for a moment, his eyes glinting like fireflies. Then, he began to yell. "Stop!" he screamed. "Don't do it, Daphne! Come back here!"

Kristine had no clue who Daphne was, but she also didn't want to stay and find out. She dove back through the muddy hole, scraping a wrist against the metal grate.

She heard thumping footsteps, heavy breathing. Panic put her in motion.

She yanked the taxidermy body up, leaning it against the wall. Behind her, she spotted a hand, then a head probing into the mud pit as well. Two, blazing eyes fixated on her. A deep, growling voice flooded the space. "Stop, Daphne—or I'll have to punish you!"

She squeaked, leaning the body against the edge of the mud pit. The figure behind her was struggling to fit through the grate—and she heard huffing and growling, like from some sort of animal.

With the body leaning against the muddy wall, she took a quick hopping step, then jumped, gasping, her spine tingling, her back prickling with horror.

She clambered up the corpse, desperately. Pushing off its shoulders, climbing past its arms. She shoved off the same elbow and the arm snapped off completely.

With a yell, she nearly tumbled, but her hand shot out, latching onto a thick root protruding from the wall, beneath the top of the hole.

She heard a loud *bang!* And the muddy wall to her right exploded with dust and debris.

"Get down!" the voice screamed behind her.

But she knew if she stayed, she'd end up like the poor fellow she was now using for a ladder. She'd grown up rock-climbing, grown up scaling the unscalable. Her fingers scrambled against mud, one hand still gripping the root. Her feet pushed off the man's shoulders now and, gasping, shaking, she lunged *up*.

Her fingers caught the branches on the top of the pit. A strangled sob of sheer joy pulsed from her lips.

She heard another loud *bang!* And felt sudden pain along her left side, scraping her ribs. Her eyes fluttered as she dangled, hanging from the branches. With a herculean effort, she pulled herself up, scrambling with gasping breaths over the top of the pit.

Branches shifted from her shoulders, leaves fell away, fluttering back into the hole. No sunlight—she'd been mistaken. The moon now stared down at her.

Nighttime.

She heard more cursing behind her. Her eyes widened, and, gasping, in pain, her ribs on fire, she rolled to the side *fast.*

Another bang. It missed her.

Gasping, head pounding, she struggled to her feet, whimpering as she did. Sharp stones gouged into her feet, and blood dripped down her leg and ribs.

"Come back, Daphne!" the voice screamed, forlorn. "*Please*, I'm sorry!"

She didn't reply, limping rapidly now, hurrying towards the trees. Ahead of her, she spotted a creek meandering through the trees, parting around a thick boulder. At the same time, she heard thumping footsteps behind her. A long pause, and then a distant echoing sound of hands against metal.

A ladder?

Her heart jolted. He was coming for her still.

She yelped, trying to sprint, but collapsing from the pain. Her feet were scraped up, her side on fire, her head pounding so hard she thought she might throw up.

She needed to hide. To hide! But where?

The trees? No...

Too dark to see. Too much pain to think. She did the only thing she could think of and took two stumbling steps and flung herself in the creek.

It was like she'd suddenly embraced ice.

Freezing cold surrounded her, washed over her. Her wounds pulsed in agony; her eyes sealed shut in the cold. The streaming, frigid liquid caressed her, caught her hair, dabbed at her nose and mouth, looking for some sly way to sneak into her lungs.

The overwhelming cold pressed in on her, dark spots dancing across her eyes. The sway of the water began to carry her like driftwood as her consciousness threatened to fade.

CHAPTER TWO

Ilse crouched by the doorway, the rough grain of the frame against her cheek. The scent of smoke and gunpowder lingered on the air. She could feel her adrenaline pulsing and she kept her firearm gripped in both hands.

The gun still felt awkward in her grasp. It was too heavy, and she never quite knew where to point it. Now, though, as she gripped it, she forced herself to focus. Another huffing breath, summoning what nerve she had, and then she burst through the ajar door, shoulder first.

The door slammed open as she catapulted into the dark room. No lights—the windows blocked out and boarded up. She frowned, aiming towards sudden movement.

Shit. Just a rotating fan. More movement.

She tried to whirl to her left, but it was too late.

Someone tackled her from the side, sending her clattering to the ground. She huffed, shoulder throbbing in pain where it hit the concrete. She scrambled, trying to maintain her weapon, but the man on top of her was far stronger. Fingers grabbed her wrist, holding it tight. Another hand tried to cover her mouth, holding her down.

As she struggled in the dark, her head on concrete, her hair swishing across her sweaty forehead, other memories slowly surfaced... Memories she'd long wished she could forget.

Little Hilda Mueller... She could feel the way her father held her down. The way he'd screamed in her face, spittle speckling her small cheeks. Could feel the way her ear had bled and the way her other siblings in the dark watched and whimpered. She'd grown up in a small house in the Black Forest of Germany, along with her brothers and sisters—tortured by her father before escaping as a child. A horrible past—one she'd been fleeing most of her life. But now, for the first time, she wasn't running. She was preparing.

Ilse's eyes flashed, snapping back to the present.

It took her a moment to realize her aggressor now had her gun and was pointing it against her forehead. The aggressor breathed heavily, one arm extended where he pinned her wrists above her head. He pointed the gun at her forehead and then whispered, "Bang." He lowered the gun, shaking his head and released her. “Nice try, Beck, but you let incidentals distract you.” The man got off her, calling out, “Lights!”

Suddenly, the small, concrete room was illuminated by bright fluorescent bulbs. Half the back wall was missing, replaced by glass, allowing the instructors to watch the trainees from the viewing platforms. This glass partition faced the back portion of the large warehouse they practiced in. The FBI training center had shooting ranges in the warehouse and an obstacle course complete with a towering wall along the southern end.

The small stone house, with the boarded windows had a couple of civilian cardboard cut-outs turned towards the glass viewing booth. Ilse had been faced with the civilians in previous training exercises.

This time, though, when faced with a live body, she'd choked.

The man above her extended a hand. Agent Alvarez had a handlebar mustache and silver-streaked bangs. He waited expectantly until she gripped his rough palm and then he helped her to her feet, reaching out to dust off her shoulders.

“What happened when you saw the fan?” he said. “You made it pretty far.”

Ilse just sighed, rubbing at her nose, and trying to suppress the flash of memories that had surfaced during the exercise. This wasn't the first time she'd frozen during the physical combat session.

Instructor Alvarez crossed his arms over his barrel chest. “Probably pushed a bit too hard,” he said. “It's a tiring exercise, I get it. Maybe best we take a break before another shot.”

Ilse could feel her stomach twisting, could feel the glare of the lights around her beating down on her. The last thing she wanted to do was to admit to Alvarez that it wasn't tiredness but trauma that had distracted her. PTSD wasn't exactly considered a strength in the FBI agent's handbook.

Alvarez glanced at her, his bushy mustache bristling. He stared at her from beneath his dark eyebrows. “Don't worry about it, Beck,” he said. “It's just one test. You aced the mental portions yesterday if I hear right from Gracie.”

Ilse tried to smile, but the expression died on her lips. She gave a hesitant little shrug. “I guess so,” she murmured.

Her eyes trailed towards the viewing room beyond. She spotted a couple of men and one woman watching the small room. When her gaze landed on a lanky, thin-framed man wearing a baseball cap, she went stiff.

Agent Tom Sawyer had been watching. She hadn't realized he'd arrived yet.

Sweat-slicked, panting, her memories still swirling about, Ilse felt sick to her stomach. Agent Sawyer had pulled a lot of strings to get her this far. He'd called in more than one favor, and from what she'd heard, Sawyer didn't have too many friends left in the agency.

And now she was going to ruin it all.

Tom met her eyes, dipping his head once. She winced, but instead of waving in greeting, she just shrugged apologetically and glanced away. When she looked back, Tom was talking with the other man inside the viewing platform. Ilse knew this fellow was Supervising Agent Rawley, one of the head honchos at this particular training facility.

Agent Rawley wasn't as tall as Tom, but he was well proportioned, like a college athlete, despite his silver hair. He had a muscled frame and wore half-framed glasses perched on his Roman nose. Rawley exchanged another few words with Sawyer, and Ilse's heart hammered.

If anyone would've known what she'd actually been thinking, trapped on the floor, it would have been Sawyer. He knew she froze up sometimes. Did he know what she'd been thinking? Would he be able to guess? Was he telling Rawley right now?

Ilse felt panic setting in, felt her hand close around the hem of her sleeve. Just then, Supervising Agent Rawley pressed a button by the window. A crackling voice filled the house over a speaker system.

"Dr. Beck," Rawley said, his silver eyebrows low over his piercing, blue eyes. "I'd like to speak with you, please. In the back office."

Alvarez winced and gave her a comforting little pat on the back. "I'm sure it's fine," he murmured beneath his breath. But his tone suggested the opposite.

Ilse let out a long, gusting sigh. She'd been worried this day would eventually come. She'd tried her best in the physical assignments. And while she was fit, and even trained ju-jitsu, she sometimes froze up when in high-stakes situations. The mental portions of the training and assessments had been easy enough.

But now, the static of the speaker still crackling in the air, Rawley's blue gaze fixated on her, Ilse felt like a bug beneath a microscope.

Would the supervising agent fail her in front of Sawyer? Perhaps not. He seemed tough but fair in his dealings with the agents under him. Perhaps that's why he'd called her to the back office.

To fail her in private, to help her save some face.

But still, failing, of either variety, simply wasn't an option.

Breathing heavily, the sweat against her arms now cold all of a sudden, Ilse turned towards the door, exited the small training house and began to maneuver through the warehouse towards the offices in the back. Rawley hadn't emerged yet from the viewing room, which meant she'd have to take the long walk on her own and then wait in isolation for the supervising agent to follow.

She couldn't fail. Not with everything on the line...

But right now, it didn't seem like she had much of a choice.

CHAPTER THREE

Ilse sat in one of the leather arm-chairs by the small, office door. The office rooms didn't even have ceilings but were rather an amalgamation of flimsy plywood walls with even flimsier doors.

Now, her eyes darted up at the sound of approaching footsteps. Her gaze traced the perfectly polished penny loafers and neatly pressed suit pants of Rawley. The SA didn't so much glance at her as he reached the thin, balsa wood door, pushed it open and stepped inside. He only paused long enough to call, "Come in, please, Dr. Beck," before proceeding into the room himself and allowing the door to close.

Ilse let out a long breath, still sitting in her leather chair. She murmured quietly, so only she could hear, "Doss. Blackouts. Eleven victims. Major depressive disorder. Poison." One of the soothing memory tricks she'd picked up over the years. Morbid, perhaps? Dark, certainly. But also effective where she was concerned. Ilse had long ago realized not to question an effective measure. The human psyche was nearly impossible to entirely predict.

Her breathing had regularized by now, and as she pushed out of her chair, she let out a long sigh, glancing in the direction of the small house in the center of the storage facility.

No sign of Agent Sawyer or Alvarez. No sign of the woman who'd been with them.

A slow prickle crept up Ilse's spine. At least none of them would have to watch this train wreck. She turned with a premonition of doom towards the balsa wood door, pushed at the flimsy wood and entered the small, cramped office space.

A single ceiling fan missing two blades dangled above a cheap, assemble-it-yourself black desk. The only expensive item in this room was the computer on the desk, which Agent Rawley was closing slowly, his eyes fixed over the lip of the machine as Ilse entered.

While he sat, there were no other chairs in the room. An intentional design to make trainees uncomfortable? An oversight by the interior decorator for the FBI who was clearly on a budget?

Before she could ponder this, standing now, facing the desk, Rawley spoke.

“I won't take much of your time, Dr. Beck,” he said, quietly.

She didn't wince, but she wanted to as if preparing for a blow. She swallowed and then, lunging at the momentary pause, the words escaped her lips before she'd realized she was speaking. “I'm sorry,” she said, quickly. “But I really think, if you give me another chance, I can do better. I know you should fail me. But I feel... feel *led* to join the FBI. I'm committed. With a few more weeks of practice, I'm sure—”

She went quiet as Rawley held up a single hand with a black wedding ring. He frowned briefly, his silver eyebrows dipping low. He cleared his throat and said, “I'm not here about your training, Dr. Beck. Apologies. I'm here about your other profession...”

She hesitated now, one hand nervously scratching at the back of her wrist. The tattoo band wrapped around it like the loop of a manacle, the ink reading: *“Take captive every thought.”* She watched Rawley, hesitant now, frowning as he seemed to be choosing his next words carefully. They knew she froze up during physical training. Surely, they knew... Didn't they?

What did he mean, though, this was about her other profession? Her work as a therapist?

Rawley looked at her, his ice-chip blue eyes unblinking. “I noticed you're still working your old job,” he said, cautiously. “Is this true?”

Ilse felt her expression flicker. She frowned, but then tried to hide it by coughing into her hand and glancing off to the side.

Carefully, she said, “I am. And...well, if you don't mind me saying, umm, *sir,* I was told it would be fine for me to continue my work with my clients. They—well, to be frank, they need me. I'm not able to cut ties. If that's what you want, I suppose all I can say is thank you for the opportunity, but—”

“Dr. Beck,” Rawley interjected, quickly. “You have it all wrong. I'm not trying to cause trouble for you. I—well, in fact, I'm here to ask for your help.”

Now, Ilse went still. She blinked, staring at the FBI supervisor. “Help?”

“Yes, Dr. Beck. Your help. It isn't strictly by the book, seeing as you haven't officially passed training. But we're on a bit of a time crunch.”

“Help with what?” She shifted her weight from one foot to the other, still standing in front of the flimsy desk.

He leaned in, folding his arms together, and somehow still not wrinkling his suit. “We have a woman who was the victim of a brutal attack in Olympic State Park. Are you familiar with the peninsula's forest preserve?"

"Yes, of course."

"This woman won't talk to police. Or FBI. Or even doctors."

"I—I see..." Ilse's eyes slowly widened. "And you'd like me to speak with her?"

"You are a licensed counselor, yes?"

"A trauma therapist. Yes, sir. I'd be happy to do what I can. When would you like—"

"Right now, Dr. Beck. Like I said, we're on a time crunch. We have reason to believe this woman's attacker isn't done yet. She may have escaped, but others might not be so lucky. She's in a hospital in the city, waiting." Rawley was already pushing out from behind his table, moving around the furniture and heading towards the door again. "I'm glad to hear you're amenable." He paused, glancing back at her now. "The woman won't speak to *anyone.* So we're sending you alone. You'll have a chauffeur of course. Agent Sawyer volunteered."

Ilse swallowed, nodding quickly. "I've worked with Tom before," she said. "That's fine. And you'd like us to leave now?"

"He should be outside, waiting in the car as we speak," Rawley replied. He made as if to move through the door, but then his expression flickered into a frown. He glanced at Ilse, and in a quiet tone, as if worried he might be overheard, he murmured, "Agent Sawyer is effective in the field. But he's single-minded. Be careful. Tom knows how to catch a killer. But sometimes, he's willing to pay too high a cost."

Ilse stared at Rawley's expression, her mind whirring, trying to catalog his meaning.

Was he warning her? She'd known that Rawley and Sawyer had something of a history but she hadn't yet picked up on the nature of their relationship. She'd heard, once, that Agent Sawyer had punched his previous field supervisor. Had that been Rawley?

All of these questions whirred by, but the instructions were clear: they needed to leave now and speak with the victim. She wasn't being fired. In fact, thanks once again to Agent Sawyer, she was getting involved.

"Thank you, sir, I'll be on guard," Ilse said, nodding once. Then she slipped past Rawley, through the door and, without glancing back, moved to the single exit to the warehouse which was guarded by two agents and a metal detector. She picked up her pace, moving away from Rawley and away from the training obstacle course.

CHAPTER FOUR

Ilse settled next to Agent Sawyer in the sedan with tinted windows. She'd grown accustomed to his reckless highway driving and buckled quickly.

"You good?" Sawyer said, glancing at her. The thin-framed agent had sandy-hair visible beneath the brim of his baseball cap. His green eyes reminded Ilse of deep forests and poison ivy. His fingers tapped against the steering wheel as he pulled from the parking lot outside the warehouse, up the long, winding road to the highway.

As they picked up speed, Ilse replied, "I'm fine. I—I just got distracted back there. That's all."

"Mhmm," Sawyer said, nodding once. His fingers were calloused and stained with what looked like dried glue or varnish. Normally, he smelled of sandalwood and sawdust. Now, though, still in his usual flannel shirt, he had the faint odor of aftershave.

"Rawley didn't tell me much about the case," Ilse said, grateful for the opportunity to switch topics. "What do you know as of yet?"

Sawyer's fingers drummed against the wheel. "Victim's head wound could've killed her," he murmured. "We think she was either camping or rock-climbing before she was attacked. Covered in cuts, and wounds, bleeding—her bare feet were a mess when they found her."

"They? Who found her?"

"A ranger," Sawyer said. He winced. "Said she was naked and near freezing."

Ilse leaned back further in her chair, resting her head and closing her eyes, allowing her mind to wander. "Visible signs of sexual assault?" she murmured, eyes still closed.

"Don't look like it," Sawyer replied.

"So then why naked?"

Another grunt, followed by more quiet and the sound of the tires beneath them whirring against the asphalt.

Ilse opened one eye, glancing towards Sawyer. He was frowning beneath the brim of his cap, staring at the road ahead. His fingers were tight against the wheel, and again, in the same way he'd looked back in the viewing room, he seemed tense, distracted even.

She swallowed, frowning, but then quietly said, “Is everything alright with you?”

Sawyer grunted, glanced at her and then nodded once. He returned his attention to the road, and the two of them dwindled into silence for the remainder of the trip to the hospital.

***

Ilse winced as the hospital's sliding glass doors swooshed open, allowing them entrance. The familiar scent of cleaning fluids and ammonia lingered in the air. She thought of another hospital, this time back in Germany. Katarina Mueller, her sister, had been housed at that particular caretaking facility. Ilse winced, remembering the meeting with her baby sister, remembering the way Kat had kept saying things about “penance...” She'd wanted Ilse to visit their father.

But the old man was behind bars, in a prison near Freiburg. Ilse fidgeted, her skin prickling beneath the air conditioning above the sliding glass doors.

Did she really want to visit her father in prison? She couldn't imagine how that conversation would go. He'd been taunting her, or helping someone taunt her, at least. The postcards from towns she'd visited as a child had started showing up in her mailbox only a few weeks ago.

Each of the postcards had simply read: *Hilda Mueller.*

A name she'd tried to leave behind her, along with her past.

But this endeavor had proven fruitless. She couldn't outrun her history. She'd determined, eventually, she'd have to face it. To find out who was messaging her. What her father's involvement was. What had happened for those three weeks she'd been missing, following her escape from the horrible home. And, perhaps most of all, who had been her father's accomplice for all those years?

Her sister, Heidi, before trying to kill her, had mentioned their father hadn't lived alone upstairs. Ilse still wasn't entirely sure what any of it meant.

But she knew why she'd taken Sawyer up on his offer to work with the FBI. If anyone could prepare her, help her track down the accomplice, find out the truth of the taunting postcards, it would be the Bureau.

Next time, she'd return home prepared.

The chill air from the air conditioner above the door slowly faded as she followed Sawyer deeper into the hospital. The lanky agent seemed quieter than usual, if such a thing was even possible.

"Which floor?" she asked.

Sawyer, in response, simply pushed the up arrow on the elevator door. He waited; then, once it *dinged,* stepped into the carriage with Ilse. He pushed the button to the fourth floor.

As the elevator doors closed again, sealing both of them in the compartment, Ilse shot another askance glance at the agent.

Tom wasn't acting like himself. Though always quiet, he seemed more tense than normal; his frown now seemed a permanent fixture of his face.

But she decided against prying. If he wanted to talk, he would.

She was here to speak with someone else entirely. And now, she felt the walls closing in. Pressure—unlike pressure she'd felt before. Was the FBI testing her? She hadn't done well in physical portions of training, but this was her domain. Was Sawyer here to take notes, to look over her shoulder?

Ilse could feel her stomach twist.

She couldn't think like that, though. She was here to *help.* That was simple. With all her clients, everyone who came to her, her job was to help. She had to remember that. External factors were secondary; the patient alone was what mattered most.

They stepped onto the fourth floor, and Sawyer didn't wait, already hurrying down one of the halls, beneath a sign above the door which read, "ICU."

A nurse, inside the door, frowned, holding up a hand. "Hang on," the woman said. "You're not supposed to be—"

"FBI," Sawyer growled. "Where's the Olympic victim's room?"

The nurse blinked, mouth half open as she tried to process. Then, her demeanor changed, and she let out a long sigh, pointing down the hall. "Second door on the left. I'm not sure she's in the speaking mood, though, agent..." She trailed off, allowing Sawyer to fill in the blank.

Which he didn't. He just brushed past the nurse, still hurrying, and Ilse, shooting an apologetic wince towards the nurse, hastened after him.

Once they reached the indicated door, though, her attention moved from Tom's strange behavior, and instead shifted through the glass door, fixating on the woman in the hospital bed.

It was hard to discern her features beneath the number of bandages wrapped around her head. The woman's entire skull seemed encased in cottony white. Her arms lay against the bed, stiff as boards, and her legs were tucked beneath a couple of sheets.

Sawyer began to push at the door, but Ilse reached out, gently pressing against his forearm.

"Let me first," she murmured.

Sawyer frowned and for a moment it seemed like he might protest, but then, at the look on Ilse's face, he lowered his hand, and stepped back, crossing his arms as he leaned against the wall facing the door.

Ilse bit her lip, but then murmured, "Actually, would you mind standing out of view of the window? I don't want her to think she has an audience."

This time, instead of hesitating, Sawyer nodded dutifully, still as quiet as a grave and moved a few feet up the hall, standing in shadows now, out of the line of sight from the hospital bed. He swallowed, for a moment, his face strangely pale. "Call if you need me," he said quickly.

Ilse flashed a grateful smile and then turned back towards the door.

Her smile died as she pushed into the hospital room.

As the door swung shut behind her, Ilse just stood there, staring at the bed and the woman with the head bandage. Along her arms, Ilse spotted other, smaller bandages or patches, all of them covering more superficial wounds, no doubt. Scrapes and scratches from her ordeal. Ilse felt her throat tighten briefly, a welling of empathy rising in her. She knew what it was to feel helpless, alone, endangered. She resisted the urge to reach out and hug the young woman. For most her clients, Ilse often had to be careful not to let her own emotions, her own compassion, get in the way of actually *helping*.

The woman wore loose hospital clothing.

She'd been found naked, though.

Ilse's eyebrows flicked down, but she pushed aside her own emotion and stepped towards the bed, careful to make some noise to alert the woman to her arrival. Ilse cleared her throat, "Excuse me," she said in as gentle voice as she could muster. "Ma'am, hello, my name is Dr. Beck."

The woman didn't move, didn't flinch. She remained staring at the ceiling, her eyes half-shuttered. PTSD paralysis? Not unheard of. A more generic sense of despondency triggered by trauma and exhaustion? Ilse found her sense of empathy slowly nudged to the side as she considered the best way to approach the problem at hand. To help the young woman.

Ilse reached the bed, but stayed near the foot, far from the woman's face. Ilse hoped by providing her personal space, she might allow the woman a bit more comfort.

She stood at the foot of the bed now, watching the bandaged woman.

For a moment, Ilse glimpsed vestiges of herself in the survivor. An escapee, found in the forest, traumatized...

Ilse's own memories flitted back. *Run! Run!* Her siblings had screamed behind her. They'd helped her through the window in the basement. They'd watched as little Hilda Mueller had raced towards the trees. She'd made it. She'd escaped.

But she hadn't returned for three weeks. Three weeks of horror for the others in the basement.

What had happened? Why hadn't she returned?

Ilse still couldn't remember. She breathed shallowly beneath her breath, trying to focus again. "I work with trauma victims," Ilse said, quietly, more to herself than the woman in the bed. "I was wondering if I might be able to help. If not, that's fine too. I can leave."

No response.

Ilse nodded slowly, moving even further back until her shoulder blades pressed against the cool wall behind her. "It's been a while since I've visited the Olympic Park—so much rain forest and mountains..." she said, quietly. "I hear it's very beautiful."

The woman on the bed continued staring at the ceiling, her eyes half hooded. Her fingers twitched on the bedspread next to her, her bandages shifting against her hospital gown.

Ilse looked up at the tube light in the ceiling, considering the situation for a moment. Silence didn't scare Ilse; silence was often an effective tool. Silence, with two people in a room, was also a type of invitation.

But the woman on the bed didn't seem ready or willing to start speaking, even in the inviting silence.

So much about her situation reminded Ilse of herself. Escaping some horror in the woods, lost in a forest, traumatized...

Ilse's own memories had been vague outlines more than anything... She'd forgotten much of her escape, of that forest... She hadn't wanted to speak with anyone about it either.

Dr. Donovan Mitchell, her mentor, had been the first person to get her to open up. She'd audited some of his classes, out of sheer interest. He'd noticed her, called out her talent. He'd personally started tutoring her, counseling her. A story that could have ended in an escort off of a university campus with college security had instead ended in a career path for Ilse.

But she could still, vaguely, remember that first meeting in his office. He'd invited her in, his eyes kind, his prosthetic arm resting against the desk. No desire to hide his flaw. No shame at his injury.

The sheer vulnerability of the man, with his crinkled eyes and Santa Claus beard had sparked something in teenage Ilse. He'd taken a piece of paper, held it in his hand and murmured, "*This is the person who hurt you.*" He'd let her stare at the paper, frowning in confusion. *"This represents all they are. Can you see them on it? Hear them?"* He'd fluttered the paper and it had made a crinkling sound.

At the time, Ilse had thought it strange, but later on, she'd learned more about emotional regulation therapy, especially with experimental models. Dr. Mitchell shared a similar philosophy to Agent Sawyer. The most successful therapists weren't scared to miss the shots they took. This allowed them to try many angles.

Emotional regulation didn't usually involve some piece of paper. And yet, on that day, he had identified, then grounded her thoughts and emotions from internal construction via an external representation. Namely the paper.

Then, he'd crumpled it and tossed it away.

Ilse looked down at the bed then, frowning once. She slowly approached a small desk next to a beeping screen with the woman's vitals displayed. A pad of paper with cramped handwriting rested on the desk.

Ilse picked up the pad, tore of a single piece of lined, yellow paper, and held it up, murmuring, "This is the man who hurt you," she said.

It felt silly at first. She glanced towards the door, but no one was watching. Just another shot. If she missed, no harm no foul.

"This is the man who hurt you," she repeated, a bit louder. "Can you hear him? See him?" She fluttered the paper, the same way Dr. Mitchell had back in his office. To counter discriminating thoughts, one had to present an alternative narrative.

So Ilse said, "He's no longer a threat. The FBI is already narrowing in." This was technically true. It was the reason they'd sent her and Sawyer to the hospital.

She then, slowly, crumpled the paper, moved over to the trash can and tossed it in the wastebin by the door.

She returned to the bed. "He can't hurt you anymore," she murmured. "We have another agent outside these doors. Security throughout the hospital. And I will *not* leave until you ask me to. Would you like me to leave?"

She remembered Dr. Mitchell's prosthetic arm resting on the table.

Ilse frowned briefly and murmured, "I was once hurt by a man, too. I also got lost in the woods..."

The woman didn't react.

Ilse continued, "I was locked in a basement for the first seven years of my life. Trapped. I thought I'd never heal—never get better. But I have."

Still no response.

Ilse continued, "My only regret...," she paused, her voice hoarse all of a sudden, "Is how long it took me to get help. Three weeks... Three weeks late. If I'd reacted sooner, I would have been able to help others... I got lost, though. From what I remember..." Ilse trailed off.

A pause, and then, a frail, croaking voice murmured, "I wasn't lost."

Ilse's heart skipped, but she didn't react, keeping her expression gentle, considerate. "Oh?" she said.

The woman turned, slowly, wincing, the scrapes and cuts along her face scabbed over now, but clearly still painful. She looked at Ilse, eyes still half hooded. "I know that park," she murmured. "What's your name?"

"Dr. Beck," Ilse said, softly. "What's yours?"

"Kristine Swallow," the woman returned, wincing. "You're with the FBI?"

"I'm a therapist. But yes, I do work with them sometimes."

She stared off again, at the ceiling, her eyes wide. "It...it was cold," she murmured, wincing. "I—I still see them. Unblinking, motionless, frozen in time." She shivered now, one hand bunching against the blankets.

Ilse leaned in, watching with a concerned frown.

"Them? Others were with you?"

"Dead," she sobbed. "All dead. Frozen. Stuffed. I think." She hyperventilated now. One of the monitors next to the bed started beeping softly.

"Like mannequins in a window—frozen, set up..." She continued and Ilse tried not to let her confusion show, just letting the woman speak for a moment. Ilse had placed herself between the trashcan with the balled-up paper and Kristine.

"The water was so loud," the young woman said, still breathing rapidly, her nostrils flaring now. The sheets bunched in her fist caused her knuckles to turn the same pale color as the fabric. "Mud at my back... so, so cold. They were frozen. Frozen!"

Her voice increased in volume and Ilse softly interjected. "The others were frozen?"

"And the dead fox!" The woman yelled. "He shot it! I heard it!"

Ilse winced. "The man who hurt you? He killed a fox."

She winced, shaking her head, glancing towards the trashcan, dazed while murmuring, "He—he can't hurt me anymore?"

She phrased it as a question.

Ilse decided to try a different track. "You found your way to a ranger," she said. "You mentioned you knew those woods."

"Yes. Mile marker 35," she said. "Near where I was climbing."

"You're a rock climber?"

She tried to nod, but then flinched, letting her head go rigid against the pillow instead. Her eyes were wide again, the beeping from the machine continued to rise. The woman swallowed and began to whimper. "I—I think he's going to come for me again. Him and those horrible friends of his. They were frozen! Frozen!"

Ilse blinked, trying to track this. A traumatic episode triggered by an auditory cue, perhaps?

"I... I can't," she sobbed. "I can't think... It's all stuck in my head. I—I don't want to keep doing this... I don't...," she swallowed, sobbing again. "This isn't worth it anymore," she murmured beneath her breath. "None of it. I just want to make it stop."

Ilse frowned at this last phrase, hesitant. "What do you mean, Kristine? Make it stop how?"

But the woman was still shaking and sobbing, her eyes haunted.

Ilse pivoted, keeping her voice firm but gentle, "How about you count with me, hmm? Let's count back from one hundred by fives. Would you be okay with that? I can start. One hundred. Ninety-five... And then?"

But the woman wasn't interested in focusing her emotions. She was still breathing heavily. And now, the beeping was so loud, Ilse could barely think. The door to the hospital room suddenly flung open, and the nurse from earlier hurried in. "Out!" the nurse barked. "Please, get out! Out! Her pulse is spiking." Ilse heard a beeping sound of a pager; she watched the nurse brush past and begin to fiddle with one of the machines. The nurse shot her another, furious look. "Get *out*!"

Ilse nodded, wincing and retreating, heading straight to the door. Her heart panged for Kristine and for the horror in her eyes. She wanted to reach out, to hug the woman, to tell her it was all going to be okay.

But she'd made a promise. She'd said the FBI was closing in.

The best thing she could do for Kristine now was to find the man who'd hurt her. The man and his "frozen friends." Whatever that meant.

Ilse winced, stepping back out into the hall and letting the glass door swing slowly shut behind her. The beeping went dull again, and Ilse began to move towards where Sawyer still leaned against the wall in the shadows. Carefully, she pulled out her phone: a dumb, flip phone. She didn't trust technology from the last decade.

Carefully, lifting the device, she placed a call. Only as her hand held the phone to her cheek did she realize how horribly her fingers were trembling. Quickly, she switched hands, shoving her other palm back in her pocket and turning away from Sawyer.

"Dr. Beck?" came the reply on the other line. "Are you at the hospital yet?"

"Yes, Agent Rawley," Ilse replied, her back still to Sawyer. "I spoke with the victim."

"She spoke with you?" the boss's tone inflected higher, suggesting he was impressed.

"Yes, sir," she said, her own tone low, somber. "She was nearly delirious. But she mentioned something about a mile marker thirty-five."

"Thirty-five? You're sure?"

"Yes, sir."

"Good job. We'll have locals swarming the area within the hour. Did she mention anything about the attacker?"

"Not much, sir. She wasn't clear."

Rawley didn't so much as huff a sigh of frustration. Ever the professional, his emotions entirely in check. She could, however, picture his blue eyes flashing nearly imperceptibly on the other end of the line. Still, when he spoke, his tone was neutral. "Well, normally we don't assign trainees to active cases. But since you've established a connection with our only witness, do you think you'd be able to take this one on? You'd have to be supervised of course, with a senior agent."

"I—which agent?"

"Agent Sawyer's with you, yes?"

Ilse glanced back towards Tom, who was watching her with a slight frown. The expression, though, didn't seem to have anything to do with her. His eyes had a faraway look to them, but when he caught her watching, he tried to force a smile and flash a thumbs up.

She smiled back, a sad, hesitant expression. She lifted the phone again. "Yes sir, he's here. We can head to Olympic right now."

"Good. Get going. We have the ranger who found her waiting for us as we speak."

"We can speak with him first. We're on our way, sir."

CHAPTER FIVE

Where the concrete of the parking lot bled into the stony trail, Ilse stood beneath the wide shadows of a large pine. They'd left in the morning, and now afternoon greeted them. Wind rustled through the branches, and the kiss of summer heat warmed her cheeks. Ilse nodded politely, stepping aside as a group of tourists made their way past her, moving along the trailhead.

Agent Sawyer stood off to the side, frowning from beneath the shadowed brim of his cap. During the height of summer, some might be allergic to pollen or certain types of flowers. Sawyer, though, seemed allergic to tourists. He didn't quite scowl at them, but it was a close thing.

He rubbed at his sweaty forehead beneath his cap, and glanced towards Ilse, muttering over the murmur of the fading tourist voices. “Crowded today,” he said.

Ilse glanced around and stepped back as another group moved past her up the trailhead. She nodded politely to them as well, before sidling closer to Sawyer where he leaned against the wooden sign displaying the biking paths in Olympic National Park.

“Height of summer is tourist season,” she said, wincing. “So, it's going to be busy.”

Sawyer's frown increased in degrees. “Not great for trying to find evidence...” His scowl went even deeper. “Not great for protecting all of them,” he said, watching the two groups of tourists splitting off at a fork in the trail and moving in opposite directions.

“Let's just speak with the ranger,” Ilse replied quietly. “One step at a time.” Inwardly, she felt nervous, the same way she had on her licensing exam before becoming a therapist. Dr. Mitchell had assured her everything would be okay at the time. Now, though, there was no one to assure her.

She knew she wasn't cut out for the physical parts of being an FBI agent. But she also knew if ever she wanted to make her way back to Germany, to confront what hid there in the mist and the trees—what was buried there in that prison cell... She'd have to go prepared. Hopefully with backup. And also armed.

She swallowed at the thought, doing her best to suppress the thought stream.

Like she'd told Sawyer: one thing at a time. Right now, they had to focus on the case. Ilse had never thought she'd be allowed a case before even graduating, but she was more determined than ever to prove herself. Sawyer flicked a splinter off his flannel sleeve and raised a hand, gesturing past Ilse towards the trail. She frowned, turning as Sawyer said, “Amos Lee?”

“That's me,” a voice returned. “You the feds?”

Ilse rounded to find a man in a park ranger's green and brown uniform approaching slowly. He wore a bandanna wrapped around his head against the heat and had deeply tanned skin visible past the rolled-up hem of his long sleeves.

Ranger Amos Lee's gold and green lapel badge caught her attention, and the small, dented and rusted ATV he'd pulled up on sat on the edge of the trail. Now, pine needles scattered beneath his feet and his boots kicked up dust as he approached, slapping his hands against his legs as if to dust these off as well. His whole uniform had a thin coat of the grainy substance.

The ranger came to a halt, glancing from Sawyer's civilian clothes to Ilse's suit pants and sweater. Normally, Ilse preferred flip flops, sweatpants and anything loose and baggy. She'd compromised by wearing a professional business suit but hadn't been able to resist the sweater as well. Thin, breathable fabric made the summer heat and sunlight somewhat bearable. But though she was starting to sweat beneath the layers, she refused to remove the sweater. She couldn't quite explain why, but the extra layer felt like a cocoon of sorts—a protective shield.

The ranger settled on addressing Ilse. “Don't got long,” he said, dusting his hands off again. “Been mulching. But what can I do you for?”

Ilse glanced at Sawyer, used to the lanky agent taking the lead. But he seemed content to allow her to do the talking.

Ilse cleared her throat, adjusting once, then wincing at the sunlight through the trees, stepping back into the shadow of the large fir before speaking. “We're here about the woman you found this morning.”

“Right, course you are,” he said, swallowing some dust and spitting off to the side. He rolled his shoulders and tugged at his bandanna. “Strangest thing that. Not used to finding naked chicks in the middle of the woods.”

"That was this morning, yes?"

"Real early," he said. "I started at about two AM. Maintaining the trail and what not. Had to clear an old hollowed out behemoth. Cart off the branches one at a time. You know the shtick. Or *stick.*" He smirked at his own cleverness.

Ilse shook her head. Sawyer nodded.

Amos Lee frowned and turned, now addressing Sawyer. "Thought I was hallucinating to be honest," he said. "I don't sleep much." He tapped his forehead. "Insomnia."

Sawyer's eyebrows flicked up beneath his cap. "You found her on the trail?"

"Yeah, near mile-marker thirty-three."

Ilse glanced at Sawyer, remembering what the woman had said in the hospital. Thirty-three was two miles away from thirty-five... Had she really traveled so far at night? Ilse decided, for the moment, not to interrupt. Ranger Lee continued. "Was a pretty cold night, especially given the season. But she stumbled out from the forest, onto the trail, shaking and spitting. She saw me and her eyes went like she'd spotted some ghost." He shook his head, sympathetically, tugging at his sleeves. "Felt weird, seeing as she was, you know, starkers. But she passed out a second later, so I did what I could. Covered her in one of them fireproof blankets that's standard issue to all of us." He jerked a thumb back towards his ATV. "She was real scraped up, too," he said, wincing again. "Tried to dab some of the wounds. Had a first aid kit and everything, but... well, it was like trying to fix a dent with tape if you catch my drift."

Ilse shook her head again. Sawyer nodded once more.

"So you called paramedics?" Sawyer asked.

"That's right. Called 911, got her off the trail and they showed up about fifteen minutes later." The ranger gave a little shuddering sigh, blinking as if severing a memory. His expression turned to one of mild relief as he nodded. "Real glad to hear she's still kicking," he said. "That's real nice."

His voice shook a little bit at the end, threatening something like an emotion. But the man had tough features and labor-hardened hands. Still, she could see in his eyes that the events of that morning had gotten to him. So, instead of speaking, she went silent, waiting to see if he'd fill in the gap.

She only had to wait a few seconds, before the ranger coughed and then, stuttering, he murmured, "I-I don't mean to pry. But, are the guests safe?" He asked, leaning in and whispering this last part. His eyes shifted towards the parking lot where a couple of doors slammed as a new vehicle arrived at the trailhead.

Ilse shared a look with Sawyer, and this time the sandy-haired agent did speak. "We'll do our best to get you the answers you need," Sawyer replied. "Gotta hang tight for now. Did you have any other contact with this woman before you found her?" Sawyer spoke this last part nonchalantly, but Ilse's eyes darted sharply back to Mr. Lee's face.

The ranger, though, didn't seem to notice the shift in questioning. He still had that faraway look in his gaze, and he let out a shuddering little sigh as he murmured. "Was like a dream," he said. "A horrible dream. She looked near frozen, too," he said, quickly, as if realizing he might have left something useful out. "Think that matters? Like she was wet. I guessed she'd fallen in one of the creeks or something... Lucky it was summer. Still pretty cold, but at least hypothermia would be a low risk." He trailed off again, muttering to himself, and glancing back up the trail.

"So is that a no?" Sawyer pressed, more insistently.

Lee blinked, glancing at Sawyer. "Was that—oh, wait. No, yes. I hadn't met the woman before. Still don't know her name."

He paused again, as if waiting for Sawyer to reply to the query. But the tall agent just shook his head. He gave Ilse a look as if waiting to see if she had anything else to add, but as far as her suspicions went, though the ranger had admitted to insomnia, and was mildly socially awkward, he didn't seem guilty of anything else. Ilse just shrugged back, and Sawyer redirected once more.

"Think you can show us where you found her?" he said.

The ranger scratched at his chin, waving a hand towards the ATV. "Was a few miles in," he said. "I'll radio for another four-wheel. Just hang tight."

He moved back in the direction of his ATV, and Ilse watched as he withdrew a radio from the front seat, lifted it and his voice cracked as he began to speak.

She supposed Sawyer was right. The next step was to examine the place where the victim had been found. But with this many tourists, under the summer heat, in such a large park, she could only hope they managed to find something useful.

CHAPTER SIX

Ilse winced as, with as much gusto as with his highway driving, Sawyer pulled the two person ATV off the side of the road, behind the growling engine of the off-road vehicle in front of them. The more than million-acre national park combined a mixture of rainforests, mountainous outlooks, rocky beaches, and wild coastlines. Now, they found themselves deep amidst the trees, the salt from the ocean lingering on the air around them, though the water wasn't visible from here. Ranger Lee cut his engine, throwing one leg over the side of his machine and hopping deftly onto the isolated, muddy trail.

A second later, with less ease, but some obvious level of know-how, Sawyer also parked the ATV. Ilse's hands gripped his shoulders where she'd sat in the back of the saddle. Carefully, she eased off, and Sawyer followed a second later, both of them standing by the side of the dusty trail.

"You good?" Sawyer said, glancing at her and massaging his shoulder. "Thought you were trying to rip my arm off."

Ilse glared at him, absentmindedly brushing her hair past her maimed ear. "You speed like a maniac," she said. "I didn't know you'd driven ATVs before."

He shrugged. "I drive a lot of things. Some of them for the first time." Then, without waiting for her reply, he stepped passed her, approaching the solitary form of their guide who had crossed his arms and was waiting for them beneath the canopy of clustered branches and dewdrop leaves.

"This the place?" Sawyer said, eyes downcast, tracing the detritus and lichen and tumbled leaves. His boots crunched into fallen boughs and crisped five-point vegetation.

"Yup," said Ranger Lee, gesturing with a calloused hand to the side of the road. "See the dishevelment there?"

Sawyer glanced over. Ilse's gaze followed. She frowned, staring at the indicated incline on the side of the road. Hesitantly, she began to shake her head at the same time Sawyer said, "Yup. See it."

Amos Lee crossed his tanned arms, sighing once. "She was hesitant to come near me at the outset, you know. But after some coaxing, she relaxed—passed out near as soon as I saw her."

Sawyer looked at him. "Then you gave her the fireproof blanket?"

"That's right. See anything worth seeing?"

Sawyer looked down again at the ground, stepping away from the incline now, his eyes moving through the vegetation.

Ilse winced, reaching up and slapping at a mosquito hovering near her neck. Another blood-sucking bug began pestering at her hand, and she wagged her fingers at this one also.

The bugs seemed to be leaving Tom alone. Ilse stepped closer to him, her footfalls even louder, somehow, than his had been. Sawyer glanced at her, didn't quite roll his eyes, but then reached into his pocket and pulled out a small green bottle.

"Neck, cheeks, wrists," he said.

She caught the bottle and glanced at the front. Bug-OFF! the label read.

"Mosquito spray?" she said.

"And ticks," he replied.

Ilse winced, glancing up and around, shivering. "Ticks?" she asked, exhaling through her nose. While she lived lakeside two hours past the other side of Seattle and she was fairly acquainted with the woods, Ilse had never been much for deep forest terrain.

Now, the trees around her and the undergrowth seemed oppressive, clawing at her, encroaching on her personal space. She pulled at the collar of her thin sweater, wincing as she shifted foot to foot. Her memories tugged at her attention, reminding her of the last time she'd stumbled through the deep, dark woods. Remembering the last time small boughs had ripped at her... There had been ticks involved then, too, hadn't there? Three incidents of the nasty parasites latching onto her soft skin. Her feet had bled, teardrops had long since dried.

Ilse closed her eyes, trying to stave off the sudden jolt of memories.

Inhaling slowly, counting to four, then exhaling for five seconds, she watched as Sawyer traced a finger across the undergrowth.

"Something came that way," Amos Lee called out. "I saw it too. But trail seems too small for the girl. See those branches—broken at two feet, but at four they're still untouched."

Sawyer's eyes twitched up from the ground, but then he grunted. "She wasn't running."

"Come again?" Lee asked.

Sawyer tapped a finger against the ground. "She was crawling." He pointed. "That direction." Slowly, he stood on his feet, a finger still jutting in the woods as if accusing the branches themselves of wrong-doing. "What's over there?" Sawyer asked.

Ranger Lee frowned, rubbing at his grimy forehead with his bandanna. "Nothing," he said. "More woods. Cops and rangers have been scouring the area since this morning. They haven't found nothing neither."

Sawyer rubbed at his jaw, nodding once. He glanced through the trees a moment longer and then looked back towards Ilse. "Anything?" he asked.

Ilse, half busy rubbing the bug spray into her skin, handed the rest of the bottle back to Sawyer, inhaling the faint odor of forest and chemicals. The mosquitoes still seemed interested. She waved a hand in front of her nose, puffing a couple of breaths to send the irritants tumbling in the air.

She glanced around the woods, but nothing stood out in particular. "Kristine mentioned water," Ilse said, softly. "Is there a river nearby? Maybe a creek?"

"Water sources all over," Amos Lee replied with a shrug.

Ilse's shoulders slumped somewhat dejectedly. She shrugged to Sawyer as if to say *what* now. People, Ilse could talk with. People answered questions.

Trees just watched. Bushes and branches couldn't be psycho-analyzed. Detritus didn't recount memories.

Sawyer, ever the boy scout, seemed in his element. For her part, Ilse was already feeling miserable. She brushed at the side of her face, pushing her bangs in front of her maimed ear and shaking her head once more. The small, looping tattoo around her wrist flashed out of the corner of her eye.

Take captive every thought...

"Kristine mentioned she spotted the mile marker thirty-five," Ilse said. "This is thirty-three, yes?"

Ranger Lee nodded. He pointed further down the trail. "Thirty-five is that way. I found her here."

"Which means," Ilse said, "she traveled nearly two miles at night, trying to escape her captor."

Sawyer frowned in the direction Amos was pointing, then glanced back towards the indicated undergrowth where he'd mentioned the poor woman had been crawling in the woods, desperate and hopeless, fleeing for her life.

The broken branches led in the same direction as Amos's indicating finger.

"Think you can take us to mile marker thirty-five?" Sawyer asked, still frowning.

Amos shrugged. "You're the feds. Your call."

Ilse slapped at her arm, trying to dislodge a bug, but missed. "Yes," she said, gritting her teeth. "Let's go to thirty-five. Please."

***

Mile-marker thirty-three had essentially been in a small, off-shoot dirt path, barely traversable if not for the slick, all-terrain vehicles.

Thirty-five, however, was a different story.

As wide as a main street, though still unpaved, cops, forensic units, and unmarked FBI vehicles still crowded the shoulder of the path. Thick, rubber tires rested on pine needles and branches. Flashing blue and red lights reflected off dusty, painted metal doors.

In the distance, about a half mile up the road, beneath an awning of branches, Ilse spotted a roadblock and two hastily erected saw-horses guard by a couple of local deputies. A jogger and a biker were currently arguing with the deputies and using their frustration at the rerouting of their favorite trail to get a good look at the on-goings further up the path.

Sawyer and Ilse dusted themselves off, nodding farewell to Amos Lee as the ranger sat astride his all-terrain vehicle on the edge of the cordoned section of road.

Flashing his ID, Sawyer led the way past one of the erected sawhorses and towards the flashing lights of the rows of vehicles.

"Hey, knuckleheads," a voice suddenly shouted from further up the path, "trail is closed, get lost!"

Ilse frowned, turning along with Sawyer to witness a thick-set man who looked more like a construction worker than a cop. His features were sun-stained, and he had a brown hat, blocking out the sun, pulled high on his forehead, angled towards the blue sky and clouds above.

The man's features seemed a bit too crowded, as if a painter had been given ample canvas, but only decided to draw in the center. His eyes were too close set, his nose small, and his lips too high.

Still, the pinch-faced man was striding angrily towards them, his thick, sun-stained neck twitching with a vein fit to burst.

"Get lost!" he repeated, louder now, scowling from beneath the brown brim. "Oi, McNulty, get these assholes out of here," he shouted, waving towards one of the deputies by the sawhorse.

As the man neared, Ilse spotted the silver badge on his chest which read *Sheriff.*

Sawyer, more accustomed perhaps, to a cool welcome, didn't even respond. He looked away from the sheriff, scanning the side of the trail, his eyes flitting along the cops, rangers, and emergency responders moving through the woods in a grid pattern.

"Find anything?" Sawyer said, ignoring the man's bluster entirely.

The sheriff came to a halt in front of them, scowling. A couple of deputies were moving over now, too, frowning.

"Didn't you hear me? Hate to interrupt your super important morning jog, but trail is closed."

Ilse glanced at Sawyer, but again he seemed content to ignore the beefy sheriff. Since Sawyer didn't care to, Ilse cleared her throat and volunteered, "Sorry," she murmured, "But we're actually with the FBI."

She nudged Sawyer, who, reluctantly at these words, fished out his credentials and flashed them.

If she'd thought this tidbit of information would help anything, she'd been sorely mistaken. Instead of changing his mood, his scowl only deepened.

"Feds?" he said. "Get off my trail," he snapped. "We're doing fine without you. You can come through once I'm finished."

"Find anything?" Sawyer repeated, again indifferent to the man's temper.

The sheriff glanced at Sawyer's credentials a second time, then, reluctantly, he held up a hand, staving off the deputies he'd called to escort them away. The deputies lingered nearby, but, at least for the moment, didn't move to intercept.

"We're doing fine," the sheriff snapped. "Don't need more cooks in the kitchen."

"We're here to help," Ilse interjected.

"Right, sweetie," snapped the man. "That's what you always say before muscling in, stealing evidence, refusing to cooperate, and trampling my jurisdiction."

Ilse wasn't sure where all the hostility was coming from, but Agent Sawyer didn't seem surprised by it at all.

"This still about the case from last year?" he murmured, raising an eyebrow.

The sheriff leaned in, as if to get a better look. "This is about playing by the rules. Wait your turn."

Sawyer shrugged. “So you're saying you *haven't* found anything?”

The sheriff frowned again, his pinched features bunching even tighter. “You accusing me of something? Those are good men out there. Doing good work. We've been here since early this morning. Already six hours now. You think you can just waltz in here—”

“Never been much of a dancer,” Sawyer said coolly. “Just wondering what you've found. I'd like to help if I can.”

In Ilse's assessment, this was very even tempered of Sawyer. The sheriff seemed to pick up on this also. He let out a bit of a sigh as if leaking. But then, he pulled his hat off, rubbing at a thinning hairline. He looked away for a moment, fanning himself with the brim of his hat, and then gestured towards the searchers off the edge of the trail.

“We've been at it since early, like I said.”

“No one's accusing you of neglect,” Sawyer returned. “I was on that case last year. Your people did a good job. Things got messy—it happens.”

The sheriff let out a longer sigh, his frown fading a bit. The creases along his forehead and around his eyes suggested his features were well accustomed to this facial expression. “Yeah. Messy happens,” he said, carefully. “But that wasn't our fault.”

“I'm not here about bygone cases,” Sawyer said. “I'm here because a young woman was found wandering naked through the woods and mentioned other victims. Just trying to help.”

Again, Ilse was impressed by the calm in her partner's voice. The sheriff at this last part seemed to ease a bit. His posture loosened; his clenched hands went limp against his thigh. Instead of scowling at Sawyer, now, he was frowning in the direction of the trees. “We've scoured the area,” he muttered. “Every root, every twig. Nothing.”

“Nothing?” Sawyer asked.

“Not anything. I—I don't know what to tell you. Our victim might've been attacked, but she may have just hallucinated the rest,” the sheriff said, wincing. He rubbed the back of his head and then replaced his hat, his eyes cast in shadow once more. “No sign of a hidey-hole. No indication of other victims, or the perpetrator.”

“Nothing,” Sawyer repeated.

“Right.”

Ilse cleared her throat hesitantly. “Not to interrupt,” she said, following Sawyer's lead and keeping her tone polite, “but Kristine mentioned something about running water. She said the sound was quite loud.”

“Bah,” the sheriff snorted, “there are creeks all over the place. That's not helpful at all.”

Ilse began to frown but Sawyer shot her a look and she caught the expression before it curdled her features.

“Mind if we lend a hand?” Sawyer said, simply. “You stay in charge. I like the dirt and the woods anyhow.”

The sheriff's frown flickered again, and he glanced back towards the search parties on the edge of the trail. “You wanna follow the grid, have at it,” he said. “But like I told you, we've been up and down the area for hours. Nothing.”

“I'd just like to help,” Sawyer murmured.

The sheriff snorted, waving a hand. “Knock yourself out,” he snapped. Then, he turned, his scowl deepening. “Hey! Hey get off my trail!” he yelled, stomping now in the direction of a biker who'd slipped past the sawhorses. “McNulty, get that guy. Get him off my trail!”

With the sheriff's ire redirected now, Sawyer glanced at Ilse and jerked his head towards the side of the dirt path, between two parked paramedic vehicles.

“He seemed in a sour mood,” Ilse whispered as she followed Sawyer away from the sheriff.

“Long story,” Sawyer muttered. “FBI muscled him on a case last year. Nearby, too.”

“I see. Well... what now?”

Sawyer shrugged, glancing at her. “How sure are you about the running water?”

“I mean... she seemed certain.”

“Well... Let's see if we can find something the locals missed. Careful, watch your head.”

Ilse ducked just in time, avoiding a branch Sawyer's momentum sent whipping back. She winced, hand in front of her face now, following Sawyer off the trail and into the woods in search of the attacker's hideout, and, if they were lucky, the assailant himself.

CHAPTER SEVEN

Sweat beaded on Ilse's brow, and she had rolled up the sleeves of her thin sweater beneath the bright sun. Her expression now matched the sheriff's, though they'd long since left the trail where the cantankerous law keeper was still keeping a weathered eye.

She stepped over a churning creek dipping out of stony terrain. Already, they'd passed three similar sources of water. And each time, they'd come up with nothing.

Was the sheriff right? Were they simply chasing their tails?

Ahead of her, Sawyer pushed doggedly on, eyes to the ground, hands at his sides, palms parallel to the ground as if he were somehow stabling himself against the wind.

"Anything?" Ilse said, watching as Sawyer moved up the rocky creek-bed.

He paused long enough to scan the water, his eyes flicking along the opposite muddy bank. "I see tracks," he murmured.

Ilse's heart skipped a beat.

"Not human," he added.

Her excitement faded. "Nothing at all?"

He looked at her, tilting his cap. "Nada," he said. He gave a forlorn shrug. "Maybe we should head back."

Ilse huffed a breath, the words like a lifeline tossed over the rail. She hated the deep woods. Hated mosquitoes. But, even more than that, she hated giving up.

Ilse had never considered herself much of a quitter—she'd never been afforded that luxury, and she wasn't willing to start now.

Sawyer, as if sensing her reluctance gave a hesitant shrug. "Ground's getting rough," he said, indicating the scattered and crumbled stones. "Not much dust, not much mud. Going to be hard to track anything across this terrain."

Ilse sighed, rubbing the bridge of her nose, her brow furrowing beneath the glower of the sun. She stood, arms akimbo, trying to piece together her thoughts. Kristine had seemed certain she'd heard loud water. That's what she'd said. Maybe not a creek, then... Something man-made? Had she been near sewers?

That didn't seem to compute given the other things she'd said. The man who'd kidnapped her would have needed privacy, would have needed some sort of lair in the woods, something even the rangers and maintenance crews and bikers and joggers wouldn't accidentally stumble on.

Ilse closed her eyes, tilting her head and feeling the sun against her cheeks.

She couldn't think like a tracker. Or like a sheriff. Not, perhaps, even like an FBI agent. She'd only just started training with the bureau... But perhaps she could think like a therapist.

She didn't know trees, or rough terrain... But she did know people.

Why had the noise of the water stood out to Kristine? What had caused the auditory trigger to come to the forefront of the woman's mind when Ilse had confronted her?

She opened her eyes, shaking her head. "The auditory cue wasn't nothing," she said, doubling down. "Kristine wasn't mistaken. The water would have been near where she was taken. Close enough to drown out the other sounds." She paused long enough to make her point, listening to the creak of branches above, the twitter of birds and bugs through the forest.

Sawyer just watched her, one foot pressed against a boulder.

Ilse frowned even more deeply, drifting back to what the young woman had told her. Then, her pulse quickened. She stared at Sawyer. "Hang on," she said. "You mentioned tracks."

Sawyer waved a hand towards the muddy embankment. "Yeah. Animal. Not human."

"What sort of animal?" Ilse insisted.

Sawyer frowned but glanced at the ground again, dropping to his haunches and readjusting his perch on the stones. "Guess... Coyote," he said. "Or..." He frowned further. "Might be..."

"Fox?" Ilse guessed.

He looked up at her, impressed. "Yeah. Might be."

Ilse began to move forward now, ignoring the sweat on her forehead, ignoring the way her sweater clung to her, ignoring the heat, and the buzz of bugs and the beating sun. "Kristine mentioned her killer shot a fox," she said, her voice strained in her own ears. "Said she heard him kill it. Auditory clues, remember. A fox near a creek."

She waved a hand towards the water. "Any way to follow those tracks?"

Sawyer hesitated, glancing at the paw prints in the ground. He waved off, away from the stone terrain, deeper into the trees, further away from the park trails. “I'm good enough to go a bit,” he said. “But it'll be slow...”

“I'm not quitting now,” Ilse said, shaking her head determinedly. She brushed her hair in front of her maimed ear. “You?”

Sawyer frowned at her. “Nah,” he said.

Ilse came to a halt on the muddy embankment, gesturing at Sawyer to take the lead. “After you,” she said, careful to keep a far enough distance that she didn't accidentally trample anything important.

To his credit, Sawyer didn't sigh, didn't react in frustration. He simply bobbed his head once, rolled up his sleeves, and then hopped across the creek with his lanky gait, moving once more through the undergrowth, following some unseen trail. Ilse wasn't sure what Sawyer was looking at, so she simply followed in his footsteps, head down, eyes on his flannel shirt.

The auditory clues were important. Auditory recollection had to have meant proximity.

They were getting close.

At least, that's what she had to tell herself to take another step through the undergrowth, another step beneath the scowling sun.

***

For another hour, Ilse followed Sawyer through the undergrowth, through the woods, hastening along the edge of the creek. Now, the waterway widened. The creek became too wide to cross, but Sawyer kept doggedly on, grunting occasionally or pointing and then setting off again. It wasn't a continual gait, but rather ten steps, a long pause for a minute or so, then another ten steps.

Like this, stopping and starting, they moved through virgin forest, further from the trail and deeper into the forest.

“He shot the fox,” Ilse murmured. “He must have seen it. Or heard it.”

The hour of sunlight, moving across rough ground saw both of them sweat now. Sawyer's flannel stuck to his back, darker between his shoulder blades. Ilse's sweater sleeves were completely rolled up now. Even this, though, exposing just her arms made her uncomfortable.

“Hang on,” Sawyer said suddenly, coming to a halt.

Now, the two of them paused. Ilse heard the sound of running water and felt her heartbeat quicken. She swallowed softly, glancing around the creek and listening to the rush of liquid. Loud. Quite loud. Even louder than the branches, than the rustling leaves, than the buzz of bugs or the tweet of birds.

And there... She frowned at where Sawyer was pointing.

A hole in the side of the muddy bank, beneath a thick tree root jutting out like a terrace.

"What is it?" she said, softly.

Sawyer, though, held a finger to his lips, crouching a bit now, and staring towards the hole. "Tracks go there," he said. "Fox..."

She stared at the hole and then her eyes widened. She shot Sawyer a significant look and also lowered now, slowly.

"Think his lair is nearby?" Ilse whispered in Sawyer's ear.

He glanced at her and shrugged, the scent of his aftershave faintly disguising the smell of sweat. He tipped his baseball cap back and began to move cautiously along the creek towards the indicated hole.

"The water is loudest here," Ilse whispered. "Louder than it was back that way," she murmured, pointing from where they'd come. "The ranger said she was soaking wet when he found her. Means the creek had to be deep."

Sawyer glanced towards the water and nodded. "Deep enough to submerge," he murmured still whispering. "Let's fan out. Careful where you step," he added.

Ilse nodded and, still hunched low, the two of them crept through the trees. She wasn't at all sure what they were looking for. Sawyer's eyes glued to the ground off to the left as he moved away from the water, through the trees, up a slight incline. Ilse's own gaze scanned the ground, the muddy bank, the trees themselves.

She couldn't be certain *what* they were looking for. Small leaves crackled beneath her footfalls, though she avoided fallen branches and boughs as much as possible, preferring to step along lichen and padded ground.

The ground cover was thick. As she moved from tree to tree, past stone and fallen logs and undergrowth, she had to rip her sweater from brambles twice. Breathing heavily, frustration mounting, she tried to keep track of the terrain, but still spotted very little in the way of anything that might indicate a killer's lair.

Others... Frozen others.

What had Kristine meant, exactly?

This area certainly wasn't cold during the day.

Ilse paused, extricating her collar from where it had snared on a low-hanging branch. She watched near the creek as Sawyer turned further inland, moving with cautious steps up the hilly terrain. She continued watching the man as he ducked under thick branch cover.

He stepped over a jagged stump. Paused, frowning.

Took another step. He thumped his foot against the ground... Hard—*harder.* Thump. *Thump!*

His frown deepened. He lifted a leg higher—

And then he yelled, suddenly plummeting as if into the ground itself.

Ilse yelped and broke into a sprint as if at the sound of a starter pistol. Sawyer was cursing and scrambling, one hand tightly gripping a thick tree root next to his arm. Half his body seemed inside the terrain as if swallowed by quicksand, surrounded by mud, detritus, and sticks.

The rest of him, his upper half, strained and he let out a groan of exertion, pulling himself with a gasp and a growl back onto the forest floor. Ilse reached him in time to grab his arm and help him to safety.

"Damn it. He covered it good," Sawyer snapped, waving a hand towards the ground.

Ilse peered over Sawyer's shoulder, both of them breathing heavily, the sound of the creek loud behind them.

Both of them now stared at the hole in the ground.

Someone had gone to great lengths to cover the hole with branches and leaves and moss.

Now, though, where Sawyer had fallen, two of the branches had been knocked aside, allowing Ilse a glimpse into the deep dark. Down a chute of mud, Ilse found her gaze fixed on a dark pit.

"I-I think this is it," she said, breathily, her voice barely a whisper.

Sawyer growled, getting slowly to his feet. "Let's hope he didn't hear me..." Then without further comment, Sawyer grabbed the same root he'd caught himself with, twisted and began to slide down the hole, into the mud pit.

He paused long enough to look at her, inching up an eyebrow. "You coming?" he whispered. Then, he shimmied further, his head ducking out of sight as he climbed into the muddy hole.

CHAPTER EIGHT

Ilse's hands strained where they gripped the muddy roots. Her fingers turned white before her eyes as she lowered herself, carefully into the pit. Her sleeves slipped along the dirt and debris, scattering pieces of earth towards the darkness. Below, she heard Sawyer cough and curse followed by what sounded like stumbling.

Her head dipped below the forest floor, following the rest of her into the pit. Strong hands gripped at her leg, guiding her until she found herself sliding onto Sawyer's shoulder.

“I gotchu, doc,” he muttered, still choking as if he'd swallowed mud. “Hang tight.”

She did just that, loosening her grip only enough so she didn't burn her hands as they slipped along the mud-scrabbled root.

Darkness swallowed her as she fell and, with Sawyer's help, loosened her grip on the root and allowed him to carry her to the ground, depositing her on a muddy floor. As she fell, the temperature dipped, and goosebumps spread across her skin from the underground cold.

Ilse blinked in the dark, her eyes adjusting to a slow, pale glow emanating from deeper in the pit, through a gap in the mud wall. Above, the sunlight trickled through the scattered branches and loose boughs placed over the hole.

“Think this is it?” she murmured softly.

In answer, Sawyer just pointed, scowling, his features pronounced and cast in shadow.

She followed his indicating finger, ducking a bit to peer through the gap in the mud wall like a window in a confessional booth.

And there, on the other side of the pit, she spotted something that made her blood go cold.

Ilse cursed, stumbling back, her feet slipping on the slick ground. Her heart hammered and her throat nearly closed up. Icy tendrils of fear probed up her spine like cold fingertips. Prickles erupted across her face, and she bit back a sudden, unprompted scream.

“Holy sh... Holy...” she began, unable to complete the expletive.

“Nothing holy about that,” Sawyer said, darkly. “And yeah. This is it."

Ilse didn't look at the agent, though, her eyes fixed on the horrible scene on the other side of the muddy pit.

Bodies, frozen bodies, just like Kristine had said, lined an adjoining room. Dead bodies, stuffed, it seemed, frozen in postures like mannequins. At first, Ilse had thought they might be just that... But mannequins didn't have those proportions, didn't have that *skin.* These were not statues.

"Let's take a look," Sawyer muttered, rolling his shoulders as if preparing for a fight. He ducked and after scraping his foot along the muddy hole a few times to widen it, he dropped to his belly, indifferent to the slick mud and squeezed through the hole. A metal grate, off to the side, scraped against stone as Sawyer pulled himself from the pit into the adjoining room filled with stuffed corpses.

Ilse's own breathing came rapidly; she stared as Sawyer's jean-clad legs wriggled through.

At first, Ilse's stomach twisted. For a moment, she felt like turning and screaming. Something about being underground... in a monster's lair.

She'd been through it herself and she wasn't sure she wanted to voluntarily face it again. Now, though, Sawyer was scrambling back to his feet on the other side of the mud pit. Growling to herself, wiping flecks of dirt and earth from her cheek, Ilse dropped to her hands and knees and also crawled through the terrain. Her hands pressed into the wet surface, her back scraping against the enclosing.

Beneath her breath, she muttered, "Brown hair. Brown eyes. Bundy. Forty-two. Thirty victims. Forty-six. November twenty-fourth."

Sawyer reached to help her to her feet, and she accepted his dirty hand, rising slowly, her own hand shaking badly as she emerged in the kill lair.

All around them, human corpses stood in grotesque poses. A couple were drinking tea, one seemed to be playing with a stuffed dog. Others were further in, leaning against walls or sitting around tables. They were dressed in outfits, accompanied by odd and eerie props. Some had hats, others wore gloves.

None of them smelled, to her surprise. Suggesting they'd been treated in a way to best preserve them.

Ilse found her heart hammering, the sound of her own breathing wild and rapid in her ears.

The room adjoining the mud pit was made of stone, like some cave or carved-out tunnel. The ground felt rough beneath her feet and a single, Turkish rug on the far end of the room was the only carpeting.

"Don't touch anything," Sawyer murmured. "Crime scene." His eyes flicked along the bodies, breathing heavily. Any moment now, Ilse half expected one of the frozen beings to bolt into motion, to suddenly charge them.

The killer had shot a fox... Was he watching them, even now? Waiting to strike?

She yelped at a sound, turning sharply towards one of the mannequins. Then, she realized what she was hearing; water echoing down the pit. Louder, even, down here, thanks to the acoustics, than it had been above.

The sound swelled and then receded, fading into the background for a moment before picking up again, louder still.

She frowned, wondering, briefly, amidst her horror, at the reason for these odd acoustics.

"Wind is catching the leaves," Sawyer murmured, watching her expression morph every time the sound did. "Muffling then not."

He glanced around the horrible hellscape, rubbing a hand across the back of his head. A couple of the taxidermy bodies were men—smaller men, with pretty features.

Most of the corpses though... Ilse realized with a shiver, belonged to young women.

"See anything?" she said, her eyes fixed on the glassy eyes of the bent, brown-haired woman playing with the small, stuffed dog.

"Need lights," Sawyer muttered. "Need forensics." He rubbed his chin, muttering, "This is going to make the news," he said, scowling. "Maybe national. Damn it. Who am I kidding—definitely national news."

"I... Not to downplay that, but maybe we should leave. Wait for forensics above," she said, shuddering. "Please."

Sawyer glanced at her, then nodded once. "Don't touch anything," he reminded her. "Let's go out the way we came in. That way might be trapped." He pointed towards another tunnel leading, ostensibly, towards another exit.

Shivering, but grateful to turn her back on the hellish spectacle, Ilse followed Sawyer back into the mud pit. He made a cradle of his hands, pressing them to his knee then nodded up towards one of the lower roots dangling down. "Think you can snatch it?"

Ilse looked up, shivering, wondering how on earth Kristine had managed without help. Sawyer was tall, strong and even with his help it was going to take some effort.

She could only imagine the courage it had taken the young woman to escape, on her own, trapped, with no one near to hear her screams.

As she pushed off Sawyer's hands, gritting her teeth as she grabbed the low-hanging root, her mind whirred. What kind of person did this? She'd never heard of something like this before. She knew most killers—had studied thousands of them. Ed Gein had been a necrophiliac, a man who stole body parts and skin from graves to make them into household items. But even Mr. Gein hadn't stooped to stuffing humans.

What kind of sickness prompted a human to kill like this?

There were a lot of bodies... More than seven she'd seen.

How long had the killer been active? How long had he gotten away with all of it?

***

Standing in the shadow of a large oak, Ilse watched as the scene now crawled with police, investigators, rangers, and forensics.

She shivered, listening to the gurgle of the creek behind them as a couple of deputies began waving their hands near a pile of old stones on the opposite side of the stream. "Over here!" one was shouting. "We found the other entrance—over here!"

It had taken fifty of them nearly a half hour to find the new entrance, even though they'd known exactly where to look.

Ilse shuddered, wondering to what lengths this killer had gone to cover his tracks.

Sawyer stood a few paces ahead of her, talking with the blustering sheriff who, despite the help they'd provided, was still scowling.

Ilse heard the red-faced sheriff mutter, "Whole section of the park is going to be shut down. Maybe the park itself—I'm waiting to hear back."

Sawyer nodded slowly, crossing his arms, his sleeves creasing. Again, he made no effort to try and muscle in on the sheriff's territory, preferring to listen for the moment.

The sheriff rubbed a hand across the back of his sweaty, shaved head. "Whoever this sicko is," the man muttered, "he's an outdoorsman."

Sawyer bobbed his head. "Knew how to cover his tracks," he said.

"I nearly fell straight through that back entrance of his."

The sheriff spat off to the side. "Not good news, that," he muttered. "He knows the park well, too. Home turf advantage."

Sawyer glanced around at the trees, wincing against the sun. He slapped at his neck where, for the first time, a mosquito ventured, finally deciding to taste someone besides Ilse.

"Hey," a voice said in her ear.

She nearly screamed, turning sharply, a hand bunching at her side.

Amos Lee, the park ranger with the bandanna, quickly held up his hands, backing off two steps. "Sorry," he said, quickly. "Didn't mean to startle you."

Ilse frowned, staring where the tanned man had postured a few paces away from a row of ATVS.

"Amos," she said, hesitantly. "Hello..?" She inflicted this word as a question.

He cleared his throat. "Oh... yeah, right. Look," he said, wagging his head and waving towards the sheriff and Sawyer, "They mentioned this guy might know the park, yeah?"

Ilse frowned. "Were you listening in?"

Amos shrugged. "Not trying to, but I just overheard."

Now, Sawyer and the sheriff seemed to have noticed the interaction and had stopped to face Amos also, both of them frowning.

"What is it?" the sheriff snapped.

Sawyer just watched.

Amos turned from Ilse, rubbing his neck. "Ah, yeah. Not to intrude or nothing, but, just..." he shrugged again in a would-be nonchalant gesture. "I happened to overhear and if you're looking for someone who knows the park..." He glanced off, wincing in the direction where a couple of other park rangers were helping to topple one of the stones near the deputies who'd found the second entrance.

"You know someone who might be of interest?" Ilse said, frowning now.

Amos glanced from her, back to the sheriff as if not quite sure where to look.

"Spit it out," the sheriff snapped.

Ranger Lee dipped his head again. "Shoot, yeah. I might, actually. You said..." He glanced towards Sawyer, wincing, "I *heard* you say that most the bodies down there are young women, yeah?"

Ilse frowned at the side of Amos's cheek. Her own expression was now mirrored by Sawyer as well.

“What about it?” Sawyer said.

“Well... Someone who knows the park,” Lee said raising a hand as if it were a scale. “Someone who makes women uncomfortable,” he raised another hand like the opposite scale and lifted his palms up and down. “We had a guy like that. Worked on the maintenance team last year.”

“A ranger?” the sheriff said, some of his irritation fading to curiosity.

“Not anymore,” Amos said. “He was, but he got fired a while back due to misconduct.”

“What sort of misconduct?” Ilse murmured.

Amos finally did look at her, wincing. “Inappropriate comments towards female hikers... Other female rangers. An allegation of harassment. Not enough to press charges, but enough to get the guy fired.”

“And you think this person might have something to do with all of this?” Ilse interjected before anyone else could redirect the question.

Amos shrugged. “Not sure. Just a thought, you know. One of the people he harassed... well, she was a friend of mine. Didn't seem right he just got away with it.”

Sawyer shared a look with Ilse, peering over Amos's shoulder.

Ilse glanced back at the ranger. “This guy have a name?”

“Yeah, yeah, George Dudley,” said Amos. “We called him Duds. But look, he was fired last year but he's still been around a few times. Kinda hard to ban a guy from a state park, you know. He sometimes still pesters rangers and hikers. If any of us see him around, we keep an eye or run him off depending. But he's still been around.”

“This George Dudley,” Sawyer said, clearing his throat, “Got an address?” This question, he directed towards the sheriff.

The pinch-faced man with the silver star paused, his fingers tapping against the brown brim of his hat, but then he dipped his head once. “Might do,” he muttered. “I seem to remember some of those harassment complaints.” The sheriff pulled his phone out, clicked through a couple of apps then paused.

Ilse and Sawyer both watched the man for a moment, but then after a second, he raised the screen, turning it towards Amos. “This the guy?”

Ilse also leaned in peering towards the face of a man with handsome, but delicate features. His eyes were twinkling as if on the verge of some joke.

“Yeah, that's Duds,” said Amos, nodding. He leaned in further. “That's his address, too.”

Sawyer peered over the sheriff's shoulder and said, “Mind sending me a copy of that?” He pulled out a business card, sliding it into the sheriff's waiting hand.

“I guess,” the sheriff said, sighing softly and glancing around the trampled forest floor. “We're busy here as it is. Let me know, though, before you arrest the creep, got it?” he said, his voice hardening.

Sawyer held up a hand. “Scout's honor.” Then, the tall agent moved towards Ilse, nodding towards one of the ATVs. “Mind if we borrow it, Amos? We need to get back to the trail.”

Mr. Lee hesitated, but then looked towards a couple of his co-workers and sighed. “Yeah. I can get a ride back. Help yourself; just leave it by the trailhead and stow the key in the lockbox on the side. Combination is 6-2-1.”

Sawyer flashed a thumbs up, already slipping into the saddle. Reluctantly, Ilse climbed on back, muttering in his ear, “Drive slowly this time.”

Sawyer's thumb lowered and he gripped the handlebars, throttling the engine and already picking up speed as they moved back towards the trail.

George Dudley. It didn't exactly sound like the name of a twisted serial killer.

Then again, if he knew the park well and had a habit of harassing woman, he certainly had a psychological profile of concern.

Ilse held onto the metal handles on either side of the ranger's vehicle as they continued to pick up speed, through the trail gouged by the rangers earlier in the afternoon. Ilse ducked low, gritting her teeth and wondering now if she was more worried about trusting her life to Sawyer's driving skills or about confronting a possible serial killer in his own home.

CHAPTER NINE

Ilse glanced through the sunroof at the thin wisps of cloud cover introducing across the sunny, summer sky. Afternoon had now turned to early evening. The journey from the preserve had taken less than a half hour. As the tires scraped against the sidewalk and Sawyer pulled the sedan to a stop, Ilse glanced through the window, past a broken mailbox. Half the mailbox post still jutted up, an accusing finger of wood, but the metal box itself lay discarded amidst overgrown weeds at the base of the post.

Her eyes drifted from the broken box towards the small house set against the backdrop of the forest preserve and a thin, wire-mesh fence distinguishing the property line.

Ilse stepped out of the car first, standing beneath the sunny, evening sky, part of her hoping the arrival of clouds heralded cooler weather.

"It doesn't look like much," Sawyer said, as he also exited the vehicle and slammed the car door. A puff of dust swirled from the asphalt with the motion, sweeping across the road.

"He's right up against the park," Ilse said softly.

"It gives him access," Sawyer replied, nodding once. The two of them stood by the car a moment longer, both of them steeling themselves for what came next.

Ilse, like Sawyer she assumed, simply couldn't shake the images.

So many bodies, frozen stiff. Most of them young women. A couple of men, also young. All of them dressed, posed. She shuddered, absentmindedly brushing her bangs past her injured ear.

From the side of the house, Ilse heard a sound like a table saw, or an electric sander. Sawyer frowned, briefly, his hand moving towards his hip.

The sound stopped, and a man emerged around the side of the house, strolling up the driveway. The man had a toolbelt and clutched a long plank of wood in one gloved hand.

For the moment, the man glanced at the wooden plank, dusting it with his free hand and muttering to himself as he did.

He hadn't noticed them yet.

"Excuse me," said Ilse, raising a hand and waving, "Mr. Dudley?"

The man jolted, dropping a hammer and raising the plank of wood like a defensive barrier. He stared at the two of them, swallowing, his eyes wide. It was the same man from the picture.

He was handsome, though small, with a slight frame. He still had the same smiling eyes she'd seen in the picture of his driver's license, but now, though his eyes were still creased with laugh lines, they were also forming a frown which fixed on Ilse and Tom.

"Who are you?" he snapped.

"Mr. Dudley?" Ilse said, carefully, "We're here to talk to you."

She hesitated, glancing at Sawyer, but again, he remained quiet, content to allow the rookie to take the lead on this one. She swallowed back her nerves, shifting uncomfortably, but trying to look professional. Trying to pretend like she belonged.

"I'm not interested in what you're selling," said the suspect, waving a hand dismissively. He ducked, picked up the hammer and then arrived at the mailbox.

With the newly cut plank of wood, he began to press it against the base of the mailbox but then paused, letting out a soft curse.

"Too wide?" Sawyer asked, innocently.

"I'm busy. Go bother the Gibsons across the street."

"Ever heard the saying," Sawyer said, making no move to comply, "measure twice, cut once?"

The man who was now finagling with the mailbox in the weeds looked up, one hand braced against his leather toolbelt. "You cops?" he snapped.

Sawyer crossed his arms. "Are you expecting cops?"

"No. You just act like cops. Like you own the place." Mr. Dudley dusted off his hands and glared at Sawyer. Slowly, he got to his feet, resting his hammer against the top of the splintered wooden post. "What's this about?"

Sawyer, with lethargic movements, removed his identification, flipped it, then lowered it again. "FBI," he said. "We're here about your job at the park."

"FBI?" he snorted. "What, they find a body?"

Ilse and Sawyer shared another look, standing at the mouth of the man's driveway. Ilse studied his expression, the twitch in the corner of his eye. His hands turned inwards, pressed tight, looking for something to do. A sign of nervousness. Nerves didn't mean dishonesty, though. She reserved judgment, still watching.

He hesitated, his sneer slipping. "Hang on, for real? They found a body?" The man dropped his hammer again, and this time it barely missed his foot. He held out his hands in placation. "Hang on," he said, quickly. "This is a mistake. I don't work there anymore."

"We know," Sawyer said.

"You were fired, yes?" Ilse said, quietly. "Do you mind telling us about the situation?"

"It wasn't much," the guy said, rubbing his jaw. "Shouldn't I have a lawyer here?"

"Would you like a lawyer?" Sawyer said.

He paused, and then replied, "I didn't do anything. Maybe you should tell me what this is about before I decide."

"Victims in the park," Ilse said, carefully adjusting her sleeves. "We heard you were terminated from your place of employment because of how you treated female hikers and staff."

He snorted, waving a hand in the air, "I'll admit I was a bit overbearing. Can you blame a guy? It's hard hunting out there. I mean, you miss a hundred percent of the shots you don't take." Mr. Dudley shrugged, flashing a smile he likely meant to be coy, but came across as simpering.

"So you admit to harassing hikers and employees?"

He scowled. "I didn't harass anyone. I was a little too forward; I got fired, and that's that."

Ilse crossed her arms. "From what we hear, that *wasn't* that, though," she said carefully. "Is it true you still frequent the park?"

In answer, he turned, extending his arms as if presenting the trees. "Kind of hard to avoid. It's in my backyard. Plus, it's not like they own the forest." He turned again, jutting his chin out defiantly.

Agent Sawyer glanced at Ilse and waited for her to speak. "So you're saying you don't know anything about the victims?"

"What victims? We talking rape? I never would. Harassment? I don't harass. I'm just a little bit forward when asking for a dame's number. There's a whole book about it. Called *Tony Red Pill's Pickup Lines*. I can give you a copy if you'd like."

Sawyer scratched his jaw. "You saying you've simply been implementing these pickup lines?"

"I'm saying," the man said, "I'm not a creep. I'm just having some fun and I haven't assaulted anyone."

"Well, Mr. Dudley," said Ilse, carefully, watching his expression. "We're not here about harassment; we're here about murder. Multiple." She didn't blink, careful not to miss his instinctual reaction. The moment she said it, though, his eyes widened, and he flinched as if he'd been slapped.

"Hang on, murder? So they *did* find a body? Shit."

"Murders," Ilse said, emphasizing the final letter. "Multiple homicides."

The man began to shake his head wildly, all signs of the smile lines turning into worry wrinkles around his eyes. "Whoa, that's heavy. I didn't hurt anyone. Yeah, I sometimes go back to the park. It's a good place to pick up athletic girls. I have a type. All consensual," he added quickly, waving a finger towards Sawyer. "I didn't hurt anyone."

"You have an alibi for the last few weeks?" Sawyer said.

"I got better than that," the man retorted with a relieved little gasp, his nostrils flaring. "I have an alibi for every night these last two weeks."

"Every night?" Sawyer said.

Mr. Dudley fished out his phone, already cycling through it. "Like I said, you miss all the shots, of a hundred well—wait, no, no, you miss a percent of the..." he trailed off, frowning. "Whatever the quote is. I do very well for myself. Not everyone thinks I'm harassing. A lot of them think I'm charming."

Sawyer frowned. He leaned in, glancing at the phone. "What am I looking at?"

"Matches," the man said. "Girls I've gone out with. You can tell the ones that'll let you take them back to your place on the first night by their profile pictures. See, the lower the blouse, the more likely. It's all down to a science. In that book. I could get you a copy if you—"

"I don't want your book. You're saying that every night this week you've been with a different woman?"

The man nodded his head quickly. "Alive," he added. "You can call all of them. They'll vouch for me. That's a lot of witnesses. When were these people hurt in the park? Couldn't have been me. I'm usually back home in my love cave. And I work six days a week. I'm air-tight, man. Air-tight."

Ilse tried not to wince at the phrase *love cave.*

"I'm going to check your alibi," Sawyer said, pointing at the man. "If any of these women deny having spent time with you, I'll be back."

The man didn't seem the least bit worried. "It's fine. They were happy to hang out, and happy to leave. All of them knew what we were getting into. Just casual. Every night this week. The week before, I had a couple of stuffy prudes. But I'm sure they'd still remember me."

Sawyer looked past the man, fixing his eyes on Ilse. She massaged the bridge of her nose, letting out a frustrated sigh. This fellow was a creep and a womanizer, but that didn't mean he killed anyone. He seemed confident his alibi would check out. Sawyer was cycling through the women Mr. Dudley had matched with, logging the women's numbers. As this proceeded, Mr. Dudley said, carefully, "Not that it's any of my business, but were any of the park rangers victims as well?"

Ilse frowned. "Is that important?

He shrugged. "I still have some friends there; I didn't hear anything about that. Which means, why would it be me? If I was angry about getting fired, trying to take something out on them, why would the rangers be fine? I haven't heard anything about any of them getting hurt."

Ilse hesitated and looked at Sawyer. The FBI agent muttered, "We can't confirm or deny details of the case."

"Look," the man said, in a wheedling tone, putting on a smile that didn't quite fit his lips, "if I were the cops, I wouldn't be looking at ex-employees. I'd be looking at those weirdos who stay camped at the park all year long. There are some real strange cookies there."

"Campers?" Ilse said, wrinkling her nose.

He glanced at her, "Not just campers," he said. "Some real nut jobs. I've seen them. Had to clean up after them more than once back when I was in the park. If you want to find some psycho killer, it'll be one of those guys. Mark my words."

Ilse shivered, not quite liking the way Mr. Dudley was looking at her. "Say," he said, slowly, "you have very nice eyes, you know that?" he said. "What are you doing tonight?"

Sawyer growled, "That's enough." He waved his phone beneath Dudley's nose. "I'll be back. If this doesn't check out, you're going to have questions to answer."

Again, the man seemed completely unperturbed. He winked at Ilse, giving a little wave. She frowned back, turning slowly and following Sawyer back towards the sedan. Already, Sawyer was cycling through the numbers and Ilse could hear the faint ring tone in the background.

"Where next?" she said carefully.

"I'll check the numbers," he muttered, quiet enough so Dudley couldn't hear. They slipped into the car, doors shutting.

"Think it's him?" Ilse said, the sound of the ring tone louder now in the closed car.

Sawyer shrugged. "Seems spineless. Seems soft."

"Is that a no?"

He didn't respond.

"Well," Ilse continued, "maybe we should check out those campsites. Just to be sure. If anyone would have access, it would be overnighters."

Sawyer's phone connected at the same time as the car started.

"Hello, Ms. Alvarez," he said, gruffly, "my name is Agent Sawyer with the FBI. I was wondering if I could ask you about a Mr. Dudley."

Ilse winced as a sudden tirade flooded the other end of the phone, and the sounds of a scorned lover filled the sedan. Asphalt crunched beneath the tires as they pulled away from Mr. Dudley's house, circling back to head towards the park entrance once more. What had Mr. Dudley meant by nut jobs? Among the campers, no less? People familiar with the park and its terrain.

Ilse folded her hands, again trying to push away the thoughts of what she'd seen in that muddy pit

CHAPTER TEN

Now, the clouds had rolled in like waves. The afternoon skies slowly dipped closer to evening, and as Ilse and Sawyer exited their car, the first hints of darkness pressed in around them, through the tall trees and along the dirt roads.

Sawyer slowly lowered his phone, scowling as he did and muttering something beneath his breath.

"Was that the last number?" Ilse asked, glancing towards the wiry agent.

Sawyer huffed, staring at his phone before nodding once. "Last one."

"Did she confirm the alibi also?"

Sawyer seamed loathe to respond at first, but then he shrugged and jammed the phone back into his pocket as if it were somehow personally offensive. "Looks like Casanova was with a girl the night Kristine was accosted. Like he said, he's got alibis for the whole week. Not all of them spoke too highly of him, but they all said he was with them."

Ilse wrinkled her nose in disgust, trying not to think too much about the womanizing ex park-ranger.

"Well," she said, facing the nearest campsite and waving a hand vaguely towards two tents, "think he's right about some of the clientele in the campgrounds? I was thinking we could do a sort of grid pattern, starting in the Southern sites and moving North as we—"

Sawyer shouted, "Hey, you, lady—I have a question!"

Ilse blinked, mouth open, caught-mid sentence as Sawyer stormed off in the direction of a young woman and young man both wearing tie-dyed t-shirts and boasting dreadlocks.

"Or we could do that," Ilse muttered beneath her breath, falling into step behind the mule-headed agent.

The young woman had blonde braids and wore spectacles perched on the edge of an upturned, celestial nose. The man had stronger features with a thick beard flecked with crumbs. Both of them smelled like cannabis and body odor.

"What's up, man?" said the woman, eyeing Sawyer up and down.

"Agent Sawyer, FBI," said Tom, not even bothering to flash his credentials. He crossed his arms, his flannel wrinkling. "I had a couple of questions."

The moment he'd said "FBI," though, both hippies frowned.

"See ya later, man," the woman said.

"Hang on," protested the taciturn agent.

"Nah—see ya, dude," said the bearded fellow.

Together, the two of them turned, strolling off, shooting the occasional look in Sawyer's direction, muttering to each other, then breaking into a series of giggles. Ilse couldn't help but notice the woman's hand kept hovering over her left pocket as if trying to hide something from view. But though Ilse noted the subconscious gesture, she didn't point it out.

They weren't here to interfere with illicit substances.

"Well," Ilse said, hesitantly, "that went well."

"Mhmm," Sawyer replied.

"Perhaps, if we take a more cautious, thorough approach, we could—"

"Hey! Hey you!" Sawyer yelled, stalking off in the direction of an older couple near a picnic table. "I have some questions."

Again, Ilse huffed a breath, rolling her eyes. She watched as Sawyer approached the elderly couple who were both eyeing him suspiciously. For her part, she turned slowly, facing one of the other tents, further up the trail.

She glanced towards Sawyer, where he was now chatting with the older man, but then began to move in the other direction, up the dusty path. Evening was quickly approaching, and while Sawyer had always proven a competent field agent, he often went with his gut rather than a plan. On top of it, he'd been acting strangely ever since they'd got this job—even back at the hospital something had seemed off-kilter with Tom.

Besides, interviewing the older couple didn't make much sense to Ilse, not that Sawyer had paused long enough for input.

The victims...

She shivered as another flash of memory reminded her of the scene back in that muddy pit.

The victims had all been young. Most of them young women.

It made sense if some deranged camper was harassing people; it would be the sort in his target demographic. So instead of joining Sawyer, Ilse set off, staying within shouting distance, but heading towards the other, orange tent she'd spotted through the trees.

As she stepped off the path, drawing nearer, she smiled politely towards a biker heading in the other direction. She waved a hand in front of her face, clearing dust and blinking against the sudden cloud, while rolling up her sweater and stepping off the trail between a cleared-out portion of flat ground.

She smelled smoke and heard the soft crackle of fire as she drew nearer. Voices arose over the sound of crackling flames. As she ducked under a prickling fir bough, she spotted *two* campsites instead of one.

On one side, a middle-aged man and a couple of kids were toasting marshmallows over a low fire. A woman stood off by a miniature wooden cabin Ilse hadn't spotted from the road. The woman was laughing and taking pictures of her family where they crowded around the fire.

On the other side of the clearing, past a small green number "4" painted on a post jutting from the sand, a second campsite was in worse shape. A few scattered chips bags lay jutting against an old stone along with some crushed cans.

The woman and her family by the fire seemed to be giving this second campsite a wide berth. Ilse stepped along the flat ground, moving away from the camping family and heading in the direction of this next site.

She avoided a smashed beer bottle, slipping past a rocky protrusion. Now, she saw the orange tent she'd spotted earlier. A small, slumping affair suggesting whoever had assembled it didn't have much experience. Another fire was going in this campsite—or, perhaps, *attempting* to go. Mostly, it was smoke and what looked like sticks picked up from the ground.

The smoldering sticks in the fire pit were surrounded by six figures—all of them looked to be about college-aged.

A few of them were drinking from more brown bottles, while two of them were smoking something, passing it back and forth.

Ilse couldn't quite make out what they were saying as she drew nearer. But the low mumble of voices gave way to a sudden peel of laughter.

"Are you for real?" one of the boys was saying, taking another long drink and then letting loose a burp.

"Gross," said a girl who was sitting further off from the others, shoulders slumped, hands clasped in front of her. She wore a small, pink beanie low over her eyebrows, nearly hiding her eyes.

"Hey," the boy with the bottle said, suddenly waving the glass container towards Ilse. "Who are you?"

Ilse waved, clearing her throat. She glanced towards the joint and said, carefully, "I'm helping out the park with some questions."

"Yeah?" the girl in the beanie said. "What sorta questions?"

"We're looking for anyone who might have been harassing campers. Especially young women," Ilse said, carefully, her eyes flicking from one of the young campers to the next.

The man with the bottle frowned and shot a quick look towards a second young woman next to the fire. She tugged at her straw-colored braids and wrinkled her nose. A subconscious gesture, but one that signified disgust. She folded her arms in a defensive posture, and twisted, ever so slightly, allowing her back to rest against the rigid wooden log they were using as a bench.

Ilse zeroed in on the young woman, waiting patiently, allowing her attention and the silence to serve as query.

The young man kept staring at the woman with the straw-colored hair. At last, she coughed, still staring at the fire and murmured, "I know a guy that's been like that," she said, frowning.

Ilse leaned in, careful not to get too close lest she spook the camper. Behind her, Ilse heard the sound of slowly approaching footsteps. She glanced back to see a scowling Agent Sawyer approaching up a dusty road. Carefully, out of sight from the young woman, she raised a hand, holding it up to hold Sawyer at bay.

The taciturn agent hesitated, but to his credit, he went still on the side of the dirt path at the edge of the camp. A couple of the children in the adjacent campsite were shooting looks towards Sawyer, but the tall agent flashed them a reassuring and rare smile. He remained standing in the shadow of the trees, inclined in Ilse's direction, but waiting on her call.

For her part, Ilse just listened.

"I—there's an old fart that comes around here a lot," the young woman ventured, hesitantly. She shifted again, some of the flecks of wood and moss scattering behind her with the motion; her shadow stretched out in the soft flames, extending towards the orange tent behind the group.

"Oh, yeah," said another one of the young women. This girl had a shaved head and a tattoo of a small black rainbow over one cheek. "I remember that creep," she said, wagging her head. She took a sip from her own bottle and then tossed the empty container into the fire. "The weirdo kept trying to talk to me by the well."

The girl with the braids wagged her head. "Exactly. Same with me. He once followed me into the woods, kept staring at me."

"Pervert," muttered the young man with the bottle, leaning protectively towards the girl.

Ilse cleared her throat hesitantly. "I don't mean to pry, but did he say anything?"

The young women shared a look, shrugged, and glanced back at Ilse. "He asked me for my number," said the one with the tattoo. "Just kept asking even after I told him to scram. I yelled at him—usually that's enough to get the skeez-balls running, but it only seemed to encourage him. He said something like, 'I like it when they struggle.'" She shivered, her face making an expression like sucking lemons. "That's when I ran."

"Did he chase you?" Ilse said, her heart pounding.

But now the woman seemed irritated by the line of questioning, glancing around and realizing her friends were all listening and staring at her. She scoffed. "It wasn't anything. The weirdo couldn't keep up. Didn't chase. Besides, if he had..." She reached into her pocket and pulled out a flip knife, holding it in front of the fire. "It would've gone bad for him."

The first girl crossed her arms again, sighing. "That's horrible," she muttered. "He didn't chase me, but he kept making kissing sounds when I was trying to go to the bathroom. I saw his shadow under the door. I got so worried I called Jeb."

The young man with the bottle nodded. "I remember that. I was going to bust his ass, but when I got there, the weirdo was gone." He scowled. "But I heard from another guy that the old weirdo bothers a lot of people."

"Do you have a name for this man?" Ilse asked, carefully, glancing between the campers.

"Calls himself Jeffrey," said the man. "That's it. No last name. He camps outside the grounds. Not technically allowed, but when rangers move him, he just heads right back. He's close enough to a rental spot that they've pretty much given up on trying to relocate him."

"Jeffrey?" Ilse said. "Do you know which campsite he's near?"

"Thirty," said Jeb without blinking. "I checked when I heard how he treated Sam." He put a protective arm around the girl with the braids. She shivered and leaned in, staring at the fire again.

Ilse nodded slowly. "Thank you," she murmured. "Sorry for asking.

Have a nice evening. And..." she hesitated. "Stay near each other, tonight. Alright?"

With those ominous words and another nod of farewell, which wasn't returned, Ilse rounded and moved off through the forest in the direction of Sawyer. The agent stared at her from beneath his baseball cap as darkness crested the horizon, moving from late afternoon to deep evening. The sky above streaked with black ink-like stains, and beams of moonlight were caught and filtered by thick clouds still rolling across the horizon.

The last thing they needed was a rainstorm, but the weather on the Olympic Peninsula could be somewhat unpredictable at times.

"Anything?" Sawyer said as Ilse drew nearer.

She stepped over a tangle of roots, moving back in the direction of the dusty path. "Campsite thirty," she said, quietly, her eyes darting towards one of the wooden signs at the trailhead numbering the campsites. She frowned, then pointed off to the left. "That way."

Sawyer fell into step, allowing her to take the lead up the trail, under the cover of mounting night. "What's at campsite thirty?"

"A guy named Jeffrey, apparently. He's known around the campsites for creeping on young women."

Sawyer's jaw went rigid, and Ilse noticed one of his hands bunched at his hip. The hand released a second later, though, his fingers spreading and pressing against his shirt. He let out a soft breath but didn't reply. Again, Ilse was struck by some of her partner's odd behavior over the last few days.

As they moved up the old, dirt road, she glanced at Sawyer and said, softly, "Is everything alright with you?"

Sawyer just grunted, refusing to look at her, keeping his eyes on the road ahead.

"I'm not trying to pry," she said. "I just want to make sure you're okay."

"Doc, don't do your thing with me. Get it? I'm not a patient." Then Sawyer frowned, picking up the pace and marching further along the trail, past the occasional RV under a canopy of trees, or along a row of tents hidden amidst the forest on flat ground.

Ilse sighed, picking up her pace now to keep up with the recalcitrant man. He was right, though. He wasn't her patient, nor was he a suspect in a case. And yet, sometimes, Ilse found it difficult to engage with people in any other capacity. She knew he was behaving oddly, but she still couldn't quite place why. She remembered on the last case they'd taken, with a serial killer cutting people up and organizing their body parts into a gruesome display of lettering, he'd mentioned how much he hated when children were involved. One of the bodies had been displayed at a high school.

Now, he seemed similarly troubled.

She glanced at Tom, studying his back as he stalked ahead of her. What sort of man punched a superior agent and yet was good enough at his job to be reassigned instead of arrested? What sort of man could face gruesome killers and monsters without blinking, and yet balk at some cases rather than others?

He was a strange mixture, and Ilse found it equal parts sad and fascinating.

"Not here," Sawyer said, suddenly pulling up.

Ilse, lost in her train of thought, nearly bumped into the tall agent. She hesitated, then glanced down to the twin numbers poking out of the trail, attached to a metal wire. *30.*

She stared past Sawyer at the flat, empty camping area. "Right," she said, quietly. "According to the campers back there, he sticks near the campsite, but tends to set up deeper in the forest, off the designated area." She hesitated, glancing around. "I'm not sure which direction—"

"This way," Sawyer said suddenly, his eyes glued to the trees.

Ilse couldn't see what Sawyer did. The way she felt with people and their thoughts, Sawyer seemed to manage with terrain. A broken branch or scattered leaves to Ilse didn't mean much, but to Sawyer it was the same as a nervous tic, or an auditory-triggered memory cluster.

Now, he stalked across the campsite, over the dusty ground. He made a beeline towards a gap between the trees. Only then did Ilse notice the tire tread in the ground. "What's that?" she said, staring at the single wheel mark moving along the dirt.

"Wheelbarrow," Sawyer said without batting an eye.

He snapped off a branch, tossing it aside in order to prevent it from whipping back and striking Ilse. He moved under the branches, along the dusty path, heading further into the dark forest. Ahead, the moonlight was now filtered by clouds and branches, leaving them in darkness. A small flashlight emerged from Sawyer's belt, the long, white beam extending through the trees and catching bark and branches in long, eerie shadows.

Ilse's breathing quickened as she followed the FBI agent further into the darkness.

"Ah, there we are," he murmured, ducking a bit lower, like a hunter at the sight of prey.

Ilse followed suit, staring through the branches as she followed Sawyer along the make-shift path cleared by the wheelbarrow. It took a few seconds longer for her to spot what he had.

There, amidst another clearing, deeper in the woods than any of the other campsites, she spotted a small lean-to made of sticks and beams with branches for a ceiling. A small, cold firepit, without a whiff of smoke, suggested it hadn't been used in a while. A long line of laundry, though, stretched between two trees above a grimy hammock suggested the off-grid campsite was still in use.

"Think this is it?" Ilse murmured.

In answer, Sawyer raised his flashlight, aiming towards the lean-to. "FBI!" he called. "Jeffrey?" he said, louder. "Hello? Is anyone there? FBI!"

No answer.

Ilse felt a slight shiver along her spine, wincing as she did. The two women back at the campground had seemed certain this man was a threat. She had heard the fear in their voices, seen the protective posture of the young man. Whoever this Jeffrey was, he clearly hadn't made friends with the other campers.

Sawyer kept his flashlight fixed on the lean-to. "FBI!" he said, louder now.

Again, there was no response.

As they drew nearer, stepping into the clearing, a faint smell of mold and sweat reached Ilse's nostrils. The odor of body stench emanating from the lean-to also suggested the campsite was still in use. She wrinkled her nose, the same way Sam had back at the campsite, and watched as Sawyer approached the lean-to, flashing his light through gaps in the branches.

"Anything?" Ilse said, her voice hoarse, her feet braced as if for sudden motion.

Sawyer, though, kept his hand hovering near his weapon. Instead of answering, he flashed his light through the lean-to again and shook his head. "Just a cot. No one's home." Sawyer began to turn, but then hesitated, frowning.

"What is it?" Ilse said, staring.

Sawyer reached out, one hand tugging at a branch and then he pulled something free, holding it up for Ilse to see in the flashlight beam.

Ilse blinked in confusion, but then her eyes widened.

“Is that hair?” she said.

A long lock of frayed, blonde hair dangled from Sawyer's hand, wrapped around a stick. “Just jutting through the wall,” Sawyer murmured. He placed the stick back, wiping his hand off on his jeans before aiming the flashlight in the direction of the laundry line Ilse had spotted.

“He's a creep for sure,” Sawyer said after a moment.

Ilse turned, following the direction of the indicating light beam. There, hanging from a laundry line, she spotted a couple of shirts and some old pants. But also, amidst the laundry, she spotted bras and panties. Lacy, frilly underwear. Some of the underwear, with little stenciled teddy bears, suggested they might have belonged to a child.

Ilse shivered, staring at the creepy collection, feeling her heart skip a beat.

“Well,” Sawyer muttered. “Not looking good for Mr. Jeffrey,” he muttered. “Normal for creeps out in the woods to collect female underwear?”

Ilse winced, swallowing once and staring at the laundry line which swayed on the faint breeze.

“It doesn't look good,” she said, softly.

“Yeah?” A voice suddenly called. “Doesn't look good sneaking around a man's house, either, does it? What the hell do you two think you're doing?”

Sawyer's flashlight beam whirled, and Ilse spun with it. A man was stepping from behind the lean-to, a weapon clutched tightly in one fist, aiming towards both of them.

Sawyer's own hand darted towards his firearm, but the man with the gun clicked his tongue. “Ah, shit—no you don't, I'll ventilate you if you try. Who the hell are you? And what are you doing sneaking around my home?”

CHAPTER ELEVEN

Ilse's heart hammered and felt like it was trying to migrate to her throat. She felt a sudden urge to scream, summoned from somewhere deep in her psyche. Standing in a forest, threatened by a predator, she was reminded of her own memories. Her breathing came rapid and ragged.

The man, though, didn't much resemble her father. This fellow was poorly kept, with stringy, oily hair which hung past his shoulders. He had a thick beard and an untrimmed mustache. His clothing looked days old with mud-stains, frayed at the hem. His eyes were sunken in his face, and he kept the gun pointed at Sawyer's head. He raised a pale hand, flicking his fingers to the side. "Get away from my house," he snapped, growling as he did. "Get—get!"

Ilse shot a look at Sawyer; she breathed in, out, exhaling longer than she inhaled, trying to calm her racing nerves. Sawyer, though, didn't back down at all. He kept his hand on his weapon, glaring at the fellow. Ilse felt exposed—wishing they'd allowed her to carry a firearm. But she still wasn't technically allowed until she was approved as an agent.

"FBI," Sawyer said, firmly. "I'm Agent Sawyer. This is Dr. Beck. Are you Jeffrey?"

"I don't give a shit who you are," snapped the wild-haired man. "You're trespassing."

"I'm FBI. *Federals*," Sawyer insisted.

"And I'm a guy with a gun," snapped the man. "Now get the hell back before I cut you down."

Ilse felt another shiver. The man seemed serious. He didn't seem to care whatsoever about the FBI, as if the acronym itself were unfamiliar to him, or irrelevant.

Sawyer glanced towards the underwear dangling from the wash line, his eyes skipping past the one with teddy-bear printing. His eyes hardened and he looked back at Jeffrey. "I'm not going to warn you again," Sawyer said, scowling into the barrel of the gun aimed at his head. "Drop it and get on the ground before I make you."

"Sawyer," Ilse said, carefully, wincing. "Maybe we should just—"

Jeffrey interrupted. "I told you to get the hell back!" he screamed, taking a step forward and now jamming his gun between Sawyer's eyes. "Are you dumb? Get back! Back! Back!"

His voice rose in volume as he spoke and increased in pitch until he was practically screeching the word. His eyes widened; his nostrils flared. His unkempt, grimy features stood out in the faint beam of Sawyer's flashlight which still angled off to the side.

Sawyer though, seemed to have decided the best course of action here was to out-stubborn the man. It was as if someone had installed a rod of iron in Sawyer's spine. The lanky agent stood stiff-backed, defiant, chin raised to meet Jeffrey's knuckles. He didn't even blink as he stared down the barrel of the gun.

"I said last warning," Sawyer murmured. "And I'm a man of my word."

Ilse spotted it before their adversary did. Sawyer's hand tightened again; his body braced. In a second, Ilse knew, despite the gun at his head, he was going to try something rash.

She winced, felt her stomach drop towards the vicinity of her feet. If she didn't do something, Sawyer was going to get himself shot.

"Wait—wait," she said, quickly, also raising her voice, also increasing the pitch. Partly because she was also frightened, but partly because in therapy, *joining* with someone could often alleviate tension.

She held up her hands, taking an intentionally slow step back, away from the man's lean-to. Sawyer hesitated now, glancing towards her.

Jeffrey's eyes flit from the agent to Ilse. "I said get back!" he screamed.

Joining didn't always mean matching the tone, but sometimes also matching the emotional output of a client. Or, in other cases, matching the emotional demands. Rather than mirroring, joining was about matching energy levels or emotional expectation in both demeanor, body language, and tone.

Now, Ilse shrunk in on herself, folding her arms, ducking her shoulders, hanging her head, making herself as small as possible. Mostly it was subtle, but anyone paying attention would have seen the obvious effort. Still, at the same time, she said, in a much quieter, docile voice. "We're sorry for coming so close to your home," she said. "We didn't mean to intrude. We just wanted to talk with you." She didn't quite meet Jeffrey's eyes, realizing that he refused to make eye contact as well. She kept glancing off to the woods, away from his house.

Sawyer seemed on the verge of clobbering the guy still. But the gun was still raised.

“I told you to get back!” the man said, still loud.

“Sawyer,” Ilse said, yelling also. “Sawyer, get back!” She commanded, matching the tone, the energy of the camper.

Sawyer gave her a hard look, but at the earnestness in her gaze, he finally sighed, his hand relaxing. He slowly raised his hands and took a step back.

“Good,” snapped Jeffrey.

“Good!” Ilse repeated. “Leave the man's house alone,” she demanded.

Sawyer took another step back, joining her on the path. Ilse kept glancing off to the side, refusing to make eye contact. “Jeffrey,” she said, quietly, in as calm a voice as she could muster, “we need to talk to you. Could you please let us talk to you? It doesn't have to be here. We won't trespass. We can go somewhere else. Would you do that?”

The man hesitated, his gun still hovering. His eyes kept widening then squinting, never quite looking either of them in the face. He breathed heavily, his chest rising and falling in rapid motions beneath his grimy clothing. He reached out, poking at the tangled mess of blonde hair jutting from his wall, readjusting it in some pattern unfamiliar to anyone but himself.

As he did, his gun lowered slightly.

Sawyer began to move, but Ilse held out a hand.

“Could we talk to you?” Ilse said softly.

The man lowered his weapon completely now, tucking his pistol back into his waistband now that both of them were far enough away.

“We can talk. Not at my home. This is my home. Go away.”

“That's fine,” Ilse said, quickly. “That's fine. Just—could you come with us? You'll need to leave the gun here.”

The man frowned, scowling at her, one hand twitching back towards his weapon.

Sawyer, though, seemed to have had enough of Ilse's method. “Nice try, doc,” he muttered. Then, his own weapon leapt into his hand, and he barked, “Hands in the air!”

The man's eyes widened, his fingers scrambling on his half-lowered gun. “No!” Ilse yelled, matching his tone from earlier. “We won't enter your house. We won't! We won't!”

His hand froze, he licked his lips. Sawyer's firearm aimed towards the man's chest—fixating center mass. Jeffrey licked his lips again, his eyes wide.

"Not here. No trespassing," he said, shaggy eyebrows flicking up beneath an equally unkempt fringe.

"Not here," Ilse insisted, nodding. "Not here. Please. Just lower the gun. We can talk somewhere else."

Sawyer took another step back from the man's house, another step away. But he kept his weapon raised. Ilse also retreated another step.

Jeffrey watched their feet against the detritus. He breathed a soft little sigh of relief the further they stepped away from his home. Then, carefully, he raised his hands. "Alright," he murmured. "We talk. But I come to you. Don't come near my home."

***

Jeffrey sat in handcuffs across from Tom and Ilse, glaring at the metal table. Once they'd managed to get him away from the house, Sawyer had disarmed and cuffed him. The man had fought something fierce, like a cat in an alley.

Sawyer had proven stronger, though, and now, after a call to the sheriff's office, they found themselves sitting in Interrogation Room Two.

The chairs were soft, plastic—the table bolted to the floor. The light above beat down on them. Jeffrey kept shooting reproachful scowls in Tom's direction, occasionally rubbing at his cuffed wrists and muttering something beneath his breath.

"That's not an answer," Sawyer snapped for the second time in as many minutes. "What were you doing with women's underwear in your home? Whose hair was that?"

"Ugly, yes. He is. Very, very ugly. And annoying. And stupid," Jeffrey was muttering beneath his breath, staring at the table as if he were speaking to his forearm.

"Excuse me?" Sawyer insisted.

"Awful voice," murmured Jeffrey. "Gross and awful. Ugly voice. Piece of shit." He giggled to himself a moment later, twisting in the seat, his cuffs straining where they interlocked against the table, rattling in their fixture.

"Are you talking to me?" Sawyer said, frowning, leaning in now.

But Jeffrey kept giggling beneath his breath, again refusing to meet Sawyer's gaze.

Ilse watched from where she sat next to Sawyer, across the table.

She waited a moment longer and could feel Tom tensing next to her. Then she reached out, placing a hand on Sawyer's forearm in a calming gesture. She spoke, her tone soft, soothing, addressing her words to Jeffrey.

"I'm sorry we trespassed in your home," she said quietly. "Thank you for coming to talk with us here."

The man tilted his head, not quite meeting her gaze. Instead of muttering beneath his breath, though, he said, louder, "Not nice to trespass pretty-faced lady. Not nice. You're nice though." He smirked, not looking at her face, but certainly looking almost everywhere else. He even ducked his head beneath the table to try and look under it at her.

Ilse shifted uncomfortably but refused to let this ogling deter her.

Sawyer's fist tensed, but she kept her hand on his wrist, still soothing. Clearly, Jeffrey suffered from paranoia, and some form of developmental disorder. The way he spoke to himself, the way he tilted his head as if listening suggested, perhaps, he might have some level of schizophrenia also, though it was far too early for her to suggest that diagnosis.

Still, this man was not well.

He lifted his head from staring at her legs beneath the table and looked up again, smirking, though not at her. "Not nice to trespass," he said again.

"No, no it isn't," she murmured. "Like I said, I'm sorry we did." She ignored his creepy behavior entirely, instead endeavoring to establish rapport. He wouldn't talk to Tom, but he seemed, at least partially, willing to communicate with Ilse. He kept shooting askance glances at her form, occasionally openly staring at her chest or her arms.

After another round of this open ogling, Sawyer slapped his hand on the table. "Cut it out," he snapped.

The man jolted as if he'd been shot, his head whipping up, staring at the ceiling now. He swallowed, his throat constricting as he glared unblinking at the lights. He murmured to himself, beneath his breath but loud enough for the agents to hear, "Yes... Yes he's a real asshole. Hers? I don't know about hers."

"Hey," Sawyer said, louder. "I'm warning you." He began to rise to his feet.

But Ilse caught his arm, guiding him back into his chair, patting him on the arm.

"Jeffrey," she said, softly, staring directly at him, refusing to rise to the bait of his behavior or comments, “While I'm sorry we trespassed in your house, I was wondering how long you'd been there? You seemed quite familiar with the place.”

He grunted, his head rolling on his shoulders, his long greasy hair shifting across his chest. “That's my home,” he said, his cuffs rattling again. He shrugged his shoulders, a stain near his lapel rising with the motion into the naked light above. “Been there a couple of years.”

Ilse blinked in surprise. “Years?”

He frowned at her, bobbing his head once. He drifted off, staring at her cheek now, his eyes tracing to her chin and hovering there.

“Two years is a long time,” Sawyer murmured beneath his breath. “Are you familiar with other parts of the park? Ever been to mile marker thirty-three?”

The man snorted beneath his breath, muttering, “Don't leave home much, do we? Don't gotta car.”

Ilse cleared her throat. “So you haven't been to mile marker thirty-three?”

He grinned, flashing a gap-toothed smile. “Nah. Haven't left my home in a long while. What would I want with the other side of the park? Did you know this place is over a million acres, hmm? Take a man ten lifetimes to cover it all.” He wagged his head. “Nah. I like my neck of the woods. You shouldn't have trespassed.”

Ilse glanced sidelong at Sawyer who was still glaring at Jeffrey. Ilse's own thoughts were likely traversing similar terrain. On one hand, Jeffrey hardly seemed together. And like he'd said, it didn't appear as if he owned a vehicle. Then again, his fingerprints weren't showing up in the system either, nor did he have any ID when he'd been arrested.

Now, the creepy forest-dweller was staring at Ilse's chest, openly, licking his lips.

She remembered now why she so often wore sweaters. Rising to her feet, she turned towards the door. A sudden scrape was followed by a grunt of pain, though, and she turned back to see Sawyer had yanked on the man’s cuffs, jerking him forward until his chest bounced off the table.

“Oops,” Sawyer said, dryly. “My bad.” Then he also arose, leaving the table.

Jeffrey glared daggers at the retreating form of Agent Sawyer as Ilse led him out into the hall, ignoring the occasional glance in her direction.

“Sorry about that,” Sawyer said, instantly, when they emerged in the hall of the sheriff's precinct.

Ilse sighed but shook her head. "I've dealt with worse than that on the weekly sometimes. Forget about that. What do you think of him as a suspect?"

"Don't like him. He's a piece of shit."

"Yes, but do you think he's likely behind the murders? Behind that lair we found?" Ilse shivered, swallowing at the memory.

Sawyer rubbed the back of his head, muttering beneath his breath, but then shrugged. "He's got no alibi. Too isolated. Also, clearly he gets his rocks off being a creep. Underwear back at his little hovel says he's got some screw loose."

"Yes, true. But…," Ilse winced, shaking her head. "He's paranoid, clearly. But I think he was playing up the angle, too. He knows what he's doing. His mannerisms changed when we got him from the woods to the precinct. Clearly socially inept, but that's not the same as antisocial personality disorder."

"What does that mean in human speak?"

"I mean...," she trailed off, huffing once. "I don't think his psychology matches our killer's. He's the sort of guy to make snide comments or ogle women around the campground, but he doesn't have the type of psychosis that matches the extreme degree of these crimes. For one, he allowed you to arrest him. For another, like you said, his gun wasn't loaded."

"So you think he's more bluff than bite?"

"That's exactly what I think. I think he's a lonely man in the woods. I think he has social development issues, and a clear issue with women, but that's not the same as..." She trailed off, allowing the silence to fill in the blanks.

"We didn't find a vehicle," Sawyer said. "He doesn't have one registered. To get from the campground to mile-marker thirty-three would be a bit of a trek just on foot. Especially to do so routinely..."

"Careful—you're starting to sound like you don't think it's him either."

"I sure as hell intend on keeping him in there as long as we can… Just in case... But...," Sawyer winced.

"But?"

He pulled his baseball cap off, fanning his face for a moment, then muttered. "Think it's time to call a meeting with the sheriff's deputies assigned to this. Some rangers are coming through also in case we need a search team."

“How will that help?” Ilse frowned, pushing off the wall and following as Sawyer began to lead down the hall once more.

“Not sure—that's up to you,” he called over his shoulder.

She frowned, skipping to keep up. “Hang on, what do you mean?”

“You're the shrink, doc. You know the psychology stuff. Someone's gotta lead the meeting.” He paused long enough to pat her on the shoulder and wink. “Might as well be you, yeah? Here, through there. Told 'em to wait in the conference room.”

Ilse briefly wondered when on earth Sawyer had the time to coordinate all of this. She frowned, wondering if one of his quick, five-minute bathroom breaks earlier had just been an excuse to ambush her with *this*.

She swallowed, staring after Sawyer as he entered through the glass door, stepping into the conference room and holding the frame ajar so she could follow.

Inside, she spotted a few deputies, a couple of rangers and even a forensic team, all waiting, glancing curiously towards the door.

Her heart hammered, worse, even, than when Jeffrey had pointed the gun at them. Public speaking—worse than a gunshot as far as she was concerned.

Still, perhaps Sawyer was right. They needed some direction, needed to narrow down the psychology of the killer. She'd just have to make sure she didn't make any mistakes. A lot was riding on this.

They'd kicked over the killer's hornet's nest, found his lair.

Which meant he'd either lay low for a while, hoping the storm would pass...

Or...

If they were unlucky, he'd react with aggression out of a sense of vengeance. They'd taken his lair, so he'd take something back...

She shivered, stepping into the conference room and feeling all eyes on her.

CHAPTER TWELVE

More deputies entered the room as she spoke, and Ilse felt the shivers along her spine spread to her fingertips. She shifted nervously, dusting at the bangs over her maimed ear and glancing askance around the room, trying to both make eye contact and not stare at anyone in particular.

This, gauging by the number of law officers in the room, was an all-hands-on-deck sort of situation.

Now, she stood next to a white board, a black marker in one hand and an eraser in the other. She hadn't found a use for either, but they provided a tactile sort of comfort.

Now, more than fifteen sets of eyes fixed on her, as if the entire precinct had shown up to watch her squirm.

Still, she'd seen Dr. Mitchell lecture in class before. As a TA, she'd once had to present his notes to the class herself. This wasn't so different, was it?

Not really. Except lives were on the line. And, plus, if she was wrong about anything, Sawyer would regret the day he invited her to train as an agent. Supervising Agent Rawley would probably fire her in an instant.

Still... She couldn't think that way. She had to focus.

Her hand tightened around the whiteboard marker; and she used it to gesticulate, swallowing again, breathing slowly and then, projecting her voice louder than she'd intended, she said, "As I was saying, in order to narrow down the psychological profile of our killer, we also have to look specifically at motivation..."

Her voice strained as she glanced around, a lump forming. She swallowed hesitantly, and it felt like the cops' eyes were boring a hole into her head. A couple in the back, near the door, seemed half asleep, arms crossed as they leaned against a glass window. Two rangers who were sitting by a coffee table both were murmuring to each other, ignoring her completely.

Still, she pressed on, her voice rising as she did, "There are multiple potential motives available currently. Firstly, a sexual deviant. The displays are for his own pleasure. The isolated nature of the space suggests he's familiar with the terrain, and familiar with the outdoors. The time it would have taken to scout out such a thing and to create the spectacle suggests he's old enough to have fallen into this pattern, but young enough to be physically adept in doing so. Another thought might involve schizophrenic tendencies, collecting trophies for company as he lives off the land." As she spoke, slowly, she began to pick up pace, remembering similar framing conversations she'd had with clients in the past. Especially when first introducing to their victimizers. Most of the clients she worked with survived trauma specifically related to killers, or even serial murderers. Many of them often asked, *Why?* And while the why of a killer's motives weren't always clear, they were often predictable in a way.

Television shows and movies often wanted to depict serial killers as complex creatures. In a way, they almost glorified the murderers. Yet, in Ilse's experience, serial killers were pathetically predictable. Sex, power, deviancy, social isolation, delusion... Similar motives, with various combinations could be found in most cases. Serial killers were humans without self-control. Humans without the usual guard rails of compassion or conscience. Banal, often enough, in how boring their motives were.

"The case reminds me of a client of mine," Ilse said, continuing, her voice strengthening as she did. "Antisocial personality disorder coupled with sexual trauma combined to create a sexual sadist. In that particular case the killer would capture young women and keep them on the premises of his property, often boasting to them how many folks he'd killed in the past as if it somehow made him special. He fed on fear. These sorts of men often do—the only emotional reactions they're able to glean come from the fear others have. It arouses them."

A couple of the police were now paying closer attention. The rangers had stopped talking, listening.

"Older than twenty, younger than fifty, most likely," Ilse said, quietly. "Possibly a sexual sadist, or, barring that, a schizophrenic. Experienced in the forest. Experienced in Olympic Park—potentially a local. And, it's also worth noting—"

Before she could finish, though, the glass door suddenly banged open, and a new figure entered.

The man's face was streaked with sweat, but his features had paled substantially, his eyes wide, his hat tilted back. She recognized the grumpy sheriff from back on the park trail.

Now, though, instead of scowling at them, the sheriff was breathing heavily, and it looked like he'd seen a ghost.

“Culpepper?” said one of the rangers. “Sheriff, everything okay?”

The man shook his head, slowly, white as a sheet. He swallowed, passed a hand across his forehead, then, muttered, “Don't mean to interrupt, doctor. But we've been searching the park...”

Everyone turned from Ilse now, staring at the ashen-faced man.

He looked up, letting out a long breath, his eyes glazed in a thousand-yard stare. “We found another hole,” he muttered. “Another kill lair.”

Ilse felt a chill down her spine. Sawyer pushed off from where he'd been leaning against a wall. “Bodies?” he said, scowling.

The sheriff just nodded, closing his eyes for a moment and looking like he might be sick. “Yeah. I'd say so.”

Ilse's skin prickled in horror. She tried to think, her mind whirring back through all things gruesome and grisly she'd studied over her professional career. If this, indeed, was another kill cave, filled with bodies... Then the serial killer was one of the deadliest in the last decade. The news would start catching wind. Things would escalate.

She found her heartbeat pounding more rapidly now. She wasn't even a full agent yet. What if there were *more* holes? She was beginning to feel in over her head. She swallowed, though, trying to focus. This was what she'd wanted, wasn't it? To face the monsters beneath the bed? To shine a light where others wouldn't venture? Now that she had what she'd wanted, though, she wasn't sure what to do with it. Just how bad would all of this get?

The energy seemed to have been sucked out of the room. She wondered if anyone here had ever faced a case like this. A mountain of a case, growing bigger with each new discovery. Body after body, attracting more and more attention. This would go national, undoubtedly. News would swarm on the scene like vultures.

She could see it in the pallid faces around her, the nervous postures, the twitching motions. Everyone sensed the sheer gravity of this case now.

Sawyer cursed and began stalking out of the room. He paused in the doorway long enough to bark out, “We're heading over. Rest of you start putting together a report on the victims we've managed to ID.” His voice rose in volume, his teeth grit. “Don't slack here. I'm talking histories, families, tendencies. I'm talking all of it. Got me? Got me?” He said, louder.

A few of the deputies nodded, hesitantly, but when the sheriff gave them a look and a bob of his head, they pushed to their feet, nodding more adamantly.

Ilse felt her heart pound. Sawyer wasn't waiting for her. The sheriff was also now moving towards the door. But it wasn't like she could do much good stuck at the precinct. So, despite the pit in her stomach, she broke into a jog, jostling past the deputies and heading towards the slowly closing glass door where Sawyer had disappeared.

CHAPTER THIRTEEN

The son of the forest stood in one of the deeper tunnel systems he'd set up. He stood straight backed, his head tilted to the side, striking a dramatic pose in the mouth of the cave. He'd hollowed out most of the tunnel himself, venturing further from what had once been a survival bunker of some long-forgotten codger.

The son of the forest kept his eyes closed, exhaling through his nostrils, feeling the thin gust of air moving through the tunnel behind him. He reclined, slowly, one arm extended, draped over the shoulders of one of his dearest friends. His fingers trailed absentmindedly at the top button of the woman's shirt, swirling around and around as he absentmindedly murmured in her ear.

"They found our second home," he said, gently, shaking his head from side to side. The son of the forest pursed his lips, giving a dramatic sigh, then spread his other hand in front of his face as if gesturing towards some unseen horizon.

"I saved you from the purloiners of youth," he declared, his voice projecting throughout the cavern. "I saved you from their devious minds, did I not, Shaley?" He gave his friend's shoulder a little affectionate squeeze.

Not that she reacted. His friends were introverts. Not exactly the expressive sort.

Now, though, his friends crowded into his favorite home. All around him, the rigid bodies pressed against each other, or wedged carefully against the walls. He'd spent the better part of the day rushing from one home to the next, grabbing his friends and bringing them all here. He hadn't been in time for a couple of his favorite spots.

He sniffed, swallowing and feeling a tear trickle from his eye. It was never easy to lose a loved one.

He released his grip on Shaley and began to stomp between his frozen friends. "Do you hear?" he bellowed at the ceiling. "No?" he placed a hand to his ear and gave a sweeping bow. "No, of course not. They cannot hear us down here. So hidden, so deep. We are safe at last, my friends! The evil masters won't take you away now. We can't be separated! Aha! Aha!" He leaned in suddenly, catching Shaley in a swooping dip and kissing her on her cold lips.

He stood again, straightening his sweater and coughing delicately. “Oh my,” he murmured. “I don't know what came over me. Apologies, my dear.”

He adjusted his sleeves, coughed and turned from his friend.

Things would now be awkward between them. He never had been one to control his emotions. Some folks just wore their hearts on their sleeves, he supposed.

And now, that same sense of euphoria at having evaded the meddlers was slowly being replaced by a simmering rage.

It started as a pit in his stomach, but began to rise almost immediately, trickling up his throat and threatening his lips.

One hand squeezed into a fist, and he slammed it against the muddy wall, breathing heavily now. He could feel his temper swishing through him, could feel the *need* falling on him.

Those bastards were stealing his friends! Raiding his homes! Ruining his life's work.

They were robbing his youth. Desecrating the mother's designs.

No... No he couldn't let it stand. He hadn't come this far by being a coward. He'd known the trek would be an arduous one when he'd taken his first, hesitant step.

Now... Now he needed to add more friends.

To bring more of the young and youthful into the fold. More vitality and beauty. More longevity. He needed to rebuild his collection fast... Immediately.

Or else all of it would be ruined.

He scowled, reaching out and adjusting a couple more of his friends, making space between them. Once a sufficiently large portion of the muddy wall was cleared, he stared at it, then nodded once. Yes, he thought, yes, perfect. *This,* he supposed, would be the perfect spot for the next one.

CHAPTER FOURTEEN

Beneath the nighttime skies, deep in the heart of the million-acre Olympic Park, Ilse watched as flashing security lights, like lightning bugs, illuminated the forest. The ATV grumbled beneath her, but slowly died as Sawyer skid to a halt and flicked off the engine. They'd made it from the police station in the sheriff's car, but the rest of the journey into the deep woods had been on back trails and newly cut paths, using the all-terrain vehicle.

Now, with dust kicking up, the low murmur of voices around them, Ilse's feet crunched into the thick detritus-laden ground. Paramedics moved through the entrance of a small hollow beneath a large root system from an ancient oak. If the tunnel entrance hadn't been illuminated by the flashlights of multiple detectives, Ilse wasn't sure she would have spotted it herself.

With Sawyer, neck-and-neck, the two of them hastened across the forest path towards the tunnel entrance. Behind them, the sheriff cleared his throat, having dismounted his own ATV, now following them through the woods. “It's not pretty,” the man's voice sounded strained in the night.

Sawyer didn't look back, stepping over a dried-out creek bed. He did, however, venture a question. “How far is this from mile marker thirty-three?”

The sheriff sighed. “Thirty miles,” he said. “I know, because I asked the same thing myself.”

Sawyer paused, glancing back as Ilse and the sheriff also stepped over the dry creek bed. His frown deepened and his hand strayed to his pocket, pressing against where his cell phone rested as if searching for some odd comfort.

“Thirty miles?” Ilse murmured, her voice laden with the emotion scrawled across Sawyer's face. “Thirty *miles* separate the two lairs?”

Sheriff Culpepper sighed and nodded once, rubbing at his forehead with a grimy hand. “Afraid so. Going to be hard to search such a large area for any more demented hideouts.” He waved a hand towards the entrance to the lair beneath the dangling tree roots. “Only found this one based on dumb luck. Bunch of hikers been watching the news and paid attention... Not going to get that lucky again."

The jutting sections of muddy wood and bark angled low over the burrow, like the fingers of some giant creature attempting to grasp at all who drew near.

Ilse shivered, huddling in on herself as she followed Sawyer, brushing against a couple of paramedics, before entering the second lair.

Instantly, the odor of mud and wet earth filled her nostrils, along with some horrible, chemical smell. The flashlights behind them illuminated the ground, casting their shadows into the darkness ahead of them like scouts.

Ilse reached out, steadying herself against the muddy wall, but then yanking her fingers away and rubbing hastily at the side of her sweater.

"Stay close," Sawyer murmured. "It's late—light's gonna be poor. Here. Use this."

He handed her something cold and metal which she took with a shaky hand. Sawyer had to duck to avoid scraping his baseball cap against the muddy roof of the horrible tunnel.

Ilse glanced down at the item in her hand and realized Sawyer had handed her a small flashlight. Swallowing once, she clicked the light on.

Instantly, their shadows retreated as if scurrying into the dark, cramped corners.

The muddy tunnel turned into an L bend at the end of the small pathway. For the moment, nothing horrible stood out to catch Ilse's attention. She could hear her own breathing echoing harshly in her ears as she cast the flashlight about to illuminate the rest of the muddy terrain.

For his part, Sawyer allowed her to lead, guiding with the light. Perhaps he'd decided he was too large to take the lead. Or, perhaps, he simply had wanted to give Ilse some sort of field responsibility. Already, the FBI trainers knew she wasn't the best when it came to the physical portions of FBI training. Maybe this was Sawyer's small way of giving her some much needed confidence.

She glanced at the lanky man, trying to read his inscrutable expression. Sometimes it seemed as if the man only had two emotions: indifferent and hungry.

"Hang on," Sawyer said, suddenly, pointing.

Ilse turned back, rotating the light to catch the indicated portion of the tunnel.

Something jutted from the mud, buried against the side and slope of the dirt-crusted wall. Sawyer dropped on his haunches while Ilse dutifully kept the light on the spot. Agent Sawyer frowned, his fingers scraping against the terrain and then, he slowly stood up, hunching once fully erect and extending a hand towards Ilse's light.

The pink bottle was caked in mud, the label half worn.

But the remaining portion of the label was clear enough.

"Lotion," Ilse murmured. She felt a shiver down her spine. "Body lotion?"

Sawyer breathed slowly. "I sure as hell hope not," he said. He lowered the bottle back to the ground, marking the item by scuffing a small circle with his foot.

Ilse tried not to stare at the bottle of skin lotion. Perhaps it was used for preparing the bodies for taxidermy?

What if it's for something worse? A small voice whispered in her mind.

Ilse shivered, trying not to think too far down this particular path and instead following Sawyer as he once more took the lead, rounded the bend in the tunnel and came to a sudden and sharp halt.

Ilse nearly bumped into him, the flashlight beam swaying for a moment as she caught her balance. Sawyer's hand shot out, instinctively snaring her wrist and keeping her steady.

"You okay?" he murmured.

"Fine, I'm fine," she said, breathing heavily. "Sorry, I just didn't—"

Her words cut off as she stared into the room beyond. Concrete blocks intermingled with muddy walls, as if someone had started to build a bunker but given up halfway.

What drew her attention, however, wasn't the naked light fixtures or the half-finished bomb shelter. Rather, her eyes were on the *people.*

Corpses.

Six of them, in total. Her flashlight darted from one to the other, accompanying the flighty sense of horror now darting around her chest like some caged sparrow attempting to be free.

She opened her mouth, and the fear escaped her lips in the form of a small, sobbing gasp.

"Dear God," she murmured, finding the light shaking so badly that she tried to switch hands. Only then, did she realize, it wasn't the light, but she who was shaking.

The bodies were organized again, this time set throughout the room in a sort of uniform pattern. All of them seemingly young, mostly women. Only one man she could see. All of them were dressed in a different way than the first lair. Here, their garb consisted of dark cloaks and upraised hoods. The bodies were posed in contrite positions as if they were caught in prayer. Some of them were even kneeling. One of them, frozen in place, had extended hands as if prepared to embrace the horizon.

All of them faced the far wall. There, in the mud, a strange emblem buried in the dirt. The thing was made of acorn stems and pinecones. It resembled the skull of a deer, with antlers. Ilse realized a second later this was because the pinecones and acorn stems were adhered to the skull. The white, bony antlers protruding over the top of the strange skull carried small bells on the end of the horns, dangling like dewdrops towards the muddy floor.

Ilse's flashlight fixated on two of the women, their faces visible past their upraised hoods, their glass eyes staring sightless at this odd and horrible emblem buried in the mud.

Ilse shivered. "What do you think of this?"

Sawyer looked around the scene, frowning. "Seven victims," he said. "Some look fresher than the other corpses back at the first lair. Others look like they've been here a while. You're the shrink—what do *you* think?"

Ilse fidgeted, brushing one hand past her bangs and then realizing her fingers were still muddy. She winced, lowering her hand again and staring at the horrible spectacle. Inwardly, her mind whirred. *"Schizotypal personality disorder. Borderline personality disorder. Psychotic disorder. Dahmer. Blonde hair. Ninety-four. Seventeen victims. May twenty-first,"* she thought to herself, practicing her memory trick in order to focus. What did she think, indeed?

She stared at the postures of the victims, at the strange emblem on the wall. Her mind flitted back to the first scene. That other horrible lair...

Things seemed different here, though.

"I... Nothing good," Ilse murmured after a moment. She swallowed, standing rigid in the tunnel, refusing to take even one step closer to the bodies. Sawyer remained at her side.

The stench of chemicals was stronger now, along with mothballs and mud.

Ilse could feel her heart hammering, could feel a sudden nausea forming in her stomach. She wanted to turn and run screaming from the tunnel. To flee and never look back. But what would Sawyer think of her then? The FBI training would be over.

Besides, the victims here were beyond her help. But those the killer would soon take?

She owed it to them, didn't she? The same way she owed her clients.

Her whole life she'd told herself that she wanted to help people. Now there was a very real opportunity to do just that. She simply couldn't lose her nerve.

She coughed again, though the sound came out more like a squeak of air. But then, despite the faint trembling in her voice, as if she were on the verge of crying, she said, "Clearly, whoever this is, sees his cause as pious in some way. The kneeling, the religious emblem in the wall..." She stared at the horrible, horned icon, then looked at Sawyer if only to find something pleasant to turn to for a moment.

But Sawyer didn't seem to be faring much better than her. Though he was a master of the poker face, his features were paler than normal, his lips drawn in a tight, thin line.

"If some of these bodies are newer," Ilse pressed on, "that perhaps means our killer's tastes in killing have changed. He's becoming bolder. More honest with his reasons. See—no kill room here. Just a display. That pit back in the first lair—with the grate? That must be where he takes them to prepare them. After... he must bring them here." She shivered. "At least, the newer corpses." She waved a hand towards the six figures in some form of worship. "Which isn't good news for us."

"Why?" Sawyer said, his voice strained.

"This... this all is more designed. Fervent. Pious... but to what? To himself? Pious to something else?" She shivered, pointing towards the deer skull. "This guy has grown stronger, bolder in his convictions. Which means one thing..." She glanced back towards the horrible scene. "He won't take kindly to our intrusion. He'll see it as a disruption. One thing about the fanatical sorts... They don't let sin go unpunished..."

"What do you mean?"

"I... I would be surprised if our killer didn't try to make things right. To offer penance. To correct the disruption."

"You mean kill again?"

Ilse didn't respond at first, but then with a shrug she simply nodded her head and then turned, pushing the flashlight into Sawyer's hand. "I think I'm going to be sick." She stumbled back in the opposite direction.

Sawyer followed closely, steadying her and murmuring, “It's fine. There's nothing more for us until forensics gets through.”

“It's late,” Ilse said, weakly, feeling a sudden headache.

“Yeah, yeah I guess it is. I can get you back to the hotel. But... First thing tomorrow,” Sawyer said, carefully, “we need to check with our only witness.”

Ilse paused, bracing herself against the wall, one arm tensed where Sawyer tried to help hold her upright. “Kristine?” she said.

“First thing tomorrow morning,” Sawyer murmured. “We need to speak with her again.” He paused, and then, his voice raspy as if from overuse, he said, “I think you're right. I don't think this guy is going to be happy we found two of his hideouts. He's going to do something. And soon.”

CHAPTER FIFTEEN

Deli's head bobbed up and down with the sound of the French Classical music. Debussy's strings and keys wafted gently in the night as she moved down the dirt path, hands at her side, moving like pistons.

Perhaps not the most traditional workout music, but Di found that it calmed her. She liked to think when she went on her hikes. Granted...

She glanced at the sky, wincing and picking up the pace again, her arms and back slick with sweat, her breathing coming in steady puffs.

...She hadn't expected it to take *this* long.

The trees above swayed and shifted, the branches creaking as she hastened along the trail, heading back towards camp and back towards the new friends she'd made around the public campfire. She smiled at the thought of Jasper... She'd always been a sucker for green eyes.

She continued to move on, the sound of the classical music emanating from the small Bluetooth speaker clipped to her running shirt.

The grainy feeling of dirt beneath her boots had long since given way to sore and sweaty feet. The breeze beneath the cloud-covered moon was a welcome respite against the heat of her own motion.

Now, though, as she took a switchback, curling over a small stream, her eyes were met by more familiar territory. Yes... yes she was getting closer. Only fifteen or so minutes from camp now. Twenty tops.

She checked her smart watch, noting her heartbeat. 121 bpm. Not bad. Certainly in the fat burning zone, though her physique didn't have much of that left *to* burn.

Just then, as she continued moving, a branch suddenly snapped off to her left. Her heartbeat jumped. 135 bpm. Her eyes flitted up and she frowned, reaching up towards the Bluetooth speaker to lower the volume. She'd heard something, hadn't she? Or had it simply been a stutter of the recorded music?

She frowned, reaching up and slowly turning down the volume. The echo of cello and piano faded, leaving her with the sound of her own heavy breathing and the whisper of wind through crackling leaves.

"Hello?" her voice sounded soft and frail in the darkness. A faint shiver tickled up her spine. "Hello?" she tried, a bit louder now. One hand hovered near the volume control of her speaker while the other moved hesitantly towards her phone.

There hadn't been reception this far out, but maybe now...

She shivered, remembering earlier when she'd been scrolling through her phone. Her mother and both her sisters had texted her the news article about the bodies they'd found in the park. Bodies as rigid as the trees around her.

She quailed beneath the outstretched shadows of the foliage above, and picked up her pace, moving along the dirt road, fishing her phone from her pocket as she did.

Now, her music was muted; the only sound was that of her laden breath and rapid footfalls.

And another *crack!*

She yelped, turning sharply.

Crack. Crack.

The sound of snapping sticks and breaking branches. The sound of unmistakable motion in the underbrush. A scream burbled to her lips as she spotted a shadow flit from the cover of the trees and dart towards the road.

For one, horrible moment, it made no sense. The person in question was completely in the nude, streaked with mud and dirt, his eyes wild and framed by shaggy hair and a beard. He looked like a caveman as he charged, wielding a strange item; it looked like an old-fashioned walking cane, with a silver knob on the end.

She tried to flee, tried to scream. But there was no one around this late to hear her. No one at all save the man with the bludgeoning stick.

The footfalls behind her were far faster than they should have been. It wasn't like she was slow.

But he... somehow... this caveman in the woods was impossibly fast.

She heard a ragged breath, a muttering of, "Hello, my young friend."

And then something struck her across the back of the head, her skull exploding in pain.

CHAPTER SIXTEEN

As she lowered back onto the hotel bed, a whooshing sigh of relief arose from Ilse's lips. She closed her eyes briefly, head downturned as she allowed some of the exhaustion from the day to lift from her shoulders.

One hand rested against her thigh, and she rubbed at it with another, feeling a strange twinge from overuse, holding that flashlight back at the second lair. Her eyes opened at this, and she stared towards the door to her hotel room.

Shut. Locked. Bolted.

She shook her head. It was one thing to hear the experiences of her clients. An entirely separate proposition to face them in full view and HD color.

Granted, she had her own horrors to draw from if she wanted to.

Her hand trailed to the hotel nightstand, where she'd placed a small toiletries kit.

Instead of toothpaste and shampoo or the like, she only stowed two items in the small black zip-up bag. She stared at the bag for a moment, leaning back in her bed now and murmuring beneath her breath "Doss. Eleven victims. Blackouts, depression. Poison." Then, she pulled the zipped bag towards herself, unzipped it and with a surprisingly steady hand pulled out the two items within.

A small, porcelain doll of a little girl and a postcard from Germany. The postcard had been addressed to little Hilda Mueller.

Ilse's head pressed against the two stacked pillows and headboard, but her eyes fixed on the postcard and the small porcelain doll. The same sort of doll her father used to collect. The same postcard that had shown up at her mailbox back outside Seattle in her lakefront office home.

Someone was taunting her. And she still didn't know who.

Two mysteries. One in the woods of the Pacific Northwest, the other in the woods in Germany's Black Forest. No closer to solving either.

Even with her training, her years of study, Ilse felt lost in the woods again. She tried to close her eyes, tried to rest the small doll against the nightstand. As she turned, head pressed to pillow, her eyes tight, she only found more adrenaline rushing through her.

Should she call Dr. Mitchell? Donovan, her mentor, often knew how to help with even the most difficult clients. Maybe he'd have insight into the case?

She began reaching for her old-fashioned flip phone, but her eyes landed on the small, digital clock next to her hotel bed, and she sighed in frustration. Already midnight. 12:02.

She felt a slight twinge of unease in her stomach at the minute number. Increments of five, she could handle. Uneven numbers were worse. Now, staring at the 2, it turned to a 3. 12:03. A prime number. She gritted her teeth, turning away from the offensive thing, extending one hand back to grope blindly for the chain to the bedside lamp.

She turned it off, felt a spurt of anxiety, turned it on, then off again. Twice more she turned it off and on. Three. To match the number.

She wished she'd fallen asleep at midnight, exactly. Perhaps she should wait until 12:30. That would sit better...

Perhaps...

As she lay there, her mind whirring, her thoughts spinning, sleep didn't so much come as creep in, slowly, stealthily, picking its way through the shadows.

Sleep descended on her, smothering her.

With it, sleep brought bad dreams.

Memories.

Her lips hurt.

Even worse than her ear had.

They hurt so bad.

Little Hilda Mueller struggled in the muddy hole beneath the house. She tried to scream, but she couldn't. He'd sewn her lips shut, hadn't he?

The pain in her mouth was nearly unbearable. Hilda Mueller grunted and struggled, trying to rise. But already, half her legs were buried in mud. Another shovel of dirt struck her chest, staining her already off-white shirt.

"Stop struggling," the man standing over the hole snapped. "Stop it or I'll hit you!" He raised the shovel threateningly.

Hilda began to cry, shaking her head, trying to raise her hands to protect from the next shovelful of dirt. She blinked, some of the flecks getting in her eyes, some on her lips. But the thread and needle he'd used to sew her lips shut shot spasms of pain through her face.

She tried to scream again, but this only hurt more. Another shovel of dirt. Another. Another.

She struggled, kicking, trying to scramble out of the hole.

A thick boot caught her small chest, sending her back into the hole as her father buried her alive.

Just a nightmare...

A part of Ilse's mind tried to protest. Tried to wake.

Just a nightmare...

Or a memory?

Even caught between sleep and memory, Ilse felt the thin glaze of sweat across her body. She wanted to rise, wanted to call out. Wanted to wake...

But not even sleep would allow her to leave.

The nightmare had her, and it wasn't ready to let go.

The only solace Ilse found was in the thought of Kristine. The poor woman had suffered similarly. Also buried under ground. Also covered in mud and dirt. She'd escaped... Barely.

She was now in a hospital, recovering.

That's what Sawyer had said, wasn't it? First thing in the morning, bright and early.

They had to speak with the surviving victim.

Survivors.

Both Ilse and Kristine.

Survivors.

Another shovel of dirt.

Another jolt of pain.

For hours, Ilse was tormented by her own memories.

CHAPTER SEVENTEEN

Ilse tensed as Agent Sawyer maneuvered the borrowed sedan along the second floor of the hospital parking lot. Her stomach twisted in knots. The horrors of last night still flashed across her mind's eye. She didn't remember everything from her past. That particular, cruel memory hadn't been one she'd recalled. Her hand hovered near her lips, feeling the smooth skin. Just a nightmare? Ilse shivered, feeling restless. Partly from the dreams, but partly a strange sense of premonition. Everything about this case stretched her capacity. Treating a patient was one thing, but dealing with victims, another thing entirely.

Sawyer pulled to a complete stop, put the car in park and stepped out into the hospital parking lot. Ilse followed a bit more hesitantly, and, as the doors slammed shut behind them, a small beeping sound emanated in the concrete and asphalt area.

Sawyer frowned, fishing his phone from his pocket, glancing at the number then shoving the device back, deep out of sight.

Scowling, he began marching in the direction of the sliding hospital doors.

"Who was that?" Ilse asked, trying to keep up.

Sawyer didn't reply.

She picked up the pace. "Was it Rawley? Sheriff Culpepper? Is everything alright?"

Sawyer shot her a sidelong glance. "Not about the case."

"Oh?" Ilse hesitated, wrinkling her nose.

Noticing her look of confusion, Sawyer let out a little huff. "It was my wife," he said with a shrug, then he stepped through the sliding glass doors leading from the parking lot to the second level of the hospital.

Ilse stood rooted to the spot for a moment as the sliding doors did a little dance, opening, half closing, opening again as the sensors tried to determine if she was coming or going.

Now, though, standing in the parking lot, staring after Sawyer, her mouth hung open. She blinked and then, frowning, hurried through the sliding doors herself. The sound of her footsteps shifting from the quiet tap against concrete to the gentle squeak against tiled floor.

Sawyer was already leaning against a half-oval reception desk, tapping a button with a laminated sign that read "Buzz for Attendant."

"I didn't know you were married," Ilse said, coming to a halt next to the lanky agent.

Sawyer rubbed a hand against his pocket with the phone and shrugged.

She frowned at him, but supposed it wasn't like he'd concealed anything. Ilse had heard something about a divorce... or separation. She'd even pegged him as someone previously married, but she hadn't realized the woman was still in his life.

Not that it mattered.

Did it?

Why should it matter?

She crossed her arms, leaning against the counter now as well and staring down a hall as a woman in blue scrubs hurried towards them.

The woman seemed to detect Ilse's frown and she matched it with one of her own. The nurse was tall, even taller than Sawyer, with broad shoulders and a thick chin. Her uniform seemed a size too small for her large frame, but the large nurse didn't seem to mind as, still frowning, she came to a halt next to a four-wheeled desk chair behind the counter.

"May I help you?" she said, her tone polite despite her gruff appearance.

"We're here to speak with Kristine Swallow," Sawyer said. Then, almost as an afterthought, he fished his ID from his pocket and flashed it. "FBI," he added in a bored voice.

The nurse's broad-cheeked face shifted into a curious expression as she examined Sawyer's casual outfit. The jeans and flannel shirt with his ever-present baseball cap didn't exactly scream *federal.*

Still, she took it in her stride as she folded her hands and slowly leaned back into the wheeled chair. The frame of the furniture squeaked as she leaned her large arms against the marble counter, delicately adjusting a screen monitor which illuminated her face in a pale glow.

"I'm afraid that isn't possible," she said carefully.

Sawyer frowned. "FBI," he repeated, not one to mince words.

"I don't care who you are," she returned, frowning. "You can't speak with Ms. Swallow, because Ms. Swallow is no longer with us."

Ilse felt the familiar sense of premonition she'd had back in the car. Some of the images from her dreams flitted back. Buried alive. Pain in her face. The sheer horror of no escape.

Suppressing the emotions as best she could, and adjusting her sleeves, she said, "I'm sorry. Do you mean she recovered enough to return home?"

The nurse shook her head, and for the first time her expression turned to something bordering sympathetic. "I'm afraid Ms. Swallow committed suicide late last night. We found her early this morning." She shook her head, wincing. "I—I was on duty last night... I didn't hear or see anything until..." She trailed off, glancing askance, the glow from the computer screen illuminating her cheek now. She steadied herself with a breath and looked up again, her expression apologetic but professional once more. "If you'd like to speak with someone about an autopsy, I'm sure that can be arranged."

Ilse stomach felt like it had twisted in on itself. Her feet glued to the pristine marble floor. A quiet scream burbled up in her throat, and this time, she knew she could let it loose. Her lips weren't sealed any longer. Vaguely, she remembered other times her father had forced his children to be quiet. Once, he'd used super glue, another time, he'd simply gagged her.

She couldn't remember everything, couldn't picture most of the hazy memories. PTSD was strange like that.

"How did she die?" Ilse said in a shaky voice.

The nurse turned her attention from Sawyer to Dr. Beck now, examining her. "And you are?"

"With me," Sawyer interjected. "How did she die?"

The nurse kept her attention on Ilse, reading her for a moment. Ilse preferred flip-flops and sweatpants. But she wore business slacks and a dress shirt beneath her usual, dark sweater.

The nurse massaged the bridge of her nose, and now Ilse noted the bags under the woman's eyes. Clearly, this hadn't been an easy night for her either.

"Cut her wrists," the nurse said, crisply. "She managed to get her hands on a pair of scissors."

Ilse winced at the description, her mind filling with other, projected images found in her imagination and raised to the forefront of her thoughts. As an afterthought, the nurse added, "I'm very sorry. Like I said, if you want an autopsy report, I can make sure its forwarded. We should have it within the week."

Sawyer nodded, but Ilse simply hung her head, limp. She felt numb. She felt frozen in place.

Suicide.

She'd survived the horrors of the woods. The horrible killer and his frozen cadavers.

And she'd committed suicide.

Why hadn't Ilse sensed this? Is that what Kristine had meant when she'd said she just wanted to make it all stop? Why hadn't Ilse done anything?

She found her fingernails scraping against the circling tattoo around her wrist. *Take Captive Every Thought.* Why hadn't she been paying attention?

Now, the final words before being ushered from the room came shouting back. *"This isn't worth it anymore,"* Kristine had murmured beneath her breath. *"None of it. I just want to make it stop."*

It didn't seem fair. She'd fought so hard—fought desperately to survive... But on the other side of it, after the action, after battling, alone with her thoughts, she'd been left defenseless. Like soldiers returning from battle—strong, capable, deadly when in combat. When given a mission, proactive and determined...

But when left alone with their thoughts? When taken from a fight or flight situation and placed only in solitude?

Ilse's foot began tapping rapidly against the floor, her breathing coming in, out, far, far too fast. Sawyer and the nurse were now talking in low, murmured voices. But it was as if they were speaking at the bottom of a well. Ilse couldn't make out their words. She didn't want to.

What did it matter?

She was supposed to be a therapist. She was supposed to be trained to spot the warning signs.

She was the one who'd spoken to Kristine. Agent Sawyer knew it. Agent Rawley knew it. They'd all blame her.

And they were right to.

She alone had failed Kristine. She had cost Ms. Swallow her life. Why hadn't she pressed further? Why hadn't she insisted on asking more questions?

Ilse gritted her teeth, resisting the urge to bite sharply down on her lower lip. In, out, exhale, inhale, faster, faster.

She should have done more. She should have stayed longer.

She thought of Heidi. Thought of little Kat. Of her other siblings. Thought of the accusations. Three weeks she'd left them in that basement, following her escape from that horrible house at the end of the street.

She hadn't done her part then either.

How many lives had Ilse's neglect ruined? How many lives had she failed to protect?

She felt eyes on her now, felt both the nurse and Sawyer watching her.

She looked up, glancing between them and realized they seemed to be waiting for some sort of response. She swallowed back the scream and instead, as carefully as she could, murmured, “Yes?”

“Good to go?” Sawyer said, enunciating as if repeating a question.

She hadn't heard him the first time.

Sawyer's eyes were fixed on hers now. Tom was a man of gut instinct and training. He knew the woods like the back of his hand. He was dogged in his pursuit. And yet, while he might not have had Ilse's training, once he figured out someone, he seemed to be able to read them like a book.

Like he seemed to be doing now, watching her, his eyes hooded.

Instead of waiting for her reply, Sawyer gave a quick nod towards the nurse and then walked up to Ilse, hooking his arm through hers and leading her away from the nurse, back towards the sliding glass doors that led to the second level of the parking lot.

“I... Yes,” Ilse said, responding to the question on delay. She felt dazed, shell-shocked. She'd seen herself in Kristine. Buried alive, hunted by a monster, lost in the woods...

But then free. Finally free. Sole survivor.

And yet, Kristine's story hadn't ended how Ilse's had. Kristine's story ended in death.

Like so many others.

“It's the job,” Sawyer said as he pushed her gently back into the parking lot. His voice seemed hollow and thin in the spacious, concrete lot.

“I—what?” Ilse said, still half-dazed.

“The job. People die. Gotta deal with it.”

Ilse frowned, trying to understand what she thought he was saying. Deal with it? Kristine was a person... Didn't he understand? It was her job to protect these people. To help them!

“Hey, look at me.”

Ilse kept walking.

“I said look at me,” Sawyer said, gripping her arm and turning her so she faced him. He placed a hand on her shoulder, fixing her with an unblinking gaze. “It's not your fault,” he said, his voice low. “Hear me?”

She swallowed, not quite meeting his gaze. He kept his hand on her shoulder.

"Doc. Dr. Beck... Ilse?"

At her name she finally looked up, feeling tears threatening her gaze.

"It's not your fault," he said, a bit more gently. "I mean it. You can't think like that."

"I—I wasn't..."

"You were. It's not."

Ilse swallowed, puffing a breath, her shoulders rising as she inhaled deeply.

Sawyer held her gaze a moment longer, his frown flickering, but he didn't let her go. He didn't blink. He just kept his hand on her shoulder, kept staring her in the eye, but didn't speak, didn't move.

She supposed this was the taciturn agent's version of a rousing speech. Inspiration by eye contact.

She found she didn't mind, though.

She used words in her job. It was nice to find someone who didn't.

But Sawyer didn't get it, either.

He was the FBI agent. She was training. A rookie, sure. But she was a therapist first. When she failed her job, people died. She supposed Sawyer faced the same problem. But he'd done this longer. He showed up *after* people were already dead.

It wasn't the same.

Was it?

She shivered, gently patting Sawyer on the hand but using the same motion to extricate his fingers and turn to move away. The man was a strange one. Sometimes, he went hours without speaking a word. Other times, the sheer strain of sweating and exerting himself, striding through the woods seemed to give him a sense of purpose. He meant well. She knew that. The sort of man who separated, or even divorced from his wife but still kept in contact with her.

What was that about?

And why did it bother her?

She didn't want to think too much about it. Not here.

"What now?" she murmured, walking slowly back in the direction of their parked vehicle, her footsteps slow and rolling like in a funeral procession.

Sawyer cleared his throat, clicking the key so the lights flashed, and the doors unlocked. "We got some of the names back this morning. I haven't had a chance to really look through yet."

“Names?” Ilse said, frowning at him. “What names?”

“Victims,” Sawyer said. “Positive ID from the victims at that first lair.”

Ilse chewed her lip. “Oh.”

“I was going to tell you after we spoke with,” he paused, clearing his throat, “er, Kristine. Didn't want to distract you. But... well... One of the families of a twenty-two-year-old named Caitlin Ellis lives nearby.”

“You just happened to get the victims' identity and address this morning?” Ilse said, suspicious.

Sawyer shrugged and sighed. His hand strayed to his pocket, and she heard a soft rattle which she recognized as the sound of a bottle of pills.

The last time she'd heard it, Sawyer had been popping caffeine pills to stay up on a previous case. He didn't much like coffee but seemed to swear by caffeine.

“I got up early, did some of the dot-connecting myself,” Sawyer muttered. “Whatever. The information is good. We should stop by and speak with Caitlin Ellis's parents.”

“Did you sleep at all last night?” Ilse said, staring at the man.

Sawyer shrugged one, thin shoulder, striding around the hood of the car, before slipping into the front seat and waiting for her to join him.

CHAPTER EIGHTEEN

Ilse felt numb as she followed Sawyer to the front of the large, suburban house. The drive from Olympic Park's trails had passed in silence.

Her mind was still spinning from the news about Kristine, from a night of fitful sleep plagued by horrible dreams, and... on a lesser scale, from the knowledge Sawyer was still in contact with his ex-wife. This last part made the least sense. She wasn't sure why she cared. Why should she?

And yet... she found she did.

Now, as if in a daze, she followed Sawyer to a freshly painted, red, metal door. A small camera blinked above the frame, a hexagonal sticker in the front window read, "Monitored by IBC Security."

The doorbell had a thin strip of masking tape over it and a small note in neat handwriting, punctuated with a smiley face read, "Doorbell broken. Please knock."

Sawyer stood on the bristling welcome mat, letting loose a little sigh as if steeling himself and then knocked on the door, the sound resounding in the quiet, mid-morning suburban streets.

Ilse and Sawyer waited, continuing their silence from the last half hour drive from the hospital. Sawyer had even observed the speed limits out of some strange offering of commiseration.

As they waited, a voice peeled out from around the house.

"In the garden!" the voice called, cheerful. "Come on around!"

Ilse and Sawyer shared a look. The lanky, thin-framed FBI agent waved at the camera, then led Ilse down the steps and along the white, painted railing, towards a side wooden gate in the fence circling the yard.

Ilse felt the eyes of a neighbor from the second floor of the white house behind them but pretended she hadn't noticed the attention.

The tall, wooden gate clicked and suddenly opened. A woman in overalls, a bonnet, and an apron stained in dirt with a small, muddy trowel in one hand was smiling at both of them.

A man knelt near a flowerbed, on his knees, his jeans stained with dirt. The man yanked something from the ground, winced, and tossed a prickly weed into a brown, paper bag at his side. He reached to where a glass pitcher and two cups rested against the concrete patio, but instead of grabbing a glass, he took the pitcher itself and tilted it back. Ice clinked, and brown liquid sloshed as the man took a long swallow, and then he also looked over, past the woman, frowning at the new arrivals.

The smiling woman in the bonnet glanced between them. "Yes?" she said, still cheerful.

"Agent Sawyer," Tom said, with a nod of greeting. "This is Dr. Beck. Do you have a moment?"

The woman's smile became rather fixed. The man in the mud looked up, wiping his gloves and pulling them free, tossing them onto the flower bed.

"Maddie, who is it?" he called.

"Mr. Ellis?" Sawyer returned.

The man frowned but nodded.

"Pardon my husband," Mrs. Ellis said, quickly, "but he can be grumpy in the morning. He works night shifts." Her voice was pleasant but strained. She seemed on the verge of saying something else, but then caught herself. In the same would-be breezy tone, offset by the cresting frown, Mrs. Ellis said, "Can I help you Agent Sawyer? Doctor Beck?" She glanced between them.

Ilse inhaled for four seconds, exhaled for five. Then, she broke the silence, "We're here about Caitlin, Mrs. Ellis." Before the woman could leap to any unfortunate assumptions, Ilse cut in, "I'm afraid it's bad news."

The muddy trowel fell from the woman's hand, clattering against the brick pathway leading through the well-maintained garden. Mrs. Ellis stood frozen, like a garden statue, framed in the wooden gateway of her small, fenced backyard.

Mr. Ellis got to his feet, rubbing at his knee and wincing before marching over to them. He came to a halt behind his wife, placing a hand on her shoulder and leaving it there. "Is she dead?" he said, blunt.

Ilse paused, but before she could reply, Sawyer said, "Yes. We found her yesterday."

Mrs. Ellis sighed, and for a moment, Ilse thought she might break down crying. Instead, though, she turned to her husband, wiping a fleck of dirt from his cheek. Her voice quavered but held strong. "At least we know," she murmured.

The man nodded; turning aside and looking away, he sniffed. His voice shook as he said, "I always hoped... Well..." he swallowed back his emotion, looking at Sawyer and Ilse once more. "Caitlin has been missing for three years now," he said. "I suppose we knew. How... How did she?"

"George, no," Mrs. Ellis said, sharply. "I don't want to hear it."

"It was bad," Sawyer said, answering the unspoken question. He began to continue, but Ilse cut him off.

"It might be best we don't discuss details of an ongoing investigation," she said, quickly, her own voice sound small and threadbare. Ilse was struggling to keep it together herself, but she'd forgotten just how bad Sawyer could be in the gentler interviews. If she didn't keep things on track, it would go off the rails quick. She winced, trying not to imagine Tom describing in grizzly detail what they'd found. The Ellis's might think they wanted to know. But they didn't.

"I... I need to... I think I might have left the stove on," Mrs. Ellis said, stammering. She began to turn.

"Hang on, we actually have some questions," Sawyer said, raising a hand in a stopping motion. But Mrs. Ellis's own hands were trembling so badly she clasped them in front of her muddy apron, picking up her pace and hurrying back through the patio door into the quaint suburban home.

Mr. Ellis remained rooted to the spot, his eyes misty, his breathing shallow.

Sawyer frowned after the victim's mother, but then just sighed, shrugged, and glanced at Ilse.

"I'm sorry," Mr. Ellis said. "She had a stronger hope than I did that our little girl was still..." He shook his head. "Anyway. Questions? I don't have any more answers than what I've already provided. You should have a report."

Sawyer began to speak, but Ilse interjected, forcing her tone to emanate sympathy rather than exhaustion. She tried to think like Mr. Ellis. Tried to imagine what it would feel like to lose a daughter. Three years ago, he'd said. She was twenty-two when she'd died.

"She would have been twenty-five this September, yes?" Ilse said, hoping by making a personal connection with the man's daughter he would focus on Caitlin rather than his frustration with law enforcement.

Mr. Ellis coughed, but nodded, clearing his throat. "Yes. Yes, she would have been. She was... she was tough. Really tough. Took after her mother that way." He rubbed at the bridge of his nose, eyes downcast, tracing the cracks in the cobblestone path. "Everyone loved Caitlin."

“Everyone?” Ilse said, careful not to press too hard. “A lot of people have rough break-ups, or jilted lovers.”

“Not Caitlin,” he insisted, firmly. “She was... was liked. A free spirit, friendly to everyone. She just wanted to help people.” He gave a little laugh. “She had a softer, spiritual side. I can't say she got that from me either.” He waved a hand towards a dream catcher dangling from the front porch. “She loved nature. The trees...” he trailed off wistfully, almost as if he were speaking to himself now.

“That's beautiful,” Ilse said, softly. She didn't ask another question, rather allowing him to continue.

“I can't imagine why anyone would hurt her.”

“She disappeared while camping,” Sawyer said, flicking up an eyebrow.

Mr. Ellis blinked as if jerked out of a reverie. His eyes darted to Tom and he frowned. “That's right. Like I said in the report. She'd been camping on her own, in the park. She'd done it before. But after a week, we didn't hear back from her. No one found anything. We contacted the authorities, but they didn't do anything.” This last part strained his voice, sounding accusatory.

To his credit, Sawyer didn't get defensive. He just nodded once and pressed, “Was she camping alone?”

“Why? Were there others? We've been watching the news... Was that Cailtin? They said they found bodies in a cave. Was she there?” His voice became hoarse, rising in volume now.

“George,” Mrs. Ellis called from the house, where she stood in the screen door. “George come in. Come inside. I—I need your help.”

Mr. Ellis scowled at Sawyer, jamming a finger towards his chest. “You didn't find my little girl. You didn't do shit! Get out of my yard. Now!”

Sawyer held up his hands, taking a single step back, away from the wooden gateway. Mr. Ellis growled and slammed the gate, latching it. Ilse heard the sound of thumping footsteps as he moved across the garden path back towards where his wife was waiting.

Sawyer glanced at Ilse. “Report didn't say anything about her camping with others.”

“She was alone,” Ilse said, simply. “It's like we thought. The victims aren't connected. He's targeting lonely campers. Targeting people on their own.”

“He's a pervert. They like picking on the defenseless,” Sawyer growled, one hand tight at his side.

But Ilse shook her head, lowering her voice so no one else could overhear. "I—I'm not sure the motives are purely sexual," she murmured. Her mind filled with images of the second lair they'd found. The strange posing of the bodies. The pious nature of the scene. The deer skull attached to the wall like some sort of icon of worship.

"If not sexual, then what?" Sawyer said.

"I... I don't—"

Before she could reply, Sawyer's phone started chirping. A louder, more musical noise than the beeping from when his wife had called. Did his ex have a custom ring tone in his phone? Ilse's nose wrinkled, but as Sawyer lifted the device and said, "Yeah?" she watched his expression fall. A frown turned into a scowl; a glower turned into a glare.

After a moment, he lowered the phone.

"What is it?" Ilse said.

"More bad news. Another camper is missing. We need to get back to the park."

CHAPTER NINETEEN

Ilse felt her stomach turn as she ducked under the low-hanging branches outside the campsite. Her heart hammered as she recognized the campers huddled around a doused campfire. Under the sun, the college-aged kids from the night before looked even younger, smaller, huddled together. Two of them were crying, but the girl with the straw-colored braids was staring off into the distance, a numb expression across her face.

Sheriff Culpepper was there, talking to one of the young men who'd been smashing brown bottles. Named Jeb, if she remembered correctly. The kid's face was pale, and it looked like he hadn't slept a wink.

Sawyer was still stalking along behind her, but Ilse didn't wait for him to keep up, taking the lead herself this time.

The kids with the dreadlocks, the tie-dyed shirts—some looking like they hadn't been washed in a week—looked in their element beneath the trees, unbound by concrete or fluorescent lights.

Ilse reached Sheriff Culpepper to overhear the second part of a question. "...last night at one point?"

The young man, now during the day, had tightly bound dreadlocks, and a thin streak of green dye through his bangs. Jeb's features were handsome, though his chin unshaved. His clothing hung loose around him like a skater, but he had a utility knife in a sheath on his belt. The young man was shaking his head, his braids swishing wildly as he did.

The young man from the night before looked with bleary eyes off into the trees, sniffling once and then murmuring something beneath his breath as Ilse and Sawyer approached.

"I understand," the sheriff was saying, a pained expression flickering. One hand rested on his belt while the other held a small voice recorder lifted towards the witness's face.

"She... she went for a run," the young guy said, his voice shaking nearly as badly as his hands which played at his side, tapping against his upper thigh. "We were waiting for her to get back. But... but she never did." His voice cracked and he reached a shaky hand up as if to hide the sound. "I don't know who would want to hurt Deli. Maybe—maybe she's just lost?" the man said hopefully, his voice lilting with the emotion. “Maybe it isn't... well... you know.” He glanced around at the other police gathered, and his shoulders slumped.

The sheriff clicked off the voice recorder, patting the young man on the shoulder and murmuring beneath his breath. “It's going to be alright. We're already sending teams to look for Ms. Altum. We have it from here.”

Ilse had come to a halt off to the side next to Sawyer. She wasn't sure she wanted to speak with the young man. Would he recognize her from the night before? It was starting to feel like everyone she spoke to ended up suffering in some way. Her mind flitted back to Kristine on that hospital bed.

Now, a new victim... Ilse hadn't met Delilah Altum the night before, but she'd seen the way the girl's friends had huddled around the campfire, laughing, carefree in their tie-dyed shirts and tangled hair. They'd been waiting up for their friend, waiting for her to return...

And now...

“Might not be our guy,” Sawyer murmured, his voice quiet enough the sheriff and his witness—standing ten feet ahead—didn't hear.

“I know,” Ilse whispered back. “People can go missing in the forest for other reasons, too...”

A flash of memory. Heavy breathing. Her feet in pain as little Hilda Mueller stumbled into a tree, grasping it with bleeding fingertips. She swallowed back a surge of emotion, inhaled for a moment, holding the breath as if cutting off oxygen to the memory itself.

“Could be our guy,” Sawyer said, shrugging.

“Might not. Could be,” Ilse replied through gritted teeth. “Either way...”

“I've got a bad feeling.”

Ilse didn't reply to this. Sawyer was normally the one who went off gut instinct and horse sense. But this time, she couldn't help but agree. She remembered the strange premonition of foreboding back at the hospital. The emotion had only worsened.

She worked with information, experience, memory. Worked with diagnoses and patient history. Sojourning too deeply into the realm of instinct wasn't her forte. To some, her profession was little more than mumbo-jumbo, but to Ilse it was as clear as any science.

A young woman had gone missing on a night-time run following the disturbance of the killer's lairs.

The odds were against them.

Sawyer was right. Might not. Could be.

She was banking on the latter. If she was right, the killer was still active, still on the hunt.

"Are they closing the park, yet?" Ilse murmured.

Sawyer glanced at her. "Rawley is pushing for it. Shut down two of the locations where the women were taken. But the place is over a million acres. Tourists from all around coming in. There's push-back... Lot of it from the governor's office."

Ilse scowled, staring at her hand. "Just for a few days," she said.

"Like I said, Rawley is trying. We'll see. Needs state approval."

Swallowing back her discomfort and not quite meeting Sawyer's gaze, Ilse moved across the campground towards where the young man was speaking with the sheriff.

She watched for a second as the voice recorder was stowed back in Culpepper's pocket, but then she stepped in, before Sawyer could join her. She didn't need Sawyer's oversight in *everything.* Besides, Sawyer was... different than she'd thought.

Before she could trace out this line of reasoning, both the sheriff and the young man turned, glancing at her. She spotted a tear stain along the witness's eye, remembering the way he'd laughed and giggled the previous night while sitting by the campfire.

"Hello," she said, nodding her head once. "I'm Dr. Beck."

The sheriff frowned but didn't interrupt. The young man shifted a shoulder. "Jeb," he said. "I remember you from last night."

"Yes, Jeb. I remember you as well. I'm very sorry for your trouble, and I'm here to help."

"Doctor?" Jeb said, frowning. His nose wrinkled and he shot a look at the sheriff. "What's a doctor doing here?"

"I work with the FBI," she said, quietly. She glanced over her shoulder towards where Sawyer was still standing beneath the trees. He'd seemed to sense she'd wanted some distance from him. Or perhaps he couldn't be bothered to talk with a witness who hadn't actually seen anything.

Still, Ilse wasn't Sawyer. She had her own questions.

"Ms. Altum was a friend of yours?" she said, establishing a simple question if only to prompt an initial response.

He bobbed his head. "Deli was a good friend. She didn't deserve..." He hiccupped and held a hand to his lips again.

"Was she staying in the tents with you guys?" Ilse asked.

"Yeah... Yeah," he said, his voice lowering. "My tent. Shared it with Grady."

"I see. And was it normal for her to run at night?"

He scratched at his chin. Again, he shot a look towards the sheriff as if wondering if he had to keep speaking. Clearly, authority figures weren't his favorite form of company. But when the sheriff maintained his stony expression, Jeb said, "She'd go for runs a lot. But usually not that late. It isn't safe."

"Right. But tonight was an exception?"

"I—I guess so. She liked moving through nature. Was a bit of a spiritual experience for her, you know?" His eyebrows shot up and he shrugged. "It's all connected," he said. Hands splayed towards the trees. "We're one with the earth, you know?"

Ilse didn't react. She simply nodded to show she'd heard. "Is there anything else you can tell me?" she said. "Anyone who's been acting strangely around Deli?"

He snorted, pointing towards the sheriff. "We've already been over it all, lady. Nothing. I didn't see or hear nothing. One moment she was here. The next she was gone."

Ilse sighed, glancing off in the direction he'd indicated when talking about the trees. Something about this comment nagged at her. "She was spiritual, you say?" Ilse asked.

"Not religious, lady," said Jeb. "But in touch with the world. She loved the world. Get me?"

Ilse hesitated, frowning slightly. Inwardly, she felt a strange tightening of her stomach.

"I think I do," she murmured. "Thank you."

She nodded farewell and began to turn. The sheriff said something to the witness, but Ilse couldn't even make it out as she hastened back in Sawyer's direction, her feet scattering dust as she picked up the pace.

"You alright?" he said, reading her expression.

"Something spiritual," Ilse murmured. "He said Ms. Altum was spiritual in a way."

"And?"

"That's what Mr. Ellis said about Caitlin, too. The way those bodies were posed, Sawyer, in that second lair. The weird emblem on the wall... I think... I think..." Ilse trailed off, frowning now, shaking her head. "Look, I think we need to head back to the lair. I need to see it again."

CHAPTER TWENTY

"Alright," Sawyer said, his voice gruff. "We're here. What's so important?"

Ilse didn't wait to convince the man; she simply stepped through the tangle of branches dangling over the muddy hollow, moving deep into the second lair.

Now, thank heavens, the bodies had been removed.

The deer skull on the wall still remained, broken eye sockets gaping. The miry walls and floors showed telltale portions, free of dust where the corpses had been posed.

Ilse's heart pounded and her chest heaved as images darted across her mind's eye. Pictures of her father, a shovel in hand, mud striking her chest. Pictures of the smiley face of corpses her own sister had posed back in that worn farm. She gritted her teeth at this last memory. Her sister had posed bodies too. Her motive had been revenge. The victims had simply been those of circumstance for nothing more than bait.

This killer...

She glanced around the space, her brow furrowed. This killer was different.

She felt the warmth of Sawyer's arm brush against hers, listening to the soft puff of his breath as air blossomed against her cheek.

"This didn't make sense at first," Ilse murmured, staring around the place. "It—it still doesn't... But maybe that's because I'm looking at it from the wrong perspective."

Sawyer grunted. "Hmm?"

"Look, remember the figure standing there, kneeling in the mud, right? A position of contrition... I didn't understand..." she turned, looking Sawyer dead in the eyes. "I don't think this guy is motivated by sex at all."

Sawyer wrinkled his nose. "Most of the victims, Ilse, they've been young women. That means—"

"I know what it *usually* means. But this place... This isn't a lair... It's a shrine. Can't you feel it." She turned to stare at the deer skull and antlers still on the wall, one of the few remnants of the grizzly spectacle they'd stumbled on before.

“I've been looking at this all from a Judeo-Christian perspective,” she murmured. “I didn't quite connect... But this—this is something else.”

“Else? What, like another religion?”

“I—I don't know. Something Jeb said. The witness back at the camp. Spiritual but not... not a religion. Something else. Something based off the land, maybe?” She stared at the skull on the wall. “It's the only thing that fits.”

Sawyer wrapped his arms around his thin frame where they stood in the dark. He frowned, his brow darkening his eyes. “What now, then?” he said.

“Now... We need to know what we're dealing with. What all of this *really* means to the killer. We need to do more research. We need to *know.”*

“Know what?”

“The why. If he's doing this for sex... he'd bide his time. Maybe even go into hiding. But if he's doing this for something else... For a conviction. He's not going to ever stop until we catch him. We need to know. So we need to do some research.”

***

He sat perched on the lowest branch of his third favorite tree. He'd named it Motruey... Or it had named itself. The branches were as familiar to him as the hairs on his knuckles. His hands gripped the thick, wooden frame of his perch as he peered through the leaves, eyes fixated on the vehicle below.

The soft swell of music drifted through the open window, accompanied by the alluring emanation of orange light.

Shadows moved across a thin, gauze curtain. Voices murmured into the night.

He sat unclothed, streaked in dirt and mud, staring down from his vantage point at the desecration.

Even where he sat though, he watched where his hand trembled, wrapped around one of the branches. His fingers went rigid, and a little sob squeaked from his lips. He was growing weaker.

He could feel it in his bones.

Feel it in his blood.

He was growing weaker.

They had robbed his youth. Stolen his friends, and now the age came in like rolling tide, threatening to crush the shore. He was weaker now than ever. Older now than ever.

With the same trembling hand, he reached up, plucking a hair from his beard and holding it against the backdrop of orange light from the RV.

The hair was brown.

Not gray, yet... But soon. If he didn't do anything, soon.

His breathing became more rapid. Were his lungs giving in? They felt like they were... Dear god...

"Please preserve me," he murmured, one hand stroking the tree. He leaned in, his lips pressing against a wooden knuckle of the branch. He kissed it, leaving a dark stain of saliva against the tree. "Preserve me," he whispered, louder now.

The desecration of the RV, and the defiled youth within would serve as an offering.

He slipped from the branches, his nude body scraping against the rough texture. He moved with practiced ease, dropping through the tangle of leaves and boughs, landing nimbly in the undergrowth.

He stared towards the RV, inhaling, exhaling, his nostrils flaring as he knew what had to come next.

An important thing to please those whose eyes witnessed the travelings and travailing of all under branch and bough. An important thing to offer suitable gifts.

Her youth, her beauty would be a boon, indeed.

His own would return. He could feel it now.

Years of work, they'd ruined. Years they'd desecrated.

He needed to make up for it.

And now, he knew how.

One big display. One giant offering.

That would have to do.

He stepped through the undergrowth, ignoring the nettles against his skin. The pain rejuvenated him after all. The cold didn't bother him either. He stepped from the edge of the forest, hiding beneath the darkness of the cradle of shadows.

He stared at the RV, waiting, scowling. Voices, orange light, shadowy movement across thin curtains...

He could wait... If he needed to, he could wait for hours. For days.

He gritted his teeth, a soft snarl creeping from his turned lips. He didn't have hours. Didn't have bloody days.

He bent, ripping up a stone from where it was embedded in the dirt.

He aimed towards the RV and threw the stone.

A window shattered. At the same time, he bolted, sprinting from the tree cover to the front of the RV.

And then...

He waited.

Too much waiting, though... No more waiting. Now was the time for action.

He listened to the sound of cursing. Then, the voices ceased, as if someone had turned off a television. Suddenly, everything felt quiet. At least, quiet to the untrained ear. He could hear the whispers of the forest, though. A moving, living, thing. A dormant, hidden thing. A sleeping giant roused from its slumber and soon... very soon it would make its rage known against the polluters, the desecration, the breakers.

And he was the agent of this coming response.

Footsteps echoed from in the RV.

"H—hello?" a voice called into the night.

He said nothing, standing with his skin against the cool metal grill of the RV.

"Hello?" the voice said, louder.

Then, a quiet *click* as the door opened.

A face peered out into the night. A young, beautiful face. Framed in brown curls. The young woman wore a fluffy, green bathrobe and bunny rabbit slippers.

"Jason, is that you?" she said, louder.

No more voices behind her. She'd been listening to something. He remembered television, though it had been nearly a decade since he'd stained his soul with that noxious passage of time.

He waited, poised, breathing slowly as he watched around the edge of the RV.

Her eyes even swept towards him, towards where his face poked around the edge of her own vehicle. But he'd known the shadows behind him. Known how weak fake light could make a person's eyes. Her gaze swept right on past, peering blind into the dark.

"Hello?" she said, a final time. And then, she pushed the door open further. She took a step out into the night.

He waited, poised. Just another step... Just another...

She stepped into the night, shaking. One hand, he noted, clutched something silver and gleaming which she held tightly against her side. A knife?

No matter.

He'd come here for one reason.

Again, standing in the dirt, she looked around, framed in the doorway of her RV, orange light flooding the space.

He darted forward. Three, bounding steps.

She didn't even hear him until he was on her. First things first. He struck her hand with the knife.

She gasped in surprise and her weapon fell from her fingertips, gouging into the dirt.

His other hand darted in, towards that thin, smooth neck.

But as he did, she let out a half-scream, before kicking *hard,* aiming between his legs.

He grunted, pain shooting up his gut. For a moment, his grip on her throat weakened. She reached up, yelling now and trying to break his fingers free. He snarled, and she kicked again, this time disentangling and scrambling back into her RV. Stupid little bird. Trying to hide in her nest. Should have flown.

Too late.

He grabbed her ankle as she scrambled away, standing out against the night, his skin streaked with mud and blood. He yanked her back and she screamed again as her head struck the top step in her RV.

"Here, to me!" he bellowed.

She hit the mud beneath him and as she tried to rise again, tried to kick him once more, with white fire of pain still swirling in his belly, his legs wobbly, he fell on her, fists flying. Fingers then scrabbling at her soft neck.

"No," he said, simply. "Quiet!"

Another punch with one hand, a squeeze with the other. The whites of her eyes fluttered, her consciousness failing her now. The trees watched but said nothing.

The grass held her, aiding him.

The breeze whispered instructions in his ear.

Another strike. Another squeeze.

The desecrating little creature fell still.

CHAPTER TWENTY ONE

Media swarmed the police precinct as she stepped slowly out of the car, and Ilse's jaw dropped. Lights flashed; cameras jammed towards her. A swarm of cameramen and would-be journalists rounded on her, glass reflecting the bright lights.

Sawyer stepped next to her, murmuring beneath his breath. "Don't say anything. Keep quiet, let's move."

Ilse's heart hammered as she ducked her head, allowing Sawyer to lead the way back into the precinct. The flashing lights, the loud voices of the news crews caused Ilse to hunch in on herself, to tug at the sleeves to her sweater. Her hear pounded, hammering, her eyes downcast as she moved hastily after Sawyer.

Shoulders bumped her; a camera struck her cheek.

"Get back!" Sawyer snapped, shoving the offending cameraman. "Get back now!"

"Where is Sheriff Culpepper?" a journalist screamed in Ilse's ear. "What are they doing about the murders?"

"Who is in charge of this?" another voice screamed. "The people deserve to know!"

More shouted questions peppered Ilse. Twenty, maybe forty news-folk crowded like vultures around a corpse. Ilse followed Sawyer hastily up the steps, both of them brushing through the media members.

For her part, Ilse's heart pounded wildly. Her skin was slicked with sweat, her throat tight all of a sudden.

Sawyer didn't seem at all surprised by this development. Almost as if he'd endured it before. He glared at any camera pointed his way, shoving more than one lens aside as he guided Ilse up the steps. But Ilse felt small, fear rising in her. She wasn't even an agent... Did any of them know? Would Rawley pull her from the case?

"Come on," Sawyer murmured, reaching the top step and guiding her through the precinct doors.

Two officers were blocking the doors from the media, nodding grimly towards Sawyer as he led Ilse past.

The case was just getting bigger... Now, more than ever, Ilse knew she had to solve it. She *had to.*

Which meant the reason they'd returned was doubly important. They *needed* to know who they were dealing with.

***

Ilse ignored the seat directly next to Sawyer, preferring to take the chair two spaces down at the small conference room table back at the precinct. Sawyer glanced at the empty chair next to him but didn't comment before returning his attention to the computer. The faint shouts of reporters had faded now. The flash of lights mercifully gone.

Sawyer seemed relaxed again, indifferent to the gaggle of noise outside. He waited as Ilse opened the lid of the laptop Sheriff Culpepper had loaned them. Soon, she knew, she'd have to bite the bullet and get over her distrust of all things technological, but for now she didn't feel the need to purchase her own laptop. The cameras outside certainly hadn't helped.

As she settled in the chair at the other end of the oval table, her eyes already skimmed the search bar of the browser. Her heart was still hammering. The shouting voices of the newspeople ringing in her ear. She paused a moment, breathing in, then exhaling, counting in her head. The case was bigger than she knew what to do with. But she still had to play her part. If Rawley took her off, then so be it.

For now, she *needed* to know what they were dealing with.

And so, after another rattling breath, Ilse paused, considering her angles, then typed, "Nature cults."

The top two results were sponsored, which she ignored, skipping past a couple of Wikipedia entries to focus on other results. As her eyes skimmed down the page, the thoughts of the onlookers, the camera lenses faded. Her attention diverted, refocusing now.

Her eyes skimmed the blue headings and her frown deepened. None of the articles did much besides pick apart different belief systems, ranging from Wicca to more technologically averse Christian communities, like the peaceful Amish.

Hesitating, she returned to the search bar and typed, "Nature beliefs..."

This time, a new set of results displayed and again her eyes traced down the page, searching for any headings that stood out in particular.

She scanned past mentions of naturism, naturalism, or some new age movements.

She hesitated, clicking on a link that said, *Wiccan order of the woods.*

Sawyer sat in front of his own computer screen, shooting her looks every so often which she ignored. She liked the lanky agent and his down-to-earth demeanor. He seemed the sort of man who bottled his feelings, which—for someone in her line of work—often perturbed her. But now, all of this aside, she felt a distance from Sawyer. Her mind was too preoccupied to think through the reason right now. She wasn't sure she wanted to explore the nature of her emotional attachments.

After another fruitless web search, Ilse returned to the top of the page.

She paused, then typed, "Nature beliefs in Washington State."

This wasn't a matter of theory or beliefs. This was a tangible reality. Someone was *acting* on spirituality. In this case, unlike the thousands of harmless spiritualistic beliefs found in the murmurings of smoke-wreathed hippies to the culturally rooted beliefs of native tribes, this person had toxified the theories. Used them to hunt and kill others.

Which meant there would be a trail... not just some theoretical blog post. But people who actually held these beliefs. Most likely, people local to the area.

She skimmed down the results of this newest search, and then paused, frowning. She read a headline that said, "Beliefs about nature in the Pacific Northwest...," she glanced at the portion below and then sighed in frustration as it continued, "...could lead to a cure for indigestion thanks to the steaming of ginger root."

Sawyer had turned, watching her now.

She glanced over, scrolling back to the top of the search engine again. She hated computers but had been forced to learn how to use them, especially when taking long distance calls with clients. Back home, next to her wood-burning oven, she had a behemoth of a desktop. It usually took ten minutes to boot up.

Certainly not nearly as fast as this device.

"What if he's just a pervert," Sawyer said, watching her from beneath hooded eyes. She glanced at him. and he tipped up the brim of his hat, causing the shadows to lift.

"I don't think it fits," she said, simply.

Sawyer shrugged. "Would be the more likely explanation," he said.

She shook her head. "It would be the *simpler* explanation. That's different than likelihood."

"Most cases like this are because of perverts."

"Maybe... But maybe not." She shrugged noncommittally, returning her attention to the computer.

For a moment, she thought Sawyer might say something further. He was frowning as he watched her. But then he simply sighed, reached into his pocket, and pulled out a bottle of pills. The caffeine tablets rattled as he fished out a couple and popped them onto his tongue, swallowing them without water.

"Those things are bad for you," Ilse murmured beneath her breath.

"So is coffee," he retorted.

"Mind helping me look?"

He grunted and turned his attention back to his own computer, pretending to read something, but judging by the blue glow against his face he was still at the login screen.

Ilse sighed again, deciding not to press the issue. She didn't want to give him the opportunity for return fire. By now, both had picked up on the other's odd behavior, no doubt.

Ilse scanned the results on the second page and then stopped, blinking. She read a result halfway down from the top, posted on a local, community news blog.

The title read: "Violent nature cult uses beliefs to justify disturbances..."

She clicked the link, beginning to read. After a few moments, she said, "Sawyer, do you know anything about the Gaiaknights?"

He glanced up. "No. Should I?"

"A group in Seattle related to Gaianism. Apparently, they've had some run-ins with law-enforcement before."

"Huh."

She continued reading. "Organizing protests. Accosting civilians. Looks like a couple of their members beat someone up for smoking in a forest preserve."

"Yeah?"

Ilse continued nodding, scrolling to the bottom of the page. "Their leader is a real piece of work."

Sawyer had logged into his own laptop by now, it seemed, because a second later he said, "Theodore Fredrick?"

"That's the guy. Apparently, he goes by Teddy. He has a blog here, too—writes a lot of stuff. Violent stuff by the look of it."

Sawyer's brow bunched together as he read his screen. "Yeah, well, this Teddy isn't much of a snuggly animal. He's got a record."

Ilse looked over the lid of her laptop. "Violent record?"

"Mhmm. Vandalism. Assault. Threatening a police officer. Looks like he tried to blow up a construction truck back in the nineties."

Ilse sighed. "Theodore Fredrick, then... Leader of the Gaiaknights."

Sawyer shrugged. "Stupid name for a group. Think he's involved? It seems like a stretch."

Ilse winced. "The way those bodies were posed," she said, insistently, "it doesn't make sense for a sexual crime. This is spiritual. And this cult is the most active in the area that I can find. Their leader has a record." She shrugged. "It's not for certain, but it's a thread to pull on."

Sawyer massaged the bridge of his nose, but instead of complaining, he simply nodded, closed his computer and got to his feet. The sound of pills was replaced by the jangle of keys as he fished these out of his pocket and began moving towards the shut conference room door. His hair ruffled beneath his upraised brim under the vent over the doorway. He turned, glancing at her.

"Guess there's only one way to find out."

"Do you have an address for the guy?"

"I can get it on the way. Let's go see what Teddy's been up to recently."

CHAPTER TWENTY TWO

Ilse mirrored Sawyer in her unwillingness to speak as they drove towards the southern boundary of Olympic Park. The silence pressed around them, and Ilse's hands clasped tightly in her lap in front of her. Partly, she'd gone quiet out of discomfort. She knew she was behaving oddly. Knew that in part it was due to her sense of guilt where Kristine was concerned. A cloying, stomach churning sensation filled her with dread.

But also, she didn't know what to make of the lanky agent. He was still in contact with his ex-wife. He'd been acting strangely ever since the start of the case.

Why?

Those questions flitted away, the apprehension replaced by a sheer tangle of nerves in her gut as Sawyer pulled them along a poorly constructed street, towards a tract of land with no visible house. A sign out front read, "Trespassers will be shot!"

Sawyer pulled the car onto the side of the road, the front wheels smooshing down strands of long, untamed grass. The yard ahead of them didn't look so much like a yard as an untended field. No one had mowed in months, by the looks of things.

On either side of the tract of land, Ilse only spotted trees.

No other houses nearby.

Mr. Fredrick's home was set right against the southern boundary of the park. As close to nature as he'd managed to get.

"Where's the house?" Ilse murmured, peering through the overgrown land, along the dusty trail leading from the broken asphalt road.

Sawyer clicked the keys from the ignition, slipping out of the car and standing at attention as he surveyed the land. She watched as wind ruffled his hair beneath the brim of his hat, and his flannel shirt, across his thin frame, shifted with the rising breeze.

For a moment, Ilse resisted the sudden urge to remain in place—unwilling to move. The car was safe. The car was protected. She liked being on the move. And if not that, then isolated away from others. She thought of her lake home. Thought of the forest she'd called home.

Still, coming here had mostly been her idea. "Ridgway, Utah, forty-eight victims," she murmured, quietly enough so Sawyer wouldn't hear. Then, calming herself with the memory trick, she slipped out of the car and waited as the breeze caught her as well, cool and caressing against her cheek. Her stomach was now twisting so badly she thought she might throw up.

For his part, Sawyer didn't seem phased. He scanned the land for a moment, through hooded eyes, then with a faint nod, he pointed. "There it is," Sawyer muttered. "Illegally parked trailer."

His hand moved to his hip as he strode passed the "Trespassers will be shot" sign, unhooking his own firearm before taking the dusty path.

Ilse had no qualms about letting him lead as he guided the two of them up the trail and towards the small trailer home she hadn't spotted from the road.

Sawyer took surefooted steps, seemingly as at ease as he'd been talking to Mr. and Mrs. Ellis. Ilse felt her heart pounding so loudly she was worried her chest might explode.

The trailer home was pressed against the forest, amidst an overgrown tangle of weeds and low-hanging branches, intentionally shielded from close scrutiny.

"Mr. Fredrick!" Sawyer called. "FBI."

They waited for a moment, and Ilse was grateful for the chance to catch up to the long-striding investigator. As she did, though, he didn't wait long. When no answer was forthcoming, Sawyer shrugged one shoulder and approached the side window of the trailer. He stepped through some nettles, careful to catch the offending barbs against his thick jeans, before stepping on his tiptoes and peering through the back window.

He frowned.

"What do you see?" Ilse asked. "Is he in there?" she said, whispering so quietly, her lips buzzed.

Sawyer just shook his head. "Animals," he said after a moment. "Dead."

"Dead animals?" Ilse's eyebrows went up. "Like taxidermy?" She was catapulted back to their last case, when they'd found similar animals in a small shack in the woods. That time, the animals had belonged to a man lopping body parts off teachers.

Maybe her hunch would prove right after all. "Anything else?" she whispered.

But Sawyer seemed to have seen enough to pique his curiosity. He rounded the front of the trailer, moving towards the door. “Fredrick!” he called, louder now.

No answer.

Sawyer puffed his cheeks, stretched for a moment, as if he had all the time in the world, standing in front of that horrible trailer, hidden from the road by weeds. And then, he took two quick steps and drove his foot *through* the flimsy trailer door.

Sawyer grunted, catching himself and cursing as he tried to disentangle his leg from the hole he'd punched. Ilse hurried over, but before she could help, Sawyer pulled himself free, reached up and in and pulled on the handle from the inside of the trailer.

A *click.*

And the fragile, abused door slowly opened, revealing a dark room beyond.

A rotten stench of preserving fluids and sweat met Ilse's nose and she gagged, breathing rapidly at the ground, her eyes tracing the dust particles and stray stones scattered across the floor.

Still heaving rapid breaths, she tried to straighten, feeling the blood rush from her face.

Sawyer was already halfway into the trailer. Ilse hesitated... Was this protocol? Legal? Was *anything* Tom did protocol? She half opened her mouth to protest. Too late.

He was already in the trailer.

Cursing, she forced her legs to move, though they felt frozen in place. She stepped behind Sawyer, into the small space, peering around now, past his dusty flannel.

Indeed, he'd been right.

Animals.

Foxes, birds, a couple of does and one buck all lined the walls, marble, glass eyes staring dully out at her from their frozen postures. The taxidermized animals were of shoddy workmanship, with missing tufts here, gaping slice marks there.

The animals weren't the only cause for alarm, though.

Ilse spotted a strange trail of thick, brown beads dangling from a ceiling fan which had been left on, causing the item at the end of the beads to circle around and around and around.

A skull. Human, by the look of it. Plastic? Or real.

Whoomp. Whoomp. The skull scooped air, repeating the sound as it swirled around the small space, above one of the deer.

Ilse's eyes darted to the buck's antlers. Four points only... She wasn't sure what the rule was on hunting young bucks, but she doubted someone like Teddy Fredrick cared.

"Mr. Fredrick," Sawyer called again, his voice carrying through the space.

But again, he received no answer. Only then, did Sawyer glance towards Ilse. "Creepy place," he murmured.

"That's the understatement of the year," she replied, still, whispering.

A small living area gave way to a kitchen which moved back to two doors. Likely a bedroom and a bathroom. The door to the bedroom was open, revealing a mat on the ground, and not much else.

Bathroom? Ilse mouthed towards Sawyer, inflecting the question with her eyebrows.

Sawyer nodded, one hand still on his weapon as he sidestepped along the narrow hall, a hand extended in front of him to guide the way. There, in the dingy darkness, without hesitating, he knocked rapidly against the bathroom door.

"FBI! Open up!"

He waited. But no response came. Sawyer tried the handle and it clicked, swinging open into the hall. A mirror on the inside of the door reflected an image of a grimy, tiled bathroom.

Empty.

Sawyer wrinkled his nose and pushed the door shut. He peered into the bedroom, but then called, "Clear!"

Ilse felt her heart quiet a bit. Her rapid breathing came back into check. Her eyes moved to the skull whipping around from the beads on the fan, and that's when she spotted the red lettering carved into the ceiling itself, behind the fan, as if it had been written before the ceiling unit had been installed.

The letters simply read. *We, who come from dust, owe the mother of earth our flesh...*

Ilse felt her pulse quicken as she re-read the words. All of this, even the skull—was it tied to this man's strange cult?

She shivered as Sawyer approached, his footsteps creaking against the old, faux-tiled ground. "Guess I was wrong," he said, reaching up and pulling off his cap to fan his face. He winced. "You were right," he added.

"I—I guess so," Ilse murmured. "But where is Mr. Fredrick?"

Sawyer looked around again, shrugging. "Hate to think it... but the guy seems like a hunter." He winced.

"You think... you think he's off hunting?" Ilse said, shivering as she did.

"Could be. Or may—"

Before Sawyer could finish the sentence, his phone began to beep. He frowned, fishing the device from his pocket. The strangely technological noise seemed so out of place surrounded by hunters' trophies, and glimpses of vegetation and overgrowth through the many windows.

"Yeah?" Sawyer answered. He paused, listening and frowning. "You sure?" he said.

He shut the device down, slipping it back into his pocket, frowning even further as he began to move back towards the door. "Guess he really is hunting," Sawyer said, a bit more energy and acerbity to the words. "Bastard took another."

"Wait, what?" Ilse said, a pit in her stomach. She stepped carefully over a stuffed fox, wincing as its bristled tail rubbed her calf.

"Another girl was taken," Sawyer said, standing in the doorway now and smacking a hand *hard* against the door frame. Normally this was more emotion than the investigator showed in front of others.

"A different girl? A second one?" Ilse said, struggling to comprehend.

"Yeah. A big fight near an RV. But he got her. That's two now. Back-to-back."

Ilse's hands trembled as she approached the door, pausing long enough to let Sawyer take the lead out onto the dusty ground. "The killer is escalating," she said, sensing the rage simmering beneath Sawyer's tensed muscles and gritted teeth. Her own emotions were now haywire. They were late. So, so late. Another body. Again, she was off in the forest somewhere... Too late to bring help. Too late to do anything.

She swallowed, stopping the trail of thoughts as she did. Take captive every thought... that's what she always told herself, wasn't it? It wouldn't help either of those women if she fell apart now.

Besides, they weren't dead yet. At least, so she hoped.

She needed to think, though. To put herself in the mind of—

Suddenly, a scraping sound arose from the bedroom.

Ilse and Sawyer both turned as one, faces angled sharply towards the startling noise.

Ilse stared, wide eyes like saucers. Her mouth hung half open, her tongue dabbing her bottom lip, but not lifting, frozen like the rest of her as she poised to hear another sound.

Just the wind. Just a mistake. Had she really—

Another scraping sound.

Ilse cursed as Sawyer pushed sharply past her, careful not to bowl her over, but hardly gentle either. His gun had now found its place in his hands, and the taciturn once-eagle scout stalked up the hall in a shooter's crouch, weapon pointed forward.

She couldn't help but notice how the man didn't hesitate, didn't think to plan. He simply acted on instinct. The squaring of his shoulders communicated more confidence than she'd ever felt.

"Fredrick," Sawyer called, "FBI! I'm warning you, come out with your hands up."

Another scraping sound, louder now, from the back room.

Ilse's mind filled with images of unkempt forest-men with weapons waiting behind the door frame. Just waiting for Sawyer to emerge.

She resisted the urge to shout, to call a warning. All she could do was watch, rooted to the floor, staring at where Sawyer—gun raised—stepped into the bedroom.

CHAPTER TWENTY THREE

She stood frozen place, nearly biting her lip, but then, Sawyer's form went stiff... Then slumped. He lowered his gun, pointing it towards the floor and reached up, wiping a forearm across his forehead.

"What is it?" she called.

"Chickens," he called back.

Ilse wrinkled her nose and Sawyer bent over and reemerged, lifting a small cage, the size of a dog kennel. Except instead of canines, this kennel housed chickens. Three of them. By the looks of things, two were still sleeping, while one had been woken by their voices and was moving around on the metal floor, its talons scraping against the ground.

Sawyer cursed, lowering the kennel, carefully, and stowing it back behind the door. Some water sloshed from a drip nozzle onto his shoes, but he ignored it, shooting one last look through the room.

Ilse didn't wait to watch. She felt like she was going to be sick and hastened out of the nose-twitching trailer, stepping into fresh air, amidst weeds and trees, inhaling deeply as she escaped that horrible place. The *whoompf* sound of the skull on the fan still echoed in the space behind her, and she walked away from the trailer far enough until the noise also faded into the background.

Then, hands on her knees, she breathed at the ground, in, out, trying not to scream. She'd thought they were being snuck up on. She'd thought Sawyer was going to get shot...

"Damn it," she muttered. "Damn it!" she said louder now.

None of this changed the news. Another woman taken. Two now taken within a twenty-four-hour period. The killer was escalating. Not only that. But if he'd attacked this second victim outside her own RV, it meant he was getting brazen, too. Not just striking on the trails, or in the deeper forest, but in the campgrounds also.

That didn't bode well for the next twenty-four hours.

"Damn it!" she repeated, screaming now, and feeling her throat constrict from the effort. She wasn't a loud person. She rarely raised her voice. And yet now, something felt right about the shout. She yelled again, incoherently, abandoning words for a moment to simply scream at the ground.

She heard movement behind her but didn't bother to look. Maybe Sawyer could keep his cool in situations like these. Maybe he'd think she was weak—and maybe he was right. But Ilse wasn't used to this. To any of it.

She missed her home office. Missed her clients. Missed dealing with those who she knew were safe, who she could help piece back together over the course of years.

Years, dammit. Not twenty-four hours.

Sawyer was built for the fear. Built, somehow, to withstand it. He had a switch—she'd seen him flip it. Shutting off his emotions, calculating, thinking, then acting on instinct. She glanced back now, breathing heavily, her voice hoarse.

Sawyer was moving around the trailer, stomping through the weeds, checking under the RV. Looking for another lair, most likely. But even Ilse could have told him he wouldn't find anything. Not here.

The killer had hidden the rest of his victims in the park. He liked keeping his work away from his home. This time, there'd be no exception.

Sawyer spat to the side after peering beneath the front of the trailer and finding nothing. He straightened and looked at her. "We need to shut down the park," he said. "State prevention or not... Rawley's not doing it. Half-assed effort. That's it. We *have* to shut it down."

Ilse inhaled, grateful he hadn't commented on her screaming. She swallowed, trying to soothe her throat before nodding once. "Guess so," she murmured.

"I'll call the rangers on the drive," Sawyer said, trampling some weeds and moving back towards her. He clutched a piece of paper in one hand—it looked like a flyer.

"The drive where?" Ilse said. "Back to the park?"

Sawyer shook his head, though. "Nah. They've got boots all over those woods. I found this."

He reached her and wagged the flyer beneath her nose. Ilse took it, frowning, and examining the text. Her eyes scanned the top heading, *"Meet the Gaiaknights—join the mother's army."*

"That's this guy's religion," she murmured. "He wrote about it online, too."

"Violent by the looks of it," Sawyer said, scanning a couple of the lines further down the document. "But look there," he said.

Ilse's eyes darted to the bottom of the paper, and then she went still.

"Meetings," she murmured. "This is an invitation to meetings..."

"Yeah. And look when the meetings take place."

She stared at the time. 7:00 PM. Then at the day. Wednesdays. "That's today," she murmured. "Tonight." She looked up. "Think he'll be there? After all of this?"

Sawyer shrugged. "I'll get the rangers to shut down the park. They'll already have law enforcement swarming it. Rawley will send in help. It'll give us some time to try and find this guy in his element. My guess... He's either hiding out in that park or... if we're lucky, he'll be here."

Ilse shivered, staring at the flyer and then swallowing again from the strain she now felt in her throat.

Would he be at the meeting? Or hiding in the woods?

One way or another, Sawyer and Ilse were two steps behind. If they wanted to catch up, they had to try *something.*

"Alright, let's go. The community center—how far is that?"

"Fifteen minutes," Sawyer said. "Gonna mean we're a few minutes late. Almost seven already. I'll drive."

CHAPTER TWENTY FOUR

"Shit," Sawyer cursed, slamming the car door outside the community center and kicking the tire. "Damn fools!" He yelled. A young couple, wearing swimming hats, glanced over at him, frowning across the parking lot.

"Sorry," Ilse said, raising an apologetic hand. The couple hurried away towards the glass doors of the community center.

Sawyer still had his phone open, though, and he lifted it to his lips as Ilse watched, wincing. "You have to close it! Are you insane? This guy isn't even close to done."

Ilse waited, watching as Sawyer listened to the muffled response. And then he simply spat on the concrete and snapped, "Next body is on you? Get it? On you!" He flung his phone towards a tree in the sidewalk, where it struck the bark, spun, then landed on the mulch, screen face-down.

Ilse flinched, smoothing her sleeves and allowing Sawyer to simmer a moment, before saying, "I take it they won't shut the park down."

Sawyer shot her a look, his eyes narrowed, his jaw set. "Idiots. Morons," he snapped. "Gonna get everyone killed for some stupid politics."

He marched back over to his phone lifting it and dusting it off. The screen was cracked, but Sawyer didn't even notice as he jammed the object of annoyance back into his pocket.

"And is that their final answer?" Ilse said. She could feel her own temper rising, but Sawyer's reaction suggested a far more personal connection than Ilse had seen up to this point.

He shook his head, spitting off to the side again, and then spinning on his heel. "Sheriff and Rawley got the governor to budge on a few thousand acres... Where the bodies were found. Send in a few of the national guard to babysit. But it's not even close to enough. We need to shut the whole park down. It's political... Idiot is thinking more about tourist season than *human lives!* Bureaucrat assholes... Morons," he added a final time for good measure, with a contemptuous smack of his lips.

"Well, maybe we won't have to," Ilse said, quickly, skipping across the sidewalk to catch up. "If *he's* here..." she said quietly, trailing off. As she did, she felt a shiver up her spine, and glanced around the parking lot, searching for attentive onlookers. But besides the couple heading out for a swim, and a couple of children shouldering rolled up chess mats, no one seemed to pay them any mind.

The community center was large and made mostly of glass and white paint, surrounded by tastefully erected trees and pruned shrubbery.

As they faced the center, Sawyer calmed down enough to glance in Ilse's direction and say, "You sure you want to come?"

She frowned. "Why wouldn't I?"

"I can do this on my own."

Ilse wasn't sure if she should be offended or grateful. "Two women are missing. There's no time."

Sawyer gave her a long look, but then seemed to reach a conclusion of his own and nodded once. He began to stride up the sidewalk, moving rapidly towards the community center. Together, they took the steps towards the rotating glass doors. Four glass doors occupied the top of twelve steps, organized in a sort of semi-circle, facing the parking lot. The reflection of greenery and trees off the windows did little to soothe Ilse, following her experiences from the last couple of days. She wasn't sure she would ever look at trees the same again.

Sawyer clutched the flyer in one hand. He consulted it as he moved through the community center. A woman behind the greeting desk perked up, smiled, and waved. "Can I help you?"

"Room 24," Sawyer said, not returning her smile.

The woman's friendly expression diminished a bit, but she nodded politely and said, "I see. You're here for the speech?"

Sawyer shrugged. "Something like that. Where's the room?"

"Downstairs," the woman replied, carefully now. "Third door on the left."

Sawyer moved in the direction she was pointing towards an exit sign and two flights of stairs, one going up, the other down.

Ilse walked with Sawyer, moving twice as energetically to keep up.

"Let me do the talking," Sawyer said. "You just stay safe. There are gonna be a lot of crazies."

"Maybe," Ilse said. "Though maybe a lot of them just responded to the invitation."

Sawyer gave her a long look. "What sorts of people do you think respond to an invitation like that?"

Ilse frowned but didn't speak further as they took the stairs, curling into a dimmer portion of the community center. One of the lights above looked like it had been smashed. A couple of tube lighting fixtures down the hall flickered, casting strange shadows across the walls. Construction paper artwork lined the walls, displaying crafts made by children. The juxtaposition of the art on the walls, the flickering lights, and room twenty-four made Ilse tense.

She reached the door first, prodded on by her own flighty nerves. Her hand pressed against the metal plate securing the handle to the wooden frame. From within, she heard a voice, dull and pulsing.

She licked her lips nervously and glanced at Sawyer. He mimed pushing. She complied, opening the door, and shouldering it the rest of the way.

The two of them emerged in the back of an auditorium. A basketball hoop still occupied one side of the room. The floor was lined with paint marking the rest of the court. But the far side of the room had a small wooden stage. The second basketball hoop had been lowered and wheeled off to the side where she could see it hidden next to a stack of foldout bleachers. Metal folding chairs lined the floor, facing the stage. Nearly eighty people, maybe a hundred, sat in the chairs, all staring up at the speaker.

Ilse wasn't sure what she'd been expecting but most of the people in the chairs looked normal enough. Then her gaze was caught by the figure at the podium.

A large man, covered in dirt and grime, and wearing a T-shirt that had once been white but was now streaked with mud.

He had thick hands, which he was making use of like gavels, pounding his podium.

The man's eyes bulged in his head, beneath his close-cut hair. His beard jutted out at wild angles, twisted and streaked with mud.

The man was large enough to subdue two young women. He was also covered in dirt, suggesting he easily could have just returned from the park.

This wasn't lost on Sawyer either, judging by the way his hand went to his weapon, and he began to sidle up a gap between the chairs, towards the stage.

"We cannot sit idly by," the large man was bellowing across the room. He didn't have a microphone, and yet his voice projected. "It is our responsibility for the sake of the children. For the sake of generations to come, to honor the mother in this way."

A few of the people sitting in the front row were clapping. Others watched quizzically.

The large man spread his arms now and bellowed, "This is not a choice. It is a reality. A demand she makes of all of you. Of us."

Sawyer sidled past a couple of chairs, maneuvering towards the side of the small stage.

"We will take it by whatever means we must," the man yelled, getting himself into a frenzy now, his eyes still bulging like marbles. A few of his sycophants in the front rows were clapping. A couple of women had risen to their feet and were waving their hands towards him as if to catch his attention.

"Do you hear me?" he called.

About twenty voices replied in practiced unison, "Heard and answered!"

A few others in the seats looked on with interest. A couple of people in the very back began to rise, moving towards the doors.

"I see you leaving," the man on the stage yelled, pointing at the retreating invitees. "You abandon your post so quickly. Good. The weak shall perish. You will answer for what you've exacted on the mother. She will consume you. And we will feast. Whether it be now, in a year, or in hundred, we are growing. You cannot stop this progress! You will answer… just like the others have answered! The nation is finally taking notice, but our mission has just begun! Those not with us will suffer or pay, if not by our hands, then the mother's!"

More laughter and chanting met his words from the sycophants in the front row, a few of them even got to their feet and began to move towards the poor souls who had dared to get up and try to leave quietly.

Sawyer, though, seemed to have seen enough. The speaker's size, with his violent rhetoric, and his mud-stained clothing was enough to entice action.

"FBI," Sawyer snapped, stalking up the stage with loud, thumping footsteps. "You're under arrest." His hand rested on his weapon, but he didn't draw it yet, showing a measure of self-restraint.

"What do you want?" snapped the speaker, turning sharply.

"I just told you. Mr. Fredrick, you're under arrest."

The mud-streaked monster named Teddy shot a shifty-eyed look toward Sawyer, then glanced towards a few of his friends sitting in the front. Ilse studied his face: panic, *fear.* This was him. It had to be the killer. It took him a moment, his eyes squinting, but then he reached a decision. He shoved the podium, sending it flying toward Sawyer and then bolted.

Sawyer cursed, reeling back, tripping over a microphone stand. The large man fled, beating a retreat towards one of the exits on the opposite side of the stadium.

Sawyer cursed, recovering himself, and breaking into a sprint as well. One of the women tried to reach out and trip him, but Ilse hastened forward, yanking her hand out of the way.

The woman cursed, and Sawyer leaped over her extended fingertips, taking the stairs of the stage and bolting towards the exit where the large cult leader was slipping into a hall.

Ilse's heart pounded. She could feel eyes on her now. Could see Sawyer now slipping out into the hall as well. She tried to think. She wouldn't be able to catch them that way. The large man would try to escape to the parking lot. Even woodsmen needed vehicles. Instead of heading towards the exit door, then, Ilse turned, breaking into a sprint and running back in the direction they'd come. She took the stairs, racing past the construction paper artwork. She could hear voices behind her as some of the sycophants followed. But they didn't give chase so much as watch her flee and call after her.

Her shoulders shook, a prickle along her spine as she hastened back to the first floor, and, with squeaking steps against the clean tiles, raced back towards the four rotating doors.

"Ma'am," a voice called from behind the greeting desk. "Is everything—"

Ilse didn't hear the rest of it, sprinting into the foyer, through the rotating doors. She breathed heavily, heart pounding. She stepped out onto the steps, taking them two at a time into the parking lot, glancing around the side of the building. There was an alley connected to a portion of the community center with darkened windows, suggesting it wasn't in use during the evenings. Was that the direction he would be coming from? Ilse winced, trying to remember.

Just then, a large figure emerged from the alley. She stared, stiffened.

The man shot nervous looks over his shoulder, and Ilse could hear Sawyer shouting after him. "Stop!"

But Teddy ignored the shouts, picking up his pace. The man was like a charging bull, enormous, fast, determined. Easily fast enough to surprise unsuspecting women on a trail. He spun back around, facing the parking lot, and Ilse realize she was standing directly in front of him.

She shivered, hands at her side. For a moment she wanted to shout, but even her lips felt numb. She thought back to the debacle at the training warehouse. She hadn't gotten out of the way. She hadn't done anything except freeze.

Now, as the large man barreled down on her, images flashed through her mind. Images of a shovelful of dirt. Images of a leering face. Images of thick hands against a small neck, squeezing. Dark images, memories. She felt cold, her heart hammering wildly. She opened her mouth, to try and tell him to stop. But the words didn't even come. She needed a weapon. Needed to do something. Needed to react. But her hands were frozen at her sides. She just stood there, doing nothing. But the large man charging towards her was still shooting looks over his shoulder, and he didn't see her. If he had taken a step to the left or the right, Ilse felt nearly certain she wouldn't have had the strength to react. Now, as it was, frozen to the spot, he slammed right into her. Two hundred pounds of muscle and fat crashed into her small, thin frame. The man cursed, stumbling, but Ilse felt like she'd been hit by a house. She slammed into the concrete, feeling a sudden jolt of pain up her back. She winced, sliding and scraping across the ground. A few people gasped who were trying to unload from a sedan. A mother was shouting at two children to get back into the car.

Sawyer's voice shouted incoherently from the alleyway, but Ilse was panicking now. Large hands gripped at her, and she heard a voice cursing, "Little bitch!"

The man was on top of her, strangling her, slamming her head against the ground.

She knew she should go for his eyes, kick, bite, scratch. But she just went limp. If she fought, he would hurt her. She remembered the scissors. The pain in her ear.

No one could resist him. He hurt all of them. He always hurt them. Resistance just brought more pain.

Her head slammed against the asphalt. Black spots started across her vision. The large hand over her throat squeezed tight, and she choked, unable to breathe. She couldn't resist. She'd survive if she just pretended that she wasn't there. Eventually he would leave her alone. He always did.

Dark spots became larger. Her breath was leaving. A small, sane portion of her mind told her she was about to die. She needed to fight. Fight!

But she'd frozen again. Frozen like when she trained. Frozen. Helpless, defenseless, motionless.

Useless.

Hot breath blossomed against her cheek. Spittle flecked her face. Fingers squeezed; her vision was gone. Gasping, not breathing, choking.

Then, vaguely, as if from down a deep tunnel, she heard a loud, screeching voice, "Get the hell off her!" A violent, tidal wave of fury pinpointed on that single sentence. And then, a blurring shadow, as Sawyer slammed into the aggressor. Sawyer was thin, lanky, about half the size of Teddy. But his bony shoulder slammed into the man's ribs, sending him reeling.

The man hit the grill of a truck and ricocheted off to the ground. He didn't have a chance to rise.

"You dare—" Sawyer was saying, spluttering, but not quite finding the words to finish the sentence. He seemed stuck on sheer outrage. "You dare!" he screamed. She had never seen Sawyer so unhinged. He kicked the man on the ground where he tried to grab at Ilse again. Teddy groaned, but again tried to rise, staring at Ilse like a Doberman eyeing a slab of meat. Sawyer kicked, punched, and the large man tried to rise again, shouting incoherently. He tried to get up, to get after Ilse, but the sheer fury of Sawyer's onslaught bludgeoned him. Again and again Sawyer drove a bony elbow into the man's chin, again and again he shoved off, and kicked him in the ribs. The whole time he shook with rage. Once he was sure the man had gone still, Sawyer wasn't done. He spun around, dropping to Ilse's side. His voice softened instantly, again, flipping that switch she knew he had. "Are you okay?" he said. "Paramedics are on their way. Are you okay?"

Ilse waved away his protests, sitting up, gasping, her throat bruised. "Bruised, but fine. I'm fine." The words choked out, and Sawyer seemed relieved to hear them; he shot a look of sheer loathing towards the man on the ground, then another back at her. "I'm sorry," he said. "I was too slow."

Ilse just shook her head in disgust. "It wasn't your fault. It was me. My own stupid fault. I'm sorry."

She leaned to the side, feeling weak all of a sudden as if her body wanted to give out. Her forehead pressed against Sawyer's shoulder, and he held her there for a moment, whispering, "I'm sorry. I shouldn't have let him hurt you. I'm sorry."

There was something haunting about Sawyer's voice. Somehow, she wasn't sure those words were directed just at her. "I'm sorry," he said, his voice strained. His eyes were glazed, as if he couldn't even see her. What was the *true* source of this rage? What was the source of this grief?

She found she didn't have the mental strength to think through it right now. She rested her head against his shoulder, breathing in, out, softly, the sound of sirens in the distance slowly approaching.

CHAPTER TWENTY FIVE

Ilse's body felt like one giant bruise, but she had refused to sit out of the interrogation. Now, sitting at the interrogation table, across from mean-eyed Teddy, they were once again in her domain. Here, words, thoughts, and psychology worked. All the muscles in the world didn't matter here. Sawyer had protested, and now he sat solemnly next to her, clearly wishing she had listened. But Ilse was determined. She felt humiliated. Was she always going to freeze up in the field? Maybe this was all a pipe dream. But for now, she had a mission. The source sat across from her.

Theodore Fredrick was massaging his knuckles. He had a busted lip, a bruised eye, and he winced every time he leaned to the side. Sawyer's beating had left its marks. Teddy was still stained with dirt and mud, and the handcuffs securing his wrists to the metal table rattled every time he flexed his fingers threateningly.

"How about we start with a name," Sawyer said.

The man gritted his teeth. Teddy clearly hadn't visited a dentist in decades. He was missing a couple of teeth and those he did have were yellow, if not brown. Most of them were crooked. "How about we start with a lawyer?" he snapped back.

Sawyer said, "You've got a way with words." He glanced down at the article on his phone he'd prepared. One of the many ranting musings on Teddy's blog. "Is that why you wrote, '*the man didn't see it my way, so my red knuckles changed his mind*'?" Sawyer looked up from his phone, the cracked screen visible from across the table. The man just shrugged. "Lawyer," he said.

Sawyer glared. "You had a lot to say back at the community center. What's got you clammed up all of a sudden?"

"Law," he said, "yer."

Sawyer leaned back, massaging his knuckles. "That's cute," he said. "You like putting up a fight when the person is half your size. But now you clam up. What gives?"

"I'm beginning to suspect you can't hear me," the man said, his mean eyes narrowed. "Lawyer."

Ilse just watched this exchange for a moment, organizing her own thoughts. She wasn't used to field work. She didn't even carry a gun. Maybe she was being too hard on herself. But whatever the case, she was determined to get answers. This was her domain. If she left this room without answers, there was absolutely nothing she brought to the table. But stressing out about it wouldn't help. She inhaled for four seconds then exhaled for seven. She counted in her mind as she did. She found the breathing exercise soothing; once she had calmed herself a bit, she forced aside the thoughts of the two women that had been captured. Forced aside the thoughts of the many bodies, and the years of violence. Forced aside the thought of the man's criminal record. She needed to speak with him. But how did one speak to a brute? Not with more prudishness. Not the way Sawyer was trying. To this man, everything was about control, his own ego, and his beliefs.

"I liked your chickens," Ilse said quietly.

The man frowned.

She didn't say anything further, leaving this silence to fill the space between them.

He hesitated, but then snapped, "lawyer."

"Three of them. They seemed nice. It was a dog kennel. I was surprised it wasn't a dog. Your place was nice too. I like animals."

The man hesitated. Breaking barriers was a science, but also an art form. She had implied that she'd been in his house, invaded his privacy, but at the same time she had suggested she liked what she found. Vulnerability, willing or not, had been rewarded with praise. So what could it hurt to answer questions honestly? Vulnerability could be rewarded.

She said, "I think the fox was my favorite. Did you do them yourself?"

"What are you talking about?" he snapped.

Not an answer, but at least not a deflection this time.

"I've seen taxidermy before. Usually, most people, get someone to do it for them. It's an art form. It's very hard to do. Really hard. It takes a lot of skill. Not that I'm trying to blame you. I would totally get it if you had to hire someone to do it. Most people have to."

Another vector of attack. Pride.

And this time, he bit. "I did it myself," he snapped. "Not that you would know anything about it."

"I suppose not. You're right. It is quite amazing, though. Did you hunt all the animals yourself?"

"I do everything myself, girl," he said. "This is a war—you can't trust anybody."

Sawyer, almost imperceptibly, leaned back. A subtle gesture, but one she noticed. He just remained quiet, melting into the background, listening and allowing her to take the lead.

Ilse didn't even blink in his direction, preferring to keep sole focus. Her tone remained calm, friendly, even. "A war? That's violent language. You were saying something similar back at that meeting. I wish I could've heard the whole speech."

"Yeah? I write about it."

"I saw your blog."

"Alright. So what? I don't care what you think. Like I said, this is a war. And I'll outlast everyone. Mother will sustain me."

"Yes," Ilse replied carefully. "I read about Gaia on your blog. Gaia came before all the other gods. She's more powerful than any of them: Zeus, Odin. She's the most powerful."

He nodded now, fervently, a sudden flicker in his eyes, and his motions became more agitated. "Exactly right," he said. "Mother Earth is stronger than any of them. They don't get it. So many people around here worship dead folk. But I worship the earth itself. The same earth their gods walked on. That twenty billion years ago, creatures walked on."

Ilse nodded. "It makes sense. If you had to choose a side, why not go with the very thing beneath your feet?"

He snorted. "It's not a *thing*. She. She's the mother. She watches everything. She hears everything. And the rest of them, you, tear it down, break it, believe it." He clicked his tongue in a disapproving sound, his rotten teeth flashing. "It's sad."

"It is. Is that why you fight for her?" Ilse said, framing the violence in a positive light. Hopefully opening up another vector of conversation.

"I'll always fight for her. Your friend there mentioned my comments about red knuckles. It wasn't about being poetic. It was about doing what was right. I found the man littering in the forest. I asked him to pick it up. I was polite. He laughed at me. He wasn't laughing after I was done."

"And it was wrong for police to arrest you," Ilse said, "wasn't it? You were just doing the right thing."

"Exactly. I don't hurt people who don't need hurting. Nature is dangerous. An avalanche, flood, tsunami. But also smaller. Have you seen how predators feast on the weak? That's the way it's supposed to be. I protect. That's my job. That's everyone's job. You don't get it. None of you do."

Ilse shook her head. "I guess not. But I'd like to know, if you're being honest, then why did you escalate? I understand beating up someone over littering," she said, her voice still gentle, compassionate, understanding, "but I don't understand what you did to the women?"

She stated vaguely enough, allowing his mind to fill in the blanks. He frowned. "Did what?"

"The ones you killed. Stuffed them. Were they litter to you? Why did you kill them?"

Now, though, it was as if she'd slapped him. He leaned back also, staring with hooded eyes. His face went pale as if the blood had fled his cheeks. "Shit," he said, "that's what this is about? I didn't kill anyone."

Ilse blinked, frowning. The reaction seemed—*genuine.* She felt swallowed, watching him even more closely now, the hairs on her neck standing at attention. Why would he seem genuine? The killer wouldn't be surprised, would he? Amnesia? Split personality? Something else?

"What about those lairs?" Sawyer said, leaning in again, his posture aggressive. "Did you build them yourself? Did you find them?"

"Lairs? I don't know what you're talking about. I didn't kill anyone."

"You just admitted to violence," Sawyer said. "I've seen your record. Three assaults. Once against a police officer."

"That bastard was trying to drag me away from a peaceful protest," snapped the man. "We were going to save a maple—hundred years old. Older than all three of us by the looks of you. And they wanted to cut it down. You tell me who was in the right."

"You put him in the hospital."

The man snorted. "One punch. On a weak chin. A lot of you guys have 'em. Bitch."

Sawyer's eyes narrowed and he tapped a finger against the metal desk between them. "If you're such a hero, how come you pick on young women? You nearly killed my partner."

He snorted. "I didn't kill her. She's fine; look at her. I was just going to knock her out to get away. She was the one who tripped me."

"I don't believe you."

"I don't kill people," he snapped. "I didn't hurt any women. I don't know anything about lairs. You're insane."

Sawyer snorted at this. But Ilse felt a niggling itch along her spine again... He seemed so genuine. Truly angry, truly outraged. Also unhinged. A psychopath? A masterful liar? Was she missing something?

Before Sawyer could retort, though, a commotion erupted outside the interrogation room. Voices drifted in from the hall, and the door suddenly banged open. A large, rotund man in a poorly fitting suit, carrying a briefcase, came in. He had intelligent eyes which darted around the room, taking in the scene, and those same eyes narrowed the way his client's did. "Excuse me, but you can't be here speaking with my client," snapped the attorney

"We were just leaving," Sawyer retorted.

A couple of deputies in the hall shrugged apologetically. The lawyer was already muttering in his client's ear, and Ilse heard, "You shouldn't talk when I'm not here. Don't say anything else."

Sawyer helped Ilse up from her chair, and the two of them moved towards the hall, allowing the door to seal shut behind them.

The two deputies were standing next to Sheriff Culpepper, who was frowning at the door. "He did it," the sheriff said. "There's no doubt. That's our guy."

Sawyer nodded, along with one of the deputies. "Looks like," Sawyer said. Let him have his lawyer. Doesn't matter. We've got the bastard."

The sheriff leaned against the sealed metal door, and murmured, "We still need to find where he hid those two girls. They're running out of time."

Sawyer grit his teeth. "When can I get back in there?"

The sheriff said, "Give the lawyer a few minutes and then we'll take another crack. But look, Tom, you need to find those girls. Hear me?"

Sawyer nodded rigidly, his eyes like his posture: brittle.

Ilse was already moving, uneasy, heading away from the gathering of law enforcement officers. She'd gotten him to talk. She'd done her job. And now she felt sick. She pushed into the room at the end of the hall marked as the women's bathroom. She leaned over the sink, exhaling. She stared at herself in the mirror.

He'd spoken. He'd talked. And now everyone was convinced it was him. He'd admitted to his violence. Clearly, he was ideologically possessed.

He wasn't above violence for his beliefs. He'd assaulted a police officer over a tree, beating up a camper over some litter.

What about the two women? Were they still alive?

She breathed heavily, staring at the sink and reached down, turning one of the faucets. Hot water. Steam began to rise, fogging the bottom of the mirror.

So why was she feeling so uneasy?

She reached for the soap, hands trembling and began to wash her hands, flicking droplets against thc porcclain basin.

Something didn't add up. Something didn't feel right. She'd been so focused on apprehending Mr. Fredrick that she hadn't allowed herself to think beyond.

Her throat was bruised, her back in pain.

He was a violent man.

But he'd said he had done the taxidermy on his own animals. Why did that matter?

"Because he did a shit job," she said, answering her own question out loud.

And he had. The taxidermy had been bad. But the ones he'd done with the human bodies? Immaculate. Pristine. The postures, the dynamic stances, all of it would've taken a level of skill that hadn't been anywhere in the trailer on Mr. Fredrick's land.

He was an amateur. Whoever had stuffed the people was skilled.

She shivered at this characterization. Then her eyes darted to the soap.

She stared, heart pounding. She thought of the lotion back in the second lair. The bottle they had seen on the way in. Why lotion? There was something tender about lotion, even sensual about the postures; something that suggested the killer cared for the victims in his own sick, twisted way.

She glanced towards the bathroom door. Mr. Fredrick didn't fit that description. He didn't have the skill for taxidermy. A bone chilling thought. But a true one. He didn't have the nature that suggested any form of gentleness, friendliness. The killer cared about his objects. Cared about the corpses as if they were friends. They meant something more to him than just an obstacle against nature itself. Maybe she had been wrong.

It sickened her.

But maybe this wasn't just religious. The body lotion, the care and posing.

What if it was also sexual too?

What if she had missed it?

Both sexual and religious. That would explain something about the victims. Most of the violence Mr. Fredrick had perpetrated had been against men. The cop was a man. The litterer had been a man. But the killer was targeting young women. Mostly young women. These last two victims were women. Kristine, a woman.

Sexual and religious.

Ilse washed off the rest of the soap and then turned off the tap. Droplets dripped from her fingers against the basin and she stared into the foggy mirror. "What now?"

She spoke the words to her reflection, as if expecting a response.

Everyone in the precinct thought they had their man. They thought they had done their job.

But they were wrong.

At least, she feared they were.

Which meant the killer was still out there. The brutish Teddy had admitted to his violence but seemed stunned by the accusation of murder.

These crimes were not the crimes of a brute. The real killer was more calculating. More cynical. More purposeful.

He was still out there. With his victims. And he was escalating—they refused to close down most of the park. Another victim could be taken in the next few hours unless she *did* something.

But everyone else seemed convinced. So what could she do?

Ilse stared into the mirror, desperately thinking.

And then it struck her.

She knew what she had to do next.

CHAPTER TWENTY SIX

He didn't like when they squirmed, or when they screamed. Fear... he didn't like fear. It bothered him. He watched as his two soon-to-be friends twisted and writhed, their hands straining against the silk rope.

The silk was expensive, but he used it to avoid bruising. He stared into the cage, making a soft cooing noise as he did.

The two women kept their eyes closed, pretending they couldn't see him. But they both tried to twist free of their bonds where they rested against the cushioned floor of his cage. The cage had once belonged to an old hunter, hired by the park to take down mountain lions—he'd managed to get it from a junkyard and install it in his own home.

It was nice to be back home. The smooth walls around him, stone set in mud. A door made of bark from his favorite oak. No electricity here. No running water, save the creek two miles north. No one would come here. No one could find him.

Only those he invited were allowed entry.

Now, two such people who'd been blessed with entrance were whimpering; he watched them twist and bump against each other, freeze in fright, then begin to move again.

Neither of them could see on account of the blindfolds. The cushioned ground would protect their bodies from disfigurement or scratches.

He was a craftsman when it came to such things.

"Isn't that right, Maya," he murmured, glancing towards the kitchen table.

A gorgeous, large-chested brunette beamed at him over the table, her eyes fixed, unblinking, her hands perpetually clutching a dish which she was placing on the table. Frozen in place. He'd created her nearly two years ago. No one had noticed her missing. People got lost in the park sometimes. Other times, they got lost nearby, and he would bring them here.

Hitchhikers were his favorite. He could take his time, scoping out the offering, deciding if it fit his project.

Now, the whimpering behind him was like music. Soft, and sweet. He didn't like fear. He didn't like tears. It could ruin their faces.

Soon... though, soon it would be quiet again. His home would be quiet, just like he wanted.

He needed a few more, though, before that could happen.

He stared through the window of his home. Little more than a circlet of glass embedded in a muddy wall. They would never find his home. He'd built it last. His other attempts, his other hideouts—they'd found those. But his home...

No. They were deep, *deep* in the woods. No one came here. No one even knew how to get here; the terrain, even for the rangers was too treacherous.

Only he knew the way. And even if they did come... His home didn't stand. It seemed a part of the muddy slopes themselves, hollowed out of the hillside, camouflaged by grass and stone and root.

Camouflaged by his friend... By the forest.

"Well, Maya, soon," he murmured, patting the brunette on the shoulder. He pointed and smiled at Janice who was by the stove. "Oh, don't you get smart with me," he said, laughing. "I'll come over there and show you *clever.*" He patted Maya on the rear, giving her a playful squeeze.

If he listened, he could almost hear her giggle in delight.

He moved over to Janice, whispering in her ear, nibbling on the lobe. "Soon, my dear," he murmured. "Very soon we'll be together forever."

And this was true. Janice didn't move either, frozen, bent as she was, peering into the oven and sliding a tray of cookies onto a wire rack.

His new friends would be joined by others soon enough.

Very, very soon.

Five... Yes. He would take five. Fresh five. Fresh was important. He had to preserve them, and it took so much time to perfect his beauties. His friends. No—he'd take all five first. They'd be the freshest he'd ever worked on. *She* would be proud.

That would be the biggest sacrifice he ever made.

And then...

He licked Janice's earlobe, the cold skin delectable against his tongue. "Then I'll be immortal, my dear," he whispered. "Then I'll be here with you and Maya, and Kimber, and Nina forever... You were always my favorite." His nude form leaned against her bent-over figure, and he found a hunger rising in him.

"Yes, yes," he said, breathily. "One great sacrifice. When I have all five. Those little mewling pups won't make so much noise then. I won't wait... No, no, I won't. Tonight. I promise. I'll go again tonight, my dear. I'll find us another friend."

CHAPTER TWENTY SEVEN

"I... I'm pretty sure," Ilse murmured beneath her breath, head low as she faced Sawyer by the conference room table that they'd cleared for him. "I don't think he's our guy."

Sawyer was playing with a bottle of caffeine pills, distractedly glancing at the door and waiting for another shot at interrogating the suspect. At her words, he barely even glanced over, focused as he was on the door. "Hmm," he said.

"I'm serious," she pressed. "I don't think he's our guy. He's too brutish. And the taxidermy animals—"

"He was your idea," Sawyer murmured, still distracted. He heard the sound of a door open down the hall and shot to his feet, pushing out of the chair. He shot Ilse a long look. "I'll get him to confess. Just give me a couple of hours."

"I don't think we have that long," Ilse replied.

Sawyer sighed, rubbing at his nose. "What do you want me to do? The governor already refused to shut down the park. They're doubly unlikely to do so now that we've got our guy."

"Now that we *think* we've got him," Ilse retorted.

Sawyer placed his caffeine pills back into his pocket. He peered out into the hall and then patted his hand eagerly against the door frame. "Ah, there we are. That's my cue," he said. "Look, Ilse, just sit tight for a couple of hours."

"Sawyer, I'm telling you, it's not our guy."

Sawyer turned fully now, sparing her his attention for a moment longer. "If not, I'll find out," he said. "You did good work, doc. You got him talking—we're going to nail this bastard. Besides, we need to find where those women are being kept. If this isn't the killer... It's probably too late for them anyway."

"We need to close down the park."

"I tried. They refused."

"We need to try again."

"The rangers are back on site," Sawyer replied. "As far as everyone around here is concerned, we've got the guy." He hesitated, frowning. "If you're right though..."

"Sawyer!" A voice suddenly shouted from the direction of the interrogation room. Sheriff Culpepper was glaring out into the hall. "Are you coming?" demanded the man.

Sawyer hesitated, glancing back at Ilse.

"Now, Sawyer!" the sheriff yelled. "I have to release a statement. I need you to take the reins here!"

Ilse could feel the lanky agent at war with himself. This was not a bureaucratic man. If anyone was willing to investigate an instinct, it would be Tom. But did she really want to drag him into a hunch? That's what it was, wasn't it? She wasn't *certain.* Not at all. She sighed, half opened her mouth, but closed it again. The sheriff was now waving an arm furiously.

"Go," Ilse muttered beneath her breath. "Go—help him."

"You sure?"

"Yes. Yes. Go."

The taciturn agent just winced apologetically, straightened his posture, and stalked down the hall towards the open interrogation room door where the sheriff was still yelling.

Ilse didn't want to sit in this time.

While she wasn't *certain,* she *was* growing more and more confident she'd been right. This wasn't their guy. Which meant the real killer was out there.

She reached into her pocket, pulling out the radio she'd lifted from Culpepper's desk. She hadn't really thought anyone would listen to her. Even Sawyer knew the sum of it. Everyone was convinced they had their suspect. No one was going to want to put in more long hours, more double shifts, more overtime looking for a phantom.

Ilse had suspected it would come down to this.

Down to a choice.

Her choice.

She stared at the radio she'd lifted from the sheriff's desk, breathing in, out, heavily. The rangers had their own radios, and a couple had been loaned to law enforcement. Sawyer would have access to one when he returned.

She nodded adamantly, then bent over, pulling a pen from her pocket and quickly scribbling down a note on the back of an old receipt. Once she'd finished writing, she placed the note under Sawyer's laptop and snatched the keys for the police sedan off the table, where Sawyer had left them along with his phone so they wouldn't jab into his leg throughout the interrogation. Also... there, resting next to the keys—a knife. One of Sawyer's utility blades. She stared at this for a moment, but then swiped it also. He wasn't allowed to take it into interrogation anyway.

Ilse gripped the keys like a lifeline, pocketing the knife, then marched purposefully out into the hall. The sedan they used had a Bluetooth, detachable music radio. That would serve for the second part of what came next.

Her eyes narrowed, her countenance darkened as she picked up pace and hurried towards the precinct's exit.

***

Darkness pressed around her, and Ilse gripped the steering wheel of the vehicle. She'd grown so accustomed to letting Sawyer drive her around, she felt twitchy as she pulled into the parking lot of the night-time forest preserve. The Boat, her own, wide, luxury sedan back at the house was a much smoother ride than the unmarked police car.

But the Boat didn't have a detachable radio player.

She took this also, holding it in the same hand as the one gripping the walkie-talkie she'd borrowed, then pushed out into the night.

As she emerged in the dark, at the trailhead leading through the campgrounds, Ilse felt a weight descend on her. The darkness seemed thick, cloying. It felt tangible in her throat, against her face, in her clothes, as if it were sifting through her, invading her.

The trees around her loomed large and crooked, their branches stretched to the sky as if to claim the horizon itself.

The forest had always been a threat. She'd tried to befriend it, but it was only a tentative alliance. A non-aggression pact. One that could be broken by either party at any moment. For one wild moment, she half wondered what it might be like to burn the whole forest down.

She blinked, shaking her head and inhaling for four seconds, then exhaling for five. Her fingers probed towards the utility knife she'd borrowed from Sawyer.

Sometimes, even after all the work she'd put in, wild thoughts occurred and scared her. But Ilse knew better than to ruminate on these errant thoughts, and so she spoke to herself, out loud. “No. I won't.”

She couldn't burn, couldn't hide, couldn't evade and avoid.

Her past could only be confronted head on. She gripped the radio and the Bluetooth music player in one hand. The other had pushed the keys back into her pocket... She left her hand there, her fingers brushing the cool porcelain of the small tchotchke of the doll she'd found back at her father's old home. The half-broken thing felt equal parts smooth and fractured. Her fingers trailed against the item, then, trembling, lifted from her pocket.

The little porcelain doll wasn't going anywhere.

The same couldn't be said for Ilse.

She picked up her pace, moving past various campgrounds in the dark, the terrain looking quite different at night. She picked out huddled forms, movement. Watched some camp-goers huddled around a contained fire.

It was still packed.

She gritted her teeth, seething at it all.

If she was too late. If this was too late, then another camper would be taken. This would be all of their fault.

Most people seemed to be sleeping, or winding down, though. Tents were motionless, RV windows darkened. The rare few who were still awake occasionally shot a glance in the direction of the sound of her crunching footsteps.

Ilse redoubled her pace, heading towards the far end of the campgrounds, towards the more isolated section of the forest. She breathed in, out, trying to steady her nerves. Her hand twisted at the hem of her sweater, nervously tapping out a pattern on the fabric.

She wasn't a big runner, though she'd once been back in college. Now, she preferred ju-jitsu, practicing at her dojo outside Seattle. Only a couple of hours from the park. Not that it seemed to matter much that she trained. If she froze up every time she was accosted, then it wouldn't matter if she trained with all the black belts in the world.

Now it would be up to her to make sure she didn't freeze up.

No one else could save her if she did.

Ilse's eyes narrowed, inhaling, exhaling.

This wasn't a plan... was it?

This was suicide...

“Shut up,” she said, out loud.

She was walking herself into danger. Why not just wait for backup?

“What backup?” she replied to her own inner monologue.

In a way, she knew both the reasonable and wild parts of herself were right. It was true she was walking into danger. True this was high risk. But also true that two young women were out there, trapped or dead.

She *refused* to show up late in a forest again.

Three weeks too late last time. It had cost all her siblings. Some of them their lives.

Kristine had killed herself because Ilse had been too late.

She couldn't spend her whole life cowering in home offices or behind tough detectives. When Mr. Fredrick had slammed into her, her first instinct had been to go still. To wait, to hope he wouldn't harm her if she just complied.

She could still feel the helplessness. She'd just lay there, allowing him to choke her.

Little Hilda Mueller had cried, had wept, but hadn't moved, her lips stitched together as her father had tried to bury her alive. She hadn't run. She hadn't tried to escape.

The forest had watched, indifferent. It hadn't helped.

Ilse was sick of it. Sick of hiding. Sick of crying.

What was a life lived in fear, anyway?

No… No, she would find the missing women. She would bring them back, whether or not the rangers, or the deputies, or the FBI agreed with her.

She picked up her pace, stamping through the dusty trails until she reached one of the empty campsites at the far end of the campgrounds. Darkness was complete now. No lights from campfires, no lights from anything. The stars above glinted and winked, staring down at her. The moon caressed the horizon in a motherly glow, tender and nurturing.

She stepped over the undergrowth, ducking under low branches, moving towards the most isolated portion of campground yet. Then, she began setting up. Ilse placed the walkie talkie on the ground next to her. She then reached into her pocket, fumbling a moment, but made sure her old burner phone was turned on. She placed a call to Sawyer, but then hung up before he could reply.

That done, she pulled the car's detachable radio, setting it up in the dust and dirt.

Isolated from the rest of the camp, settling into a site without a tent, exposed, Ilse began to turn up the music. An old, staticky station, every other word to the crooning tune lost in a sea of fuzz. The music came louder, louder now.

She reached for the radio, sighing once. Then picked up the device. She wasn't too familiar with these things, but she'd spent the last two days watching the rangers use them throughout the forest. She turned the thing on, sliding the resistant button with her thumb...

Nothing happened.

Ilse stared, trying again.

The small red light remained dull. The radio wasn't working.

Ilse felt a cold chill creep up her spine. She'd taken it off a desk *not* from a charger station... In her haste, she hadn't even checked. *Idiot.* She tried the radio a final time, but try as she might, the thing wouldn't turn on. She was alone out here.

The music from her speaker pulsed louder, louder, moving through the trees, the sound of fuzz and tunes mingling with the creak of branches and rustling leaves.

***

The friend of the forest moved lightly on his feet, even in the dark. He knew these trails. He'd lived here for years after all... His two new friends waited back at home, along with Janice and Maya and the others.

They wouldn't be alone for long. Just a few more friends. A few more, then the offering of blood and flesh. Then...

He smiled to himself in the dark, his lips curling back like orange rind peeled from the fruit.

Still, tonight he had work to do. It wasn't always easy to find a proper candidate. Not just any first-fruits would do. Only those acceptable. Only those who were fitting. He'd already been on the look out for hours now. But people were more careful. Moving in packs or pairs. Hiding away from him. Hours had slipped by—no proper candidate.

He moved through the undergrowth on the opposite side of the dusty trail. The campgrounds sprawled before him. His eyes darted over tents, and mobile units and tinted-windowed sedans pulled onto the flat partitions. His eyes narrowed at the gas-guzzling beasts.

The mother alone would know what to say...

The mother would whisper instructions in his ears about the desecrators.

But a holy friend could only do so much on behalf of the woods. Sometimes, nature itself would take its course. She was in a rage, anyway. More fires, more hurricanes, more storms, more snow. She was rising from her slumber, and soon she'd have her say on them all.

But in the meantime, he would pave the way.

And he would live long enough to witness the collapse.

He spotted an older couple moving from the facilities back towards their tent. He spotted a young man playing with a small animal outside a tent. His eyes skipped from one scene to the next. He'd tried young men before, but it didn't please the mother the same way. Didn't please him the same way either.

So he moved on, ducking under boughs. Leaves brushed his cheeks, tickling against his skin. Spindly, jutting branches caught at his naked flesh, scraping over his shoulders. But he didn't mind.

He continued with practiced precision through the dark, unseen, unnoticed.

They never paid close enough attention.

He reached another campsite and heard soft laughter.

He frowned, peering through the branches, stepping closer and ducking under a tangle of vines to spot a young woman leaning back against a toppled log, waving a hand towards a young man who was retreating off into the forest on the other side of the campsite.

"Don't go anywhere," the young man called, his voice full of mirth. "Imma be right back," he said, his tone slurred.

The girl sitting on the log pulled a tuft of moss and tossed it after the man, giggling again. Her shirt was slipping coyly over one shoulder, her pale shoulder visible in the dark, catching the moon against her smooth skin.

He wet his lips, watching as the man distanced further, likely to go relieve himself in the trees. Another impetuous gesture. He didn't go into their homes, urinating willy-nilly... But not all lessons could be taught.

Some had to be seen.

He waited, breathing slowly, staring at where the young woman now huddled on the log, pulling her thin shirt close and staring off in the direction the man had disappeared.

Sometimes his friends stared at him like that also. A sort of longing in their eyes, a desperation, a need.

It felt good to be desired.

He took a step from the trees, hands flexing at his thighs.

But then...

He froze, wrinkling his nose and frowning, tilting his head even as if to sniff at the horizon.

A strange, static-filled buzz of music... It echoed through the trees, echoed across the park. A pulsing, blaring, half-fuzz tone. It grated at his ears. It mocked the forest itself.

He scowled, waiting for the sound to die...

Except it only grew louder.

He pulled up now, turning away from the woman on the log. She was also tilting her head, listening and bobbing with the music.

Though to call it music was a stretch. A horrible, screeching, thumping cacophony. The critters and creatures, the pets of the mother would flee the sound. The birds would wake. The whole habitat would be disrupted because of such chaos.

He felt his fingers twitch at his side. His eyes narrowed.

He glanced back towards the woman on the log.

But the music grew louder still, spewing like auditory sewage through his home.

He snarled, turning away from the woman on the log and breaking into a jog, heading towards the direction of the obnoxious sound.

Sometimes, he chose his new friends.

Other times their sheer idiocy chose for him.

He picked up his pace, moving fleet-footed through the trees, his naked skin kissed by breeze and bur alike. His skin was used to flagellation, his body used to the cold. Nude and dirt-streaked, he picked up his pace, using the source of the horrible, grating sound as his marker.

The campsite in question was at the far edge of the camping grounds, where the desecrators often gathered.

Now, the site in question was abandoned.

Save a single, solitary figure.

He pulled up, covering his ears momentarily with the palms of his hand to block out the horrendous noise. He tilted his head, peering through the branches at the single figure standing in the dusty clearing.

No tent.

No shelter.

A trap?

Did the desecrators come to catch him now?

Or was this a gift of the god?

Was mother looking out for his best?

The woman in question fidgeted, brushing her hair past her cheek. Even in the moonlight, it was obvious she was pretty, in a natural, sort of way. No makeup, no blush, no eyeliner.

His eyes widened. A natural beauty. The way the mother intended.

And here she was, sending out a call into the surrounding woods as if *inviting* him to find her.

This wasn't a trap.

It was a gift from the mother herself.

What could be more perfect to join the rest of his friends?

He stepped from the trees, quiet, careful, placing his feet to avoid sound as much as possible. He emerged in the clearing, his feet pressing against the dusty terrain. She still hadn't seen him. She'd blinded herself with that noise.

In the forest, at night, sound—not sight—was the best way to see. He couldn't wait to show her.

CHAPTER TWENTY EIGHT

Ilse's ears were beginning to hurt, and the walkie-talkie was still dead. Everything told her to turn and return to the more populated campgrounds. But wasn't that what she always did? Hide? Run away? She stared almost sightless in the dark at the trees around her. They seemed little more than one giant amalgam of shadow. What if he was out there? Her father. What if his face emerged from the night, leering at her, his eyes staring, his lips twisting in that horrible little smile of his? The way that sadist would smile before he hurt one of them. Her eyes began to droop as the exhaustion of the last few days caught up with her. Even with the fear running through her system, she couldn't shake sheer exhaustion. Still, the fear did keep her standing.

Maybe this wasn't worth it. Maybe she should have just waited with the others. Maybe they were right.

"Then why be scared?" she muttered to herself.

If, indeed, they did have the right killer, she had nothing to fear, did she?

But she couldn't leave now. Not with the two women still out there. They were in danger or dead. But she refused to believe they were dead until she had proof. No one came for her siblings when they were trapped. Ilse was supposed to, but even she had delayed. She still couldn't remember why. She couldn't delay any longer. The forest claimed too many secrets. She'd grown to trust the forest and despise the forest.

The killer couldn't be allowed to walk free.

Her eyes drooped again, and her shoulders sagged as exhaustion fell across her. She missed Sawyer at her side. She'd been acting cold towards him. But he'd been strange too. She wasn't sure what to think of all of that.

With Sawyer, things felt nice. He didn't talk as much as she did. For someone in the profession of gab it was a nice change of pace. He was more instinctual, spontaneous.

She felt her cheeks warm at the thought. Thoughts she rarely allowed herself to entertain. Thoughts, that even if she did consider, she suppressed. She hadn't thought a relationship was possible for someone like her. So damaged. Now, though, the thoughts seemed important, somehow. It was important to be honest, wasn't it?

Her eyes felt like lead now. She wanted to just yawn and curl up on the forest floor.

As this thought flitted through her sleep-deprived brain...

A sudden burst of movement from behind her suddenly startled her to attention. Ilse only caught a single glimpse of the wild-eyed attacker. A man, completely nude, streaked with mud and dirt and a beard and hair like a caveman came charging across the ground with wild footsteps, his eyes alight like the moon.

In one hand, he clutched a rock now swinging towards her forehead. A sudden cold flooded Ilse's system, her nerves responding to the stimuli.

Things almost seemed to slow, her mind processing thoughts as fast as the neural connections would allow. *Don't freeze. Don't free—*

Was all she could think, her panicked mind trying to fill in the gaps of the wild-eyed, wild-haired attacker. She'd frozen back in training. Frozen when Teddy had tackled her. Frozen when her father had buried her alive. Frozen again and again. She was sick of allowing her mind to root her in place. Now, in the dark, with the sound of static and music emanating around her, alone in the forest...

Forests... So familiar to her now. Something about the witness of trees, the familiarity gave her pause. The trees had tormented her—the creak and sway of their branches, their silent witness to her family's torment.

Now, they watched again, their shadows one giant monolith, bathing the ground in darkness, holding her fast.

She felt a flicker of fury in that single, suspended moment. She wouldn't allow the trees to watch again. She wouldn't set her own roots. She lifted her voice *and screamed!*

But the sound of her shout was drowned by the blaring radio.

Then, everything seemed to speed up again.

The bludgeoning rock whistled towards the back of her head, but Ilse ducked. She didn't freeze—she moved! She flung herself backwards, tripping over her own feet and hitting the dust. The wild man was on her a second later, snarling and baring his teeth as he came.

She scrambled back, fingers and feet scraping against the ground. She'd managed to attract the killer. This was him; it had to be! Her hand darted towards her pocket, gripping the knife she'd taken from Sawyer's desk.

But the second part of the plan had required the walkie-talkie. She needed to call for backup. Now, though, the thing was still dead. The battery wasn't charged. She pulled the knife sharply, trying—with a trembling thumb—to flick the blade open.

The madman was on her, though. Naked and hairy—not to mention *the stench.* Her nose itched, her eyes watered against the horrible smell as he tried to lunge at her, pressing towards her as she reeled back.

It was as if he hadn't showered in months—perhaps years.

The smell accosted her as she finally whipped the blade out of her borrowed knife. She slashed *hard.* But the mountain man reacted faster—almost like a forest creature in his speed. His large hand slapped at hers, sending the knife skittering into the dark.

Panic flooded her.

Gasping, she scrambled away from her assailant, kicking dust, plunging towards the trees. The knife? Where was it? Where—too dark. She'd lost it.

Ilse regained her feet completely and flung an arm out, dislodging a hand tight on her shoulder. Her fingers probed into her pocket, ripping out her small, dumb phone and lifting it. As she ran, stumbling forward, it was nearly impossible to navigate the numbers. Sawyer was on speed dial, though. Her fingers tremored.

The man behind her caught her again, gripping her by the shoulders and yanking her back *hard.*

Her legs continued the momentum while her body went still. Her feet kicked out like the edge of a pendulum, up over the dusty road, across the ground.

Her back slammed into the dust, and her spine twisted in pain. For a moment, she felt a flash of terror that she'd snapped her spine. But then she managed to kick, trying to re-orient herself. Black spots danced across her vision, and she heard the huffing breaths of her attacker, feeling his hands grip her shoulders while trying to hold her to the ground. Fingers moved along her arm, towards her throat.

Gasping, Ilse tried to get to her feet, kicking out his she did. But again, the man slammed her back against the dust.

"Get off," Ilse gasped, her voice weak, trembling.

Again she tried to rise, and again she fought hard fingers against her windpipe, squeezing tight. Sweat and dust intermingled across her brow, pain exploded in her chest, and she felt like she couldn't breathe. Her fingers gripped her phone in a slack grip. The device banged against the dirt at her side, she tried to lift it, but he placed a knee on her forearm holding her down. The sound of the static and the music still emanated through the trees. Even if she had managed to summon a breath to scream, if he hadn't choked the air from her lungs, she wasn't sure anyone would have even heard her.

She should have waited for Sawyer. She should have called for backup. But she hadn't been allowed any the first time. What was Hilda supposed to do? The trees were the only witnesses. At least this time she would suffer alone.

A small, more rational part of her mind wondered at this thought. Was she punishing herself? Did she want to suffer in the woods like the rest of them had?

The man who was choking her was making a shushing sound now. He was so strong. Far stronger than even his size suggested. His naked form crouched like a gargoyle above her, throttling the life out of her.

Her fingers scraped at his chin, trying to grab his eyes, or his throat. But he avoided her easily enough. Her hands were limp now. The dark spots grew wide, swallowing her consciousness.

CHAPTER TWENTY NINE

She knew she was alive because she was in pain. Ilse awoke with a pounding headache. She blinked, searing flashes of pain darting across her vision. She felt ready to throw up as consciousness slowly returned. Ilse gasped, blinking, trying to dislodge the dark spots. "Help," she managed to croak out, her voice so strained it was nearly a whisper. Her mouth felt dry, her tongue like cotton. "Help," she said, a bit louder.

And that's when she heard the movement. Ilse glanced at her hands, and realized they were zip-tied in front of her. A single band of plastic wrapped tightly around her wrists, holding them together. Try as she might, her hands were secured. She put pressure on her wrists, and the plastic bit into her skin painfully, but it didn't come undone. She tried again as the sounds came closer, with renewed fervor, but again, the zip-tie was too strong. The killer clearly had experience restraining his victims.

She was in a dark room, her back to a metal cage. Her shoulders brushed against the cage, and she glanced over, still wincing, still blinking. Two sets of eyes stared out at her, wide, terrified. Ilse swallowed back her own fear, staring, stunned. "Hello," she said, her voice raspy.

Both the women whimpered, ducking their heads and crowding further back into the cage.

Ilse resisted the urge to speak to them further. She didn't want to scare them.

She looked at the women a moment longer, despite the dark, shadowed nature of the space. A faint light came from a flickering candle on a stand made of old driftwood; the candlelight illuminated a cramped, small space, like the circular interior of a mud hut. One side of the room seemed built into the face of a cliff, with thick stone protrusions and roots jutting out of the wall. The other side had windows, covered in foliage, peering through the trees, at the night sky, catching glimpses of moonlight and twinkling stars.

Everything around them was quiet. No sounds coming through these windows except the rustle of the forest.

As for the two women behind her, in the cage that she rested against, they were both injured and scraped up. One of them had a head wound, which still bled. Crusted scabs framed the side of her face.

Delilah—Ilse recognized her from photos. The other woman had been taken from the RV. They were still alive. For now. Ilse wasn't inside the cage. Rather, she'd been placed with her zip-tied hands in front of her, her shoulders against the cage.

"Ah," called a voice from deep within the shadows. "I found the key, my dears! Here it is, indeed." The voice boomed out, strong and rich like the voice of some actor projecting their lines to the back of an auditorium.

Ilse went so still she thought she might have frozen in place. Her breath came in a quiet puff, the air angled up, tickling the inside of her nostrils. She stared into the shadows, her eyes aided only by the candle over her shoulder.

Cold needles prickled her spine, and a scream caught in her throat.

"My dears, do not be afraid," the voice called out. Now, the sound of footsteps was audible from further in the darkness.

A new shadow emerged in the black, caught by the intrepid fingers of light cast by the candle. The figure swayed in the dark, its silhouette swiping across the muddy windows, blotting out the horizon with its form as it approached.

As it neared, Ilse felt her skin crawl, her heart pounding so wildly she thought she might have a stroke. Again, her wrists strained, but the plastic band held them in place, biting and gouging into her flesh.

As the figure approached now, Ilse glimpsed past him.

Other people... frozen people.

She forgot to breathe.

Corpses. Other stuffed bodies, arranged around this new hideaway. The figure was now visible in the candlelight. The same, naked man with the mud-streaked form. His hair jutted every which way, wild and unkempt, his beard a tangle of strands like some bird nest.

His rich, thespian voice didn't at all match his appearance. Now, the whites of his eyes illuminated in the candlelight as he drew near, and his shadow cast across the frozen corpses behind him. The women in the cage whimpered and sniffled as he approached. In one hand, he held a key, which he dangled for her to see.

"Well, well my dearest Fiora," he said, nodding to Ilse. "You, of course, are most welcome here. Would you like to meet your friends, Fiora?"

Ilse swallowed, unsure if she ought to respond or not. The name didn't register. Had one of the victims been named Fiora? The killer's voice was singsong, quiet, playful even. He seemed in good humor, smile lines wreathing his eyes where the candlelight illuminated his features.

"When I saw you in the forest," he prattled on, "it gave me pause... I was quite enamored, at first sight. Certainly, I was. No—No, I'm not a liar," he called over his shoulder. Then he let out a good-natured little chuckle, slapping a hand against his upper thigh, and leaving a dark, dirty handprint against his skin. "Don't mind them," he said to Ilse, with a would-be roguish wink. He jutted a thumb over his shoulder, the key he gripped flashing. "They like to chime in at times, but really they're quite harmless."

He reached for the cage, past Ilse, the proximity of his flesh immediately sending Ilse crawling back against the muddy wall. She hyperventilated, eyes the size of saucers. His shadow fell over her, but instead of touching her, he was reaching for the padlock on the kennel. "Hush, hush, Fiora," he murmured. "It will all be okay, soon, my dear. So, so, soon. Please, shh. Shhhh."

He fit the key in the lock, but then hesitated, staring at the side of her face. All at once, the man leaned in, sniffing slowly, inhaling through his nose.

Ilse went still, not looking up, not wanting to entice any further inspection.

He leaned in closer now, his breath warm against her cheek, his body over her like some spider trapping a fly beneath it in its web. Ilse strained against the plastic bonds on her wrist, now she was bleeding. She could feel the warmth slipping down her wrists, to her elbows. Could feel the pain, jolting like fire.

She winced against it, trying a final time to tear the bonds. But the plastic only cut deeper into her skin.

She'd lost.

This had been a horrible idea. She never should have gone for training. What had she been thinking? There was a reason her siblings had been tormented. A reason she hadn't been able to stand up to her father.

She couldn't.

She wasn't equipped for it.

Now she'd come here and lost. He was going to kill her. Maybe do other things to her. And there wasn't a damn thing she could do about it. She began to exhale through her mouth now, shallow, though.

His breath still warmed her face. His face was inches from hers now, as if he were studying her face... Or, more accurately, the side of her face, near her cheek and the maimed portion of her ear.

"What is this, my sweet?" he said, growling.

Ilse winced at the tone of his words. All ice, no warmth. Something beneath the sentence suggested a slithering fury.

His grimy fingers brushed against her hair, revealing her maimed ear.

It felt like he'd stripped her naked. Ilse tried to twist her head, but his other hand shot out, grabbing her chin as if in a vice and holding her still.

He clicked his tongue and shook his head. "Pity that," he murmured. "Damaged..." he sighed. "Oh, dear. What will mother think if I bring her a damaged lamb, hmm? I suppose I'm running out of time, though, aren't I? Well, my dear, you and your damaged ear will just have to do, won't you? But I can't leave it like that... Perhaps a bit of preparation. Mother respects effort. Yes, yes, I know. Here... One moment."

He turned, scampering back towards the darkness. He fumbled around on a table in the far corner of the room, then returned a few moments later, carrying a bottle.

"Put this on," he said, throwing the bottle towards her.

It hit her in the chest with a dull *whack,* then fell to her knees. She winced, head pressed to the bars of the cage and the stone of the wall. The bottle on her lap was a beige thing and she recognized it a second later...

Skin lotion.

Her heart leapt to her throat. She tried not to look in the direction of the frozen bodies behind the killer, but it was a difficult task to ignore them.

Now, trapped in the lair, without a hope in the world, Ilse's more rational self tried to rise to the surface. Panic and fear were all well and good, but they rarely helped much. Now, as she considered her position, she knew she was doomed.

This man clearly wasn't well. He kept referring to a mother, of sorts... Gaia? His own brand of the nature cult? What sort of ailment prompted someone to wander through a forest, naked, talking to themselves?

Schizophrenia? Multiple personality disorder? Both serious conditions in need of immediate treatment. Treatment this man clearly hadn't received.

A form of OCD, judging by his discontent with her ear... Maybe not. Maybe that was a more religious angle.

Ilse swallowed, staring at the bottle resting on her lap, wanting nothing more than to throw it clear and run screaming from the muddy prison.

But the killer was staring at her now, the whites of his eyes gaping in the darkness, fixated on her like spotlights.

"Put that on yourself, dear," he said, his voice a bit colder now.

Ilse looked at the bottle again, glimpsing trails of red down her wrists from where the plastic bond had gouged deeper. Her fingers would be able to uncap the bottle, if she'd needed. But... but then what? What was the lotion for?

Once she put it on, what would he do?

The fear came back, but the rationality didn't retreat. Sometimes, fear was the most rational thing there was.

And now, Ilse knew she was out of options...

But one thing she was more accustomed to than the women in the cage... Than most folk...

Pain.

She'd befriended pain. She'd been forced to, at a young age.

Pain was not unfamiliar to her.

She gritted her teeth, growling, a loose whimper bursting from her lips as she tried to tear free of the zip-ties once more, but her thumbs caught against the plastic, and the strip gouged deeper into her wrists.

"Put it on, my dear," the man said, gritting his teeth now and hissing at her. "I mean it. Put it on!"

Ilse looked at him, trying to think desperately. How might she treat a client with MPD or borderline personality disorder? Was he paranoid? Should she soothe him? She was flying dark. Clearly, he had no aversion to violence. A violent schizophrenic, then? She couldn't feed the delusion, but neither could she reject it. A confrontation now would only agitate the aggressor.

Trembling, her voice as shaky as her hands, she murmured, "I'm sorry... You called me Fiora. What's your name?"

She spoke soothingly, quietly, hoping her words alone might calm the killer.

He tilted his head, staring at her. For a moment, it almost seemed as if he hadn't heard her. But then, he blinked and wrinkled his nose. "I mean... Thank you?" he said, hesitantly. "It is nice to hear."

She swallowed, hesitating. Nothing about his response suggested he'd heard her question.

"I'm sorry," she said. "I don't understand. Who are you?"

Now, he laughed, wagging his head up and down and pointing a finger at her. "There it is. That's what I remember. How time flies, right? Six years we've been friends. I can only imagine what the next six hold in store. But you can give me the present after—thank you for remembering. For now, though, please, just put the lotion on."

Ilse stared, stunned. He clearly wasn't even listening. He couldn't even hear her. Were delusions speaking instead of her? Was something else going on? Who was he talking to?

She shivered, feeling a root jutting from the wall against her shoulder. The leaves outside rustled louder now, the tree creaking and groaning. As it did, Ilse realized the man's smile widened. He bobbed his head in sound with the rustling branches.

"I don't know how," she said, lamely, desperately buying time. She tried to push the lotion away from herself, knocking it off her lap, onto the muddy ground, and then pushing it with her foot across the floor towards the man.

He glanced at this, back at her. He blinked, and his eyebrows rose for a moment as if surprised. Almost, strangely, as if he were seeing her for the very first time.

"Put it on," he said, a bit more insistently, his tone still friendly. Still amiable.

He shoved the bottle back towards her with his bruised and dirty toes.

She stared at the thing, swallowed, and shook her head. "I can't," she said. "Please, who are you? Maybe if you'd talk with me, I can help you. Is this about Gaia? I know Gaia. I actually just talked to a man who serves her. Are you like that too?"

The man frowned at her now, clenching his teeth for a moment and causing his jaw to become more pronounced. He nudged the bottle a bit more insistently with his dirty feet.

The women behind Ilse were both sobbing now, though clearly trying to keep the noise to a minimum. The cries of the trapped women, in the dark, wretched place, with the groan of the trees outside gave an eerie quality to the moon and stars visible outside the windows. The man's wild hair fluttered on the breeze, though not too much, suggesting the growth was caked with mud and oil.

"Put it on, please, Fi," he whispered. He nudged the bottle with his toes, gently, like a puppy probing a food dish in earnest.

Ilse stared at the thing, furiously thinking. He wasn't responding to conversation. Perhaps nonverbals were the way to go. Sometimes a therapist had to take risks. She would miss all the shots she didn't take. Just like Sawyer said.

So... she shoved the bottle away again with her foot, shaking her head wildly. “No,” she said, more insistently now. Too confrontational, though. She knew it the moment she'd done it. She'd let the fear, the tension, get to her. She'd overplayed her hand.

She'd never said *no* to him before. Not when he'd cut her ear. Not when he'd stitched her lips. Not when he'd buried her alive. Not when he'd beaten her or thrown her down the stairs. Not when he'd done those things to her older sisters and made her look away and cover her ears.

She shouldn't have said no. Her father hated no.

“No?” the man said, growling now. His shoulders hunched a bit, his eyes fixated on her, swaying like the mane of a lion about to pounce. “No?” he said, louder.

His body posture shifted nearly imperceptibly. His stance became wider, his fists bunched, his chest jutting.

“I said put it on!” He yelled, anger in his voice now. The friendly demeanor had vanished. His wide eyes gaped at her in fury.

“Please, no thank—”

He screeched, an inhuman, hyena sound. Then, he kicked her in the face, sending her head snapping back. Lights danced across her eyes, and pain exploded through her skull. Blood began to pool down her nose, across a busted lip. She felt fingers rip at her hair, dragging her from the corner and shoving her face against the floor. Her cheek pressed into the plastic of the bottle, scraping against the mud.

“Put it on! Put it on! On! On!” he screamed in her ear, holding her down. A knee jammed into her back, hard. “Put it on! The mother is watching. You won't steal my youth—whore! City whore! Steel whore! Glass and bones and windows galore! Whore! Put it on! On!”

Her ears ached from the screaming; her head pounded wildly from the pain. She wanted to fold in on herself, to wrap her arms around her knees and drift off into darkness.

But now, right now... if she stopped, she knew he'd kill her. He might even beat her to death. Perhaps that would be better than what else he had in store for her. The whimpering of the other captives now echoed louder through the cave. This only further infuriated the man.

He began to yank at Ilse's head, tilting her face, her cheek smooshed to the ground. "Want to see them bleed? Hmm? Is that it? You want to see them squeal? Alright. Alright—here we go, Fi! I could never say no to you. Let's watch. Which one? Which one squeals?"

Both women's eyes flashed in the dark. Both of them crowded back against the far portion of the cage, against each other. Their sobs were uncontrolled. One of them started screaming. A weak, desperate voice. "Help!" she croaked. "Please, someone help us! We're in here!"

The man didn't seem to care though. He knew no one would find them. How deep in the woods were they? Ten miles? Fifty?

A million-acre forest preservation... No one would hear them. Not now. Certainly not at night. They were doomed.

Ilse gasped, listening as the man used one hand to grope for the key in the lock of the cage. His other meaty fist kept her face jammed to the ground.

"Watch them die... Hmm? Watch them squeal... Yes, yes! Come now, darling!" he crowed, his voice booming again. "The spectacle is what entertains!"

He ripped open the cage door, reaching towards one of the women. Both of them screamed, both tried to kick out. He caught one of them by the leg, though. His hand snared her ankle, and he began to drag her from the dark. Again, he exhibited a herculean strength that didn't quite match his hunched form.

The woman yelled wildly, kicking, desperate, but he dragged her from the cage.

Watch her bleed?

Whatever he was about to do, Ilse couldn't allow it.

"No, no!" she yelled. "Alright. I'm putting it on. Please," she said, croaking, her voice coming out warped from the way her face was pressed to the dirt. "Please, I'll do it! I'm doing it! Watch—watch! Let her go!"

The killer froze. He looked down at Ilse, lifting his hand momentarily. His other hand still gripped the struggling, kicking woman by the ankle. No matter how hard she fought, he refused to let her go. The hand strength of a rock-climber, Ilse realized.

Bleeding, gasping, her head throbbing in pain, Ilse reached with trembling fingers towards the bottle of body lotion. Blood still trickled down from her wrists, past her fingertips, tapping against the dust and mingling with the dirt.

The agony in her wrist shot fire up her arms. But still, with shaking, blood-slicked hands she tried to undo the cap of the bottle.

"Now," whispered the killer. "Do it now. Forever she'll be with me. Forever. Don't you understand?" He leaned in now, calmer again. His lips brushed her forehead, sending a jolt of revulsion through Ilse. He kissed her, gently, nuzzling against her head. His tongue licked out as if to taste the blood from where he'd kicked her.

"Put it on, my dear," he whispered in her ear.

Ilse's stomach twisted, but at last, she managed to take the bottle cap off. At last, she managed to hold the lotion between her bound hands. The odor was fragrant, like honey.

The killer released his grip on the woman in the cage and she scrambled back to safety, bunching up and hyperventilating. Just like Ilse's siblings had done in that basement.

None of them had stood up to him.

Her father had been too strong. None of them had believed they could do anything to stop him. Perhaps they'd been right.

But what if not?

Ilse gripped the bottle between her hands, shaking, feeling the expectant gaze of the monster above her.

Maybe she couldn't do anything to save them. Maybe she was about to die.

But this time... she'd learned her lesson.

This time, even if it came with pain, little Hilda Mueller was going to do *something*. To try. Anything. She refused to suffer quietly. Not this time.

CHAPTER THIRTY

Ilse tensed, waiting for the right moment. It wasn't much of a plan, but if she could throw the lotion in his eyes, maybe she could distract him enough to get his key. Maybe, if she could help the women escape, they could gang up on the man. Three against one—the only shot she had.

She held up the lotion, and said in as innocent a tone as she could, "Is it supposed to look like this?"

He frowned, leaning in the way he had to examine her ear.

Then, Ilse burst into motion. She jerked her arms up, the motion clumsy due to the zip-tie, yet still flinging the contents of the bottle. Faster still, though, his hand shot out, catching her wrist. A deep, bellowing howl burst from his lips, "You did *what*?"

The bottle of lotion smashed against the ground, sending globs of emulsion across the floor in puddles. But he didn't even seem to notice the lotion anymore. In fact, it didn't seem as if he'd even realized what Ilse was trying to do. Rather, his eyes were glued to her bloodied wrists. He gripped her forearm, practically yanking her arm from its socket. "You did this?" he screeched. "How dare you?" His voice shook through the mud bunker and echoed out the windows. "How dare you!" he screamed, an inhuman squeal to his voice.

Now that he held up her wrists, yanking at her arm, the candlelight caught the damage she'd done to herself. It wasn't pretty. Attempting to yank her hands free, despite the pain, despite the ripping, again and again, had left deep, bloodied furrows across her skin. Cuts, dripping red, encircled her wrists. Her skin was torn, and blood pooled along her arms.

The killer looked stunned with rage. The maimed ear perhaps he would forgive. But the fresh wounds sent him into new heights of fury.

As his grip tightened, and his eyes widened in rage, Ilse glimpsed the way his free hand began to curl. She knew in that moment, no matter what she did, he was going to kill her.

But she had already determined not to take it lying down.

As he sent his fist careening towards her head, with a bellow of fury, she kicked out, hard. One benefit of a naked man: it was easier to find a good target.

Her feet caught him between the fork of his legs. The caveman let out a whooshing breath, doubling over and gasping at the ground. Strands of saliva and mucus stretched from his mouth towards the floor. He choked out a squeak of rage, but his grip on her forearm had loosened. Ilse turned, scrambling on the ground, not bothering to get back to her feet. She crawled desperately away from him, unable to get her hands quite under her. The same way Kristine had called crawled, through the trees, which Sawyer had spotted back at the mile marker. The same way the young woman had crawled onto the road, in search of a ranger. Desperate, strong, but ultimately futile.

Ilse reached what looked like a kitchen table with a sturdy wooden chair. Her shoulder bumped into a boot. The boot belonged to a foot. One of the corpses toppled, crashing down on her, and thudding into her back. She yelled in pain. Her spine was already bruised.

She continued to scramble, shouting at the top of her lungs, "Get away from me! Get back!"

The killer was howling now, letting out a seething sound as he charged her again. He tackled her from behind, his full weight pounding her small form into the dust. Something jammed into her lower back. Something crashed. She turned enough to glimpse the killer ripping an arm off the toppled corpse. Ilse stared in horror as he lifted the severed arm and began to use it to bludgeon her.

The first blow hit the ground as she jerked her head to the side. The next crashed off the thick, sturdy wooden chair, as she tried to crawl under the table for temporary cover. The chair tilted, but at the same time, landed between her arms, effectively trapping her in place. The killer yelled and yanked at the table, jamming the chair against the wall, trapping Ilse in place.

She cursed, trying to pivot, to topple the chair, but now her hands were trapped by the sturdy leg.

He was too strong anyway. Howling, he yanked her out from beneath the table, her arms extending over her head where the zip-tie caught the chair leg, holding her fast. He screamed, "You can't steal this from me! I deserve this! I will live!"

He swung the bloodless arm down on her again. This time it caught her over the shoulder. More pain. More desperate scrambling backwards. She was fighting tooth and nail. Fighting simply to survive. She couldn't hurt him. She hadn't been able to as a child either. Sometimes, dangerous men just won. But that didn't mean she couldn't fight to live. Just a few more seconds. She kicked out. Just a few more seconds. She tried to scratch at him. Blood flecked from her wrists across his face. Just a few more seconds; she screamed at him as he tried to strangle her now, throwing the arm aside and wrapping his fingers around her throat. Just a few more seconds.

And then she heard a shout. Another figure burst into the muddy room, coming from down a dark hall. A flashlight clicked on. She recognized, briefly, a man with a baseball cap and a flannel shirt. The lanky form of agent Tom Sawyer came careening out of the tunnel, screaming at the top of his lungs, "Get off her!"

Shock flooded her system. How... How had he....?

Sawyer slammed into the killer, his shoulder catching the wild man in the neck. Both of them went down hard. Sawyer was on top at first, his fingers scrambling for his gun.

But the wild man seemed familiar enough with guns to know to keep Sawyer's fingers from reaching it. He tried to snap one of Sawyer's pointers, bending it back, and Sawyer cursed, twisting. The motion, though, cost his balance, and he was sent sliding off the man's chest.

Ilse stared, stunned. How had Sawyer found her? She couldn't believe it. Now, though, she had wedged herself beneath the table, her hands were tangled up in one of the table legs, the zip ties caught by the wooden chair. She cursed, trying to pull free from where she'd dove to safety. She needed her hands. Needed to grab a weapon. She needed to help Sawyer.

The killer was like a cornered animal now, ferocious. Sawyer was full of rage. He was a man driven by his desire to protect the helpless, defenseless. But now, a wild man tried to rip his eyes out with fingers.

Sawyer was using punches. The killer was going for the testicles, for the eyes, for the fingers. Sawyer tried to reach his gun. The killer spat in Sawyer's face. He tried to bite him. Sawyer yelled, yanking his hand back. But again, this move lost his position, and the killer managed to gain the upper hand, pushing Sawyer off, and shoving him onto the ground.

"Stop!" Ilse screamed. "Get off him." She tried to jerk out from where her hands were trapped. The thick table leg had wedged against the wooden chair, which was between her arms, holding the zip-tie fast.

She didn't have time to try to move the table leg. She needed to get free.

Both men were yelling ferociously, kicking and spitting. Sawyer was still throwing punches. The man on top of him was still going for Sawyer's eyes. Then the killer changed tactics, his hand wrapping around Sawyer's throat, beginning to squeeze.

Sawyer's shouts went quiet, strangled. He was choking. In moments, he would be out as well. And then, Ilse wouldn't have just killed herself, the two women, but also Sawyer. She couldn't let that happen.

"Run," Sawyer tried to choke out. "Ilse, run," he croaked. Even now, all he seemed to care about was protecting someone else. She howled in frustration and then grit her teeth. She couldn't lift the table, couldn't disentangle the chair where it had lodged against the wood. Rather, she knew what she had to do. She had befriended pain.

She knew pain.

The killer was used to snaring people in his lair. Accustomed to using tools that would hold them fast.

But she had been in a lair in the woods before. Pain didn't scare her. Not like it did others. She'd endured so much of it, the familiarity alone bred companionship.

She howled at the sky, paused for a moment, listening to the choking sound behind her, and then didn't hesitate. He needed her help. She jammed her thumb hard against the wooden table leg. She put the full force of her body behind it, twisting until her full weight bore down on her thumb, where it twisted with the plastic band.

Her finger cracked. She nearly passed out in pain. She screamed a second later as it hit her with the full force of freezing shock. Agony pulsed up her arm, along with the trails of blood from the plastic around her wrist. She had cracked her thumb. Broken? Dislocated?

No time. That had been the easy part.

Gasping desperately, all too aware the sounds behind her were quieting, Ilse yanked her hand with the cracked thumb. Slick with blood, the plastic band stretched as it was from all her efforts, her thumb now bent at an odd angle, one hand ripped free. Again, pain flooded her. Again, she resisted the urge to scream in agony.

Gasping, desperate, she tried to push to her feet. But the moment her hand hit the ground, to brace herself, she collapsed. Her hand was unable to support her. Now, though, with one hand free, she was able to slide the other from beneath the table leg. Desperately, her vision spattered with white spots of agony, she got shakily to her feet.

Sawyer was on the ground, his face red, his hands wrapped around the fingers choking the life out of him. The killer braced himself against Sawyer, the muscles in his back visible against his skin, straining, illuminated in the moonlight. He didn't even see Ilse.

With one busted hand, full of pain, she reached for the closest weapon she could find. She pushed past her distaste, and with her free hand lifted the loose arm of the cadaver.

Nightmares would haunt her after this. But it didn't matter. They haunted her anyway. This scenario would just have to wait its turn to show up in her dreams. She charged, howling, and swung the stuffed arm towards the back of the killer's head. A metal joint, used to secure and fasten the arm to the body, struck the killer in the back of the head. He jolted. Ilse didn't wait, wheeling around and bringing the makeshift bludgeon down again. The man croaked, letting out a sickly sound. The metal in the embedded arm caught his neck and made a grizzly, crunching noise. Ilse wasn't done; she screamed, with one good arm wheeling around, hitting him again and again and again.

Red spots danced across her vision. She could barely breathe. She wanted to scream, to trample the monster. To kick him until he wouldn't rise.

A few seconds passed, and then she felt a hand ripping her arm. She screamed, trying to wheel around. But realized a second later, gasping, bent, one hand massaging his neck, Sawyer was trying to steady her.

"It's okay," he said, gasping, his voice hoarse. "It's all right. It's all right. He's done. You did it. He's done."

Ilse blinked, not quite believing what she was seeing. She tried to swallow back the horror welling inside her. Tried to swallow back tears, the fury.

She'd never been able to resist him before. She had grown up not saying no.

It felt good to say no. She hated to admit it. She also hated that now Sawyer watched as she began to weep. Her shoulders shook, and the agony in her hand only intensified the sensation. Partly from emotion, partly from sheer pain, tears streamed down her dusty cheeks, creating mud trails. She wept, and shook, and wept some more. Sawyer leaned in, pulling her close. The killer was lying on the ground, motionless, his arms spread wide as if to embrace the ceiling. The two women in the cage were crying, whispering to each other, for the first time, the sounds of their voices carrying something close to hope.

Ilse hadn't come too late this time. She'd made it. She hadn't gotten lost in the woods. She'd made it in time for them.

"It's all right," Sawyer said. He smelled of blood and sandalwood and the faintest hint of aftershave and bug spray. "It's all right," he said, gently, holding her with one arm, not too tightly, allowing her space if she wanted to push away. But she didn't. She leaned her head against him, still crying, still shaking, bleeding but alive.

At least for a few seconds more.

CHAPTER THIRTY ONE

Ilse watched Sawyer sleep across the hospital room. Soft green lines played across the screen between their beds. A thin curtain divider had been pulled back, allowing sunlight to warm the both of them through the large window overlooking Seattle.

Ilse had never been so glad to return to the city. She glanced down to where her hand was now in a cast. Only dislocated, the doctor had said.

At least there was that. Still, it would be a few weeks before she was allowed full use of her thumb again. Her face felt heavy where the bandages pressed to the cuts and scrapes. She'd been dehydrated too, so the thin IV now dripping fluids shifted, the plastic tube waving with every motion she made.

Still, with her head resting against a rough hospital pillow, she felt relieved...

They'd both lived. The two women who'd been trapped with them also survived.

"Hey," a voice said.

Ilse blinked, focusing again and realizing he was now watching her.

"You're awake?" she said, hoping he hadn't realized she'd been staring.

"Mhmm."

"I—I didn't realize. Sorry."

"Sorry?"

"I mean," she hesitated, wincing as she propped up on her good elbow. The IV tube swished, and she carefully lowered again, not wanting to dislodge it. "How are you?"

Sawyer groaned, reaching up and massaging his neck with a bruised hand. His voice was hoarse as he spoke, "Alright. Can't complain." He shrugged, but then winced at the motion and leaned back. He didn't turn, though, preferring to rest in a way that allowed him to face her between the dividing line between their beds.

For a moment the two of them just watched each other, studying one another's visible injuries.

Not all the injuries could be seen, though.

Images of the corpses in the dark, of the wild man charging them flashed through Ilse's mind.

"Did they count the bodies?" Ilse whispered. "No one told me anything."

Sawyer wrinkled his nose. "This our second day, right?" He began to sit up, groaning as he did. His baseball cap, which he'd refused to let them take, sat next to him on the hospital bed. He looked older without it, somehow. Though Ilse knew he was only thirty-six, a few years older than her.

"Yeah. Second day."

"Insane," Sawyer muttered. "I'm barely bruised."

"Rawley said you needed to stay the full forty-eight hours for observation." Ilse winced. "Sorry."

Sawyer snorted, glancing back out the window. "At least the view ain't half bad," he muttered.

"Oh. I didn't realize you liked the city."

Sawyer glanced at her. For a moment, it almost seemed as if he smirked, but he covered the expression with a cough. "You look awful."

Ilse sighed, nodding. "I deserve that. I... I'd look worse if you hadn't shown up on time."

"Ms. Altum and Ms. Farrow would look the same if not for you," said Sawyer. "But yeah... What you did was dumb."

"I... My phone?" Ilse said, leaning in now. The last time she'd asked him, she'd been half delirious, when they'd first been shuttled into the hospital. Two days had passed, with good rest and recuperation. She was thinking more clearly now. Even Ilse balked at the choices she'd made. Why had she gone off into the woods on her own? Why hadn't she left when the walkie-talkie had failed? It was almost as if she'd *wanted* to punish herself.

"Yeah, well, good thinking placing that call," Sawyer said.

Ilse hesitated. That was right... That's how he'd found her. The phone call she'd placed from the campsite. He'd managed to trace it back. Spotty coverage in the woods, but enough for the FBI to triangulate her position. That, coupled with the built in GPS of the walkie-talkie she'd taken. Even without communication function, the GPS had helped them narrow in on the phone's signal as well.

If the killer had tossed the items, or broken them...

Ilse shivered at the though.

He hadn't.

That's all she could think about for now.

"Nineteen," Sawyer said.

"I—excuse me?"

"Bodies," he replied. "Nineteen. At all lairs. They're looking for others."

Ilse shivered in horror. Nineteen dead. Nineteen people who would never see their loved ones again. Perhaps she'd arrived late after all. "What's two survivors compared to nineteen?" Ilse murmured, her voice carrying a haunted quality. Agent Rawley had personally taken the time to call her that morning. Commended her. Her first case—one of the biggest in recent memory. He'd seemed over the moon. But Ilse only felt sick to her stomach.

"Two more than zero," Sawyer retorted. He frowned at her. "Four."

"What?"

"Four survivors." He waved a hand towards his neck and Ilse's bandages. "Four. Sometimes that's all you get."

"This isn't a batting average," Ilse returned. "It's people's lives." The words were hard, but her tone was gentle. She didn't blame Sawyer... If anyone was at fault, it was her.

"Nah," Sawyer said as if reading her mind. He seemed to have good instincts where her thoughts were concerned. She wasn't sure if she liked that. He said, "It's sick twists in the woods with a boner for murder. That bastard is the one at fault. Not you."

Ilse sighed. "Did they find out who he was? No one's telling me anything."

Sawyer shrugged, glancing towards his cap. Then, he held up a finger, the white bandages standing out against his work-calloused hands. He lifted his hat, pulled his phone from beneath the headwear and lifted it. It took a moment for the screen to turn on.

As he leaned back, head against the pillow, Ilse simply watched him scrolling through the device.

After a few moments, he blinked, then turned the phone towards her. "That look like the guy?"

Ilse frowned, wincing as she leaned over the edge of her bed, peering across the gap above the tiles between them. A handsome man, with a neatly trimmed beard stared back at them.

"Who is that?"

"DNA match," Sawyer said.

Ilse gaped. "That's our killer?"

"Yeah it is."

"Is... not was... So... so I didn't kill him? I wasn't sure."

Sawyer shook his head. "They took him to a different hospital. But it's a DNA match." He turned the phone back around. "Used to be an actor, apparently. Got some sort of cancer... Went into remission then disappeared." Sawyer grunted. "Seven years ago. Went off grid."

Ilse stared, her mind spinning. "He was suffering from something," she said. "Delusions, most likely."

"Might have been a side-effect of the drugs he was taking," Sawyer said. "Some special stuff for cancer patients. Experimental shit."

"Maybe... That might account for delusions, but... But something snapped," she replied. "I could see it. The way he spoke. Like I wasn't even there. It was more than just a delusion."

Sawyer shrugged. "Some people can't face death. It breaks them before they even die. One way or another, our guy was a psycho."

"But an ex-actor turned cancer patient?" Ilse shivered, shaking her head. Remembering the sound of the bludgeon slamming into his neck. "I... It's so horrible. He was ranting about the mother... Ranting about..."

"Gaia?" Sawyer grunted, wiggling his phone again. "Looks like, of all things, our friend Teddy recognized the picture."

"What?"

"Yeah—go figure. Our killer used to go to meetings. Would get healing rituals and the sort from Teddy. Also donated heavily from what funds he had left. Teddy was more than happy to take advantage of a new soldier for nature."

Ilse felt sick. "What was his name?"

Sawyer began to reply. But then Ilse cut him off just as quickly. "Wait—no, never mind. I don't... I don't think I want to know."

Sawyer watched her once, then nodded, a strange look of respect in his features. He clicked off his phone and shoved it beneath his hat again.

Ilse turned away for a moment, staring at the blank wall at the foot of her bed.

"It... it doesn't bother you?" she murmured, her voice faint even in her ears. "All those dead? All the people we didn't help?"

She didn't look over and, in the silence, briefly, she wondered if he'd even heard. But then, Sawyer inhaled for a moment, and he replied. "It bothers me. But I've been at the job more than a decade, doc. You gotta learn to deal with it. Otherwise, it'll eat you alive... Shit. Hang on."

A sudden beeping noise emanated in the hospital room. Ilse frowned, glancing over and Sawyer picked his phone back up. He glanced at the number and then groaned. He winced in Ilse's direction, held up a finger as if to say *one second,* then lifted the device.

"Yeah?" he said. A pause. Then, Sawyer said, "Jen, I mean this the nicest way possible. Stop fucking calling me." He hung up, and turned off his phone, shoving it deep beneath his pillow as if burying it.

Ilse watched him, frowning. "Was that your wife again?"

"Ex-wife," Sawyer retorted. "Well... mostly... Kinda. As good as divorced. She's just too lazy to sign on the dotted line."

Ilse blinked. "Oh."

"Man... I hate that woman," Sawyer muttered beneath his breath. "She knows she's tormenting me by dragging it out. That's why she's doing it." He drifted off, grumbling beneath his breath.

Ilse stared at Sawyer a moment longer. She hated to admit it, but somehow, these words almost relieved her. Sawyer hated his wife. Hooray!

What an odd reaction. She thought about it for a moment, but then realized she was falling into a classic trap. Thinking her feelings instead of feeling them. She couldn't always change the way she felt—though sometimes it was possible. Most of the time, though, it was easier to just choose how she reacted.

"Damn, doc," Sawyer said, wincing as he readjusted again. "I wish I'd listened closer," he said. "Back when you were trying to tell me. You know. About Teddy."

Ilse shook her head. "Not your fault. Everyone thought he was the guy. Me too at first."

"Yeah... Well. I still wish." She was surprised to hear a note of emotion to his voice. He turned to her now, frowning. He looked at her, but it was almost as if he were looking straight through her. "I would've hated if something had happened to you," he said. A sincere, straightforward claim. None of his usual deflection or airy tone. He nodded once. "I would've *hated* it," he said, his teeth set.

She glimpsed pain in his eyes. A pain that went deep. A pain she recognized because she had her own share of it.

She watched him for a moment, and he blinked as if snapping back; he looked at her for a moment, confused, and then swallowed and said, "Dang. Glad you're kicking, doc." He smiled and flashed a thumbs up.

Ilse studied him for a moment, then collapsed back on the pillows, staring at the ceiling. She wasn't sure what to make of Agent Tom

Sawyer. But she knew she liked how it felt being around him. Not that she really had *any* experience with such things.

"Hey Ilse," Sawyer said, suddenly.

"Mhmm."

"I *do* hate the city. But I still like the view from here."

Ilse turned just in time to catch a smirk as Sawyer lowered his baseball cap on his face, tilting it back and settling in for a nap.

CHAPTER THIRTY TWO

Ilse shook her head, above the steering wheel to the *Boat,* grateful to finally have the cast off at last. Three weeks she'd been forced to wear that infernal thing. Three weeks without being able to train at the dojo.

Now, finally, freedom.

Not only that...

She smiled, glancing towards the fresh, laminated identification sitting on the passenger seat. FBI. Agent Ilse Beck.

Amazing how much easier the tactical test had been with two hands. She hadn't frozen, either. Sometimes fears couldn't be avoided. They simply had to be faced.

Ilse smiled again as she pulled up the driveway, newly graduated, her hand back in action, her spirits high. The scent of the lake, the creak of the trees around her didn't hold the same allure they so often had before.

Now, pulling to a halt on her driveway, Ilse knew she had to leave.

She'd decided a week before. She'd subconsciously chosen this place to stay mired in her past. To face her childhood again and again... To recreate a more palatable version of her own trauma. But no longer. She couldn't stay here.

With each passing day, the conviction only grew stronger. Hadn't she started packing, after all?

Even from the driveway, through the front window, between the slits in the blinds, she spotted a couple of the yellow packing boxes she'd left resting against the sofa. Her books had been packed first. Eventually, she'd have to figure out how to fit her colossal desktop into a box also.

She kicked the door and slid out of the front seat, stepping into the cool lakefront air. The trees above her stretched their arms wide and leaves curled down, fluttering on the wind towards the ground to join their fallen brethren.

Ilse stared at the thousands of fallen leaves for a moment, feeling a shiver up her spine. Then, careful to avoid the detritus, she avoided the forest floor and stepped firmly on concrete, moving towards her front door, a spring in her step, her new ID clutched in one hand.

Four weeks of recovery and relative happiness.

It was nice she'd been given four weeks.

Sometimes, that's all someone was allowed before the next thing in life came crashing in.

In this case, that *thing* came in the form of a single manila folder resting in front of her door. The moment she spotted it, Ilse slowed, one hand slipping into her pocket and placing the ID next to her wallet. She frowned as she took the bottom steps, her other hand trailing along the cold, metal rail.

The tops of the yellow boxes were even more visible from here now. But she ignored the window, her gaze fixated on the folder.

Her hand was steady as stone as she bent in front of her lake home. A home she was leaving. For good.

She picked up the folder and tore the top.

Inside, she found an unsigned Walgreen's letter... Only a single line of text and laminated photograph of Olympic National Park.

The text read, "So sorry to see you go!"

Ilse stared at the sentence, her blood going cold. With a hand shaking now, she reached into the folder and pulled out a small, cool item.

A tchotchke... Not surprising now.

Predictable in its cruelty. Meant to terrify. To remind.

A small, porcelain little boy carried a suitcase. The boy's poorly painted face beamed, his cheeks pudgy and upturned. A small hand waved in the air as if bidding farewell.

Ilse turned, her neck prickling, glancing towards the road.

For a moment, it felt as if a million eyes were watching her. She breathed in, out. Carefully, she stowed the letter and the tchotchke back in the folder.

Her eyes narrowed.

She wasn't the same little girl anymore.

She knew how to say no.

She knew how to fight.

Even if only for a few more seconds.

This time...

This time she wasn't the one who needed to be careful. She gritted her teeth, snarling at the trees, at anyone watching.

She'd trained. She had new friends. Dangerous friends. She didn't freeze anymore.

Perhaps it was time.
She needed to see him.
To face the man who'd caused it all.
She needed to return to Germany and visit a man behind bars.

NOW AVAILABLE!

NOT LIKE THIS
(An Ilse Beck FBI Suspense Thriller—Book 4)

When FBI Special Agent Ilse Beck's patients turn up dead in string of suicides, she suspects something more nefarious. Has a serial killer from her past—the one she fears the most—returned?

In this bestselling mystery series, FBI Special Agent Ilse Beck, victim of a traumatic childhood in Germany, moved to the U.S. to become a renowned psychologist specializing in PTSD, and the world's leading expert in the unique trauma of serial-killer survivors. By studying the psychology of their survivors, Ilse has a unique and unparalleled expertise in the true psychology of serial killers. Ilse never expected, though, to become an FBI agent herself.

But even FBI agents are not invulnerable, especially when targeted by serial killers. And it just may be, that Ilse herself is next on this killer's list.

A dark and suspenseful crime thriller, the bestselling ILSE BECK series is a breathtaking page-turner, an unputdownable mystery and suspense novel. A compelling and perplexing psychological thriller, rife with twists and jaw-dropping secrets, it will make you fall in love with a brilliant new female protagonist, while it keeps you shocked late into the night.

NOT LIKE THIS (An Ilse Beck FBI Suspense Thriller) is book #4 in a new series by bestselling mystery and suspense author Ava Strong. Future books in the series will be available soon.

Ava Strong

Debut author Ava Strong is author of the REMI LAURENT mystery series, comprising three books (and counting); of the ILSE BECK mystery series, comprising four books (and counting); and of the STELLA FALL psychological suspense thriller series, comprising four books (and counting).

An avid reader and lifelong fan of the mystery and thriller genres, Ava loves to hear from you, so please feel free to visit www.avastrongauthor.com to learn more and stay in touch.

BOOKS BY AVA STRONG

REMI LAURENT FBI SUSPENSE THRILLER
THE DEATH CODE (Book #1)
THE MURDER CODE (Book #2)
THE MALICE CODE (Book #3)

ILSE BECK FBI SUSPENSE THRILLER
NOT LIKE US (Book #1)
NOT LIKE HE SEEMED (Book #2)
NOT LIKE YESTERDAY (Book #3)
NOT LIKE THIS (Book #4)

STELLA FALL PSYCHOLOGICAL SUSPENSE THRILLER
HIS OTHER WIFE (Book #1)
HIS OTHER LIE (Book #2)
HIS OTHER SECRET (Book #3)
HIS OTHER MISTRESS (Book #4)

www.ingramcontent.com/pod-product-compliance
Lightning Source LLC
Chambersburg PA
CBHW030615310726
48979CB00003B/733

* 9 7 8 1 0 9 4 3 9 3 4 3 8 *